浙江工商大学
"数字+"研究生专业建设成果——教材系列

U0569852

# 代西方女性作家
# 精选
## ——短篇小说数字阅读

主编 薛春霞

浙江工商大学出版社
ZHEJIANG GONGSHANG UNIVERSITY PRESS
·杭州·

**图书在版编目(CIP)数据**

当代西方女性作家作品选：短篇小说数字阅读 / 薛春霞主编. — 杭州：浙江工商大学出版社，2024.9

ISBN 978-7-5178-5943-7

Ⅰ. ①当… Ⅱ. ①薛… Ⅲ. ①短篇小说—小说集—世界—现代 Ⅳ. ①I14

中国国家版本馆 CIP 数据核字(2024)第 003952 号

**当代西方女性作家作品选——短篇小说数字阅读**

**DANGDAI XIFANG NÜXING ZUOJIA ZUOPIN XUAN—DUANPIAN XIAOSHUO SHUZI YUEDU**

**主　编　薛春霞**

**责任编辑**　王　英
**责任校对**　张莉娅
**封面设计**　廖佳怡
**责任印制**　包建辉
**出版发行**　浙江工商大学出版社
（杭州市教工路 198 号　邮政编码 310012）
（E-mail：zjgsupress@163.com）
（网址：http://www.zjgsupress.com）
电话：0571-88904980，88831806（传真）
**排　　版**　杭州朝曦图文设计有限公司
**印　　刷**　杭州高腾印务有限公司
**开　　本**　787mm×1092mm　1/16
**印　　张**　16.5
**字　　数**　296 千
**版 印 次**　2024 年 9 月第 1 版　2024 年 9 月第 1 次印刷
**书　　号**　ISBN 978-7-5178-5943-7
**定　　价**　56.00 元

**版权所有　侵权必究**

如发现印装质量问题，影响阅读，请和营销发行中心联系调换
联系电话　0571-88904970

"She Unnames Them" by Ursula K. Le Guin. Copyright © 1985 by Ursula K. Le Guin
First appeared in *The New Yorker*, published in 1985
then in BUFFALO GALS, published by Capra Press in 1987. Reprinted by permission of Ginger Clark Literary, LLC.

The entirety of the story "Able, Baker, Charlie, Dog" from *Sweet Talk* by Stephanie Vaughn. Copyright © 1990 by Stephanie Vaughn. Reprinted by permission of Georges Borchardt, Inc. , on behalf of the author. All rights reserved.

"Who's Irish?" by Gish Jen. Copyright © [Gish Jen], [2000] Reprinted by permission of Gish Jen.

"Tiny, Smiling Daddy" by Mary Gaitskill. Copyright © 1997, Mary Gaitskill, used by permission of The Wylie Agency (UK) Limited.

# 前　言

西蒙·波伏娃在《第二性》(*The Second Sex*,1947)中指出,性属(Gender)是一种社会构建,性别(Sex)是人的生理特征。这一观念已经得到了社会的广泛认可。在一般的社会观念中,男性和女性这两种性别构成了社会基本的性属单位。每个人都是在特定的性别身份下学习和生活的,并逐渐体验自己的人生。

没有经过训练的眼睛和头脑很少会发现:生活中点点滴滴的快乐和苦恼、或大或小的日常工作和生活决断,都可能受到性别身份的影响。青春期交友、成年后的婚恋与性别直接相关。大学专业、工作类型的选择,定居地的确定,以及人际交往和思维方式的形成,也都受到性别身份和性别意识的影响。青春期对性别身份的认知,会在之后的成长阶段进一步受到社会观念中性别要求的冲击或强化,由此会产生自我认知的困惑。对于这些与性别身份相关的成长认知,有些人会欣然接纳,有些人则备受束缚;有些人会乐享其中,有些人则困惑不已。而在妥协、服从、质疑和挑战中,很多人还没有意识到这些都与自己的性别认知和性别身份息息相关。

对女性而言,女性主义运动及思潮或多或少地影响了她们的性别认知和自我期望。当下,整个社会对两性关系的认知处于新旧观念的交替之中。经济的发展和教育的普及允许更多的女性进入社会生产领域,发挥个人的潜能,实现自己的生命价值。但是,很多女性也发现,在大多数情况下,社会允诺的性别平等仅停留在形式层面。包括女性在内,很多人依旧遵从男主女次的传统。当女性的个人性别认知与社会传统观念产生分歧时,就会产生性别对抗。城市剩女、"丧偶"式育儿乃至女性不满于工作和家庭的双重要求而拒绝进入婚育等相应的社会问题也随之产生。对男性而言,刻板的性别边界让他们备受压力,难以适从。但是,因为男性作为性别差异的受益方,也并无孕育的生理功能,所以他们很难对女性的处境感同身受。占据社会主导地位的男性很少真正了解女性的需求,也很少有机会真正踏入女性的世界。因此,了解女性的心理和思想成为跨性别沟通的必要渠道。而对性别差异的了解,少不了女性与男性关系的相互建构。

在过去的几个世纪里，女性参与社会活动、追求个体发展的样板大多来自男性的经验。曾经，文学作品中对女性生活的描写也大多出自男性作家之笔。直到18世纪，女性作家的作品才逐渐出现在读者面前。女性作家通过自身的视角、感受和经验来描述女性的生活处境，这算是在真正意义上对女性生活做了完整表述。本书选取的短篇小说涉及女性从无奈顺从性别规范到主动改变社会观念的一系列生活处境及相关变化。读者可以从中看到女性从不被看见到自我觉察、从社会边缘视角向中心视角的迁移。通过对这些文学文本的阅读，读者也能够在回看女性意识历时性变化的同时，产生代入感，更为深入地了解女性多方面的生活处境。

本书大致分为“受限的智力活动”“女性的能动性”“代际关系”“爱情与婚姻”“乌托邦、反乌托邦与现实”五个主题。这些主题以历时性的方式编排，读者可以从中清楚地看到女性个体意识在不同时代发生的变化。在细节安排方面，弗吉尼亚·伍尔夫的《一间自己的屋子》(*A Room of One's Own*)和爱丽丝·门罗的《办公室》(“The Office”)在女性个体发展的空间意识方面形成呼应，《小小的、微笑的老爸》(“Tiny, Smiling Daddy”)与《艾博、贝克、查理和狗》(“Able, Baker, Charlie, Dog”)分别从女儿与父亲的视角审视父女隔阂，《谁是爱尔兰人?》(“Who's Irish?”)与《两种女儿》(“Two Kinds”)从代际差异性视角来观察文化冲突。整本书的编排为读者展现了女性意识和生活的变化轨迹。读者可以从中清晰地看到，当女性作家有机会进行自由而自如的文学创作时，她们的文字也会与男性作家的文字一样，为读者提供丰富而多样化的生命体验。女性在迂回地实现生命价值的过程中蕴藏着与男性不一样的情感策略、成长路径和表现方式，这是女性作家特有的对生命的细腻表达。

值得注意的是，关于本书的编排，特别考虑到本科与研究生阶段青年学子的专业需求。而从文学的角度进行选材，则是为了给广大学生提供一个可以进行英文文本细读的载体(二维码内容获取密码：0726)，让他们从精巧的细节中体会文字的魅力、叙述的力量。

# *Contents*
# 目　录

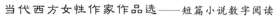

# Part One

## *Restrained Intellectual Life*

# Unit 1  *The Second Sex* by Simone de Beauvoir

## Ⅰ Introduction to the Author and the Work

Simone de Beauvoir (1908–1986) was born in Paris, France. She laid the foundation for the modern feminist movement. As an existentialist philosopher, she had a long-term relationship with Jean-Paul Sartre. When she was 21, Simone de Beauvoir met Jean-Paul Sartre, forming a partnership and romance that would shape both of their lives and philosophical belief. De Beauvoir published countless works of fiction and nonfiction during her lengthy career—often with existentialist themes—including 1949's *The Second Sex*, which is considered a pioneering work of the modern feminist movement. De Beauvoir also lent her voice to various political causes and traveled the world extensively. She died in Paris in 1986 and was buried with Sartre.

De Beauvoir may appreciate the fact that her current philosophical status reflects our changed understanding of the domain of philosophy and the changed situation of women, for it confirms her idea of situated freedom, that is, our capacity for agency and meaning-making, whether or not we are identified as agents and meaning-makers, is constrained, though never determined, by our situation. She may appreciate the fact that while her works are instrumental in pushing these changes, their lasting effect is a tribute to the ways that others have taken up her philosophical and feminist legacies, for one of her crucial contributions to our ethical and political vocabularies is the concept of the appeal, that is, the success of our projects depends on the extent to which they are adopted by others.

## Ⅱ *The Second Sex* (Excerpt)

### Introduction *Woman as Other*

For a long time I have hesitated to write a book on woman. The subject is irritating, especially to women; and it is not new. Enough ink has been spilled in quarrelling over feminism, and perhaps we should say no more about it. It is still talked about, however, for the voluminous nonsense uttered during the last century seems to have done little to illuminate the problem. After all, is there a problem? And if so, what is it? Are there women, really? Most assuredly the theory of the eternal feminine still has its adherents who will whisper in your ear "Even in Russia women still are *women*"; and other erudite persons—sometimes the very same—say with a sigh: "Woman is losing her way; woman is lost." One wonders if women still exist, if they will always exist, whether or not it is desirable that they should be, what place they occupy in this world, and what their place should be. "What has become of women?" was asked recently in an ephemeral magazine. But first we must ask: What is a woman? "*Tota mulier in utero*," says one, "woman is a womb." But in speaking of certain women, connoisseurs declare that they are not women, although they are equipped with a uterus like the rest. All agree in recognizing the fact that females exist in the human species; today as always they make up about one half of humanity. And yet we are told that femininity is in danger; we are exhorted to be women, remain women, and become women. It would appear, then, that every female human being is not necessarily a woman; to be so considered she must share in that mysterious and threatened reality known as femininity. Is this attribute something secreted by the ovaries? Or is it a platonic essence, a product of the philosophic imagination? Is a rustling petticoat enough to bring it down to earth? Although some women try zealously to incarnate this essence, it is hardly patentable. It is frequently described in vague and dazzling terms that seem to have been borrowed from the vocabulary of the seers, and indeed in the times of St Thomas it was considered an essence as certainly defined as the somniferous virtue of the poppy.

But conceptualism has lost ground. The biological and social sciences no longer admit the existence of unchangeably fixed entities that determine given characteristics, such as those ascribed to woman, the Jew, or the Negro. Science regards any characteristic as a reaction dependent in part upon a situation. If today femininity no longer exists, then it never existed. But does the word *woman*, then, have no specific content? This is stoutly affirmed by those who hold to the philosophy of the enlightenment, of rationalism, of nominalism; women, to them, are merely the human beings arbitrarily designated by the word *woman*. Many American women particularly are prepared to think that there is no longer any place for woman as such; if a backward individual still takes herself for a woman, her friends advise her to be psychoanalyzed and thus get rid of this obsession. In regard to a work, *Modern Woman: The Lost Sex*, which in other respects has its irritating features, Dorothy Parker has written: "I cannot be just to books which treat of woman as woman ... My idea is that all of us, men as well as women, should be regarded as human beings." But nominalism is a rather inadequate doctrine, and the anti-feminists have had no trouble in showing that women simply are not men. Surely woman is, like man, a human being; but such a declaration is abstract. The fact is that every concrete human being is always a singular, separate individual. To decline to accept such notions as the eternal feminine, the black soul, the Jewish character, is not to deny that Jews, Negroes, women exist today—this denial does not represent a liberation for those concerned, but rather a flight from reality. Some years ago a well-known woman writer refused to permit her portrait to appear in a series of photographs especially devoted to women writers; she wished to be counted among the men. But in order to gain this privilege she made use of her husband's influence! Women who assert that they are men lay claim none the less to masculine consideration and respect. I recall also a young Trotskyite standing on a platform at a boisterous meeting and getting ready to use her fists, in spite of her evident fragility. She was denying her feminine weakness; but it was for love of a militant male whose equal she wished to be. The attitude of defiance of many American women proves that they are haunted by a sense of their femininity. In truth, to go for a walk with one's eyes open is enough to demonstrate that humanity is divided into two classes of individuals whose clothes, faces, bodies, smiles, gaits, interests, and occupations are manifestly different. Perhaps these differences are superficial, perhaps they are destined to disappear. What is certain is that they do most obviously exist.

If her functioning as a female is not enough to define woman, if we decline also to explain her through "the eternal feminine," and if nevertheless we admit, provisionally, that women do exist, then we must face the question: "what is a woman?"

To state the question is, to me, to suggest, at once, a preliminary answer. The fact that I ask it is in itself significant. A man would never set out to write a book on the peculiar situation of the human male. But if I wish to define myself, I must first of all say "I am a woman" on this truth must be based all further discussion. A man never begins by presenting himself as an individual of a certain sex; it goes without saying that he is a man. The terms *masculine* and *feminine* are used symmetrically only as a matter of form, as on legal papers. In actuality the relation of the two sexes is not quite like that of two electrical poles, for man represents both the positive and the neutral, as is indicated by the common use of *man* to designate human beings in general; whereas woman represents only the negative, defined by limiting criteria, without reciprocity. In the midst of an abstract discussion it is vexing to hear a man say "You think thus and so because you are a woman"; but I know that my only defense is to reply "I think thus and so because it is true," thereby removing my subjective self from the argument. It would be out of the question to reply "And you think the contrary because you are a man," for it is understood that the fact of being a man is no peculiarity. A man is in the right in being a man; it is the woman who is in the wrong. It amounts to this: just as for the ancients there was an absolute vertical with reference to which the oblique was defined, so there is an absolute human type, the masculine. Woman has ovaries, a uterus: these peculiarities imprison her in her subjectivity, circumscribe her within the limits of her own nature. It is often said that she thinks with her glands. Man superbly ignores the fact that his anatomy also includes glands, such as the testicles, and that they secrete hormones. He thinks of his body as a direct and normal connection with the world, which he believes he apprehends objectively, whereas he regards the body of woman as a hindrance, a prison, weighed down by everything peculiar to it. "The female is a female by virtue of a certain lack of qualities," said Aristotle, "we should regard the female nature as afflicted with a natural defectiveness." And St Thomas for his part pronounced woman to be an "imperfect man," an "incidental" being. This is symbolized in Genesis where Eve is depicted as made from what Bossuet called "a supernumerary bone" of Adam.

Thus humanity is male and man defines woman not in herself but as relative to him; she is not regarded as an autonomous being. Michelet writes: "Woman, the relative being ..." And Benda is most positive in his *Rapport d'Uriel*: "The body of man makes sense in itself quite apart from that of woman, whereas the latter seems wanting in significance by itself ... Man can think of himself without woman. She cannot think of herself without man." And she is simply what man decrees, thus she is called "the sex," by which is meant that she appears essentially to the male as a sexual being. For him she is sex—absolute sex, no less she is defined and differentiated with reference to man and not he with reference to her; she is the incidental, the inessential as opposed to the essential. He is the Subject, he is the Absolute—she is the Other.

The category of the Other is as primordial as consciousness itself. In the most primitive societies, in the most ancient mythologies, one finds the expression of a duality—that of the Self and the Other. This duality was not originally attached to the division of the sexes; it was not dependent upon any empirical facts. It is revealed in such works as that of Granet on Chinese thought and those of Dumezil on the East Indies and Rome. The feminine element was at first no more involved in such pairs as Varuna-Mitra, Uranus-Zeus, Sun-Moon, and Day-Night than it was in the contrasts between Good and Evil, lucky and unlucky auspices, right and left, God and Lucifer. Otherness is a fundamental category of human thought.

Thus it is that no group ever sets itself up as the One without at once setting up the Other over against itself. If three travelers chance to occupy the same compartment, that is enough to make vaguely hostile "others" out of all the rest of the passengers on the train. In small-town eyes all persons not belonging to the village are "strangers" and suspect; to the native of a country all who inhabit other countries are "foreigners"; Jews are "different" for the anti-Semite, Negroes are "inferior" for American racists, aborigines are "natives" for colonists, proletarians are the "lower class" for the privileged.

Levi-Strauss, at the end of a profound work on the various forms of primitive societies, reaches the following conclusion: "Passage from the state of Nature to the state of Culture is marked by man's ability to view biological relations as a series of contrasts; duality, alternation, opposition, and symmetry, whether under definite or vague forms, constitute not so much phenomena to be explained as fundamental and immediately given data of social reality." These phenomena would be incomprehensible if in fact human society were simply a *Mitsein* or fellowship based on solidarity and friendliness. Things become dear; on the contrary, if, following Hegel, we find in consciousness itself a fundamental hostility towards every other consciousness; the subject can be posed only in being opposed—he sets himself up as the essential, as opposed to the other, the inessential, the object.

But the other consciousness, the other ego, sets up a reciprocal claim. The native travelling abroad is shocked to find himself in turn regarded as a "stranger" by the natives of neighbouring countries. As a matter of fact, wars, festivals, trading, treaties, and contests among tribes, nations, and classes tend to deprive the concept Other of its absolute sense and to make manifest its relativity; willy-nilly, individuals and groups are forced to realize the reciprocity of their relations. How is it, then, that this reciprocity has not been recognized between the sexes, that one of the contrasting terms is set up as the sole essential, denying any relativity in regard to its correlative and defining the latter as pure otherness? Why is it that women do not dispute male sovereignty? No subject will readily volunteer to become the object, the inessential; it is not the Other who, in defining himself as the Other, establishes the One. The Other is posed as such by the One in defining himself as the One. But if the Other is not to regain the status of being the One, he must be submissive enough to accept this alien point of view. Whence comes this submission in the case of woman?

There are, to be sure, other cases in which a certain category has been able to dominate another completely for a time. Very often this privilege depends upon inequality of numbers—the majority imposes its rule upon the minority or persecutes it. But women are not a minority, like the American Negroes or the Jews; there are as many women as men on earth. Again, the two groups concerned have often been originally independent; they may have been formerly unaware of each other's existence, or perhaps they recognized each other's autonomy. But a historical event has resulted in the subjugation of the weaker by the stronger. The scattering of the Jews, the introduction of slavery into America, the conquests of imperialism are examples in point. In these cases the oppressed retained at least the memory of former days; they possessed in common a past, a tradition, sometimes a religion or a culture.

The parallel drawn by Bebel between women and the proletariat is valid in that neither ever formed a minority or a separate collective unit of mankind. And instead of a single historical event it is in both cases a historical development that explains their status as a class and accounts for the membership of *particular individuals* in that class. But proletarians have not always existed, whereas there have always been women. They are women in virtue of their anatomy and physiology. Throughout history they have always been subordinated to men, and hence their dependency is not the result of a historical event or a social change—it was not something that occurred. The reason why otherness in this case seems to be an absolute is in part that it lacks the contingent or incidental nature of historical facts. A condition brought about at a certain time can be abolished at some other time, as the Negroes of Haiti and others have proved; but it might seem that natural condition is beyond the possibility of change. In truth, however. the nature of things is no more immutably given, once for all, than is historical reality. If woman seems to be the inessential which never becomes the essential, it is because she herself fails to bring about this change. Proletarians say "We"; Negroes also. Regarding themselves as subjects, they transform the bourgeois, the whites, into "Others." But women do not say "We," except at some congress of feminists or similar formal demonstration; men say

"Women," and women use the same word in referring to themselves. They do not authentically assume a subjective attitude. The proletarians have accomplished the revolution in Russia, the Negroes in Haiti, the Indo-Chinese are battling for it in Indo-China; but the women's effort has never been anything more than a symbolic agitation. They have gained only what men have been willing to grant, they have taken nothing, they have only received.

The reason for this is that women lack concrete means for organizing themselves into a unit which can stand face to face with the correlative unit. They have no past, no history, no religion of their own; and they have no such solidarity of work and interest as that of the proletariat. They are not even promiscuously herded together in the way that creates community feeling among the American Negroes, the ghetto Jews, the workers of Saint-Denis, or the factory hands of Renault. They live dispersed among the males, attached through residence, housework, economic condition, and social standing to certain men—fathers or husbands—more firmly than they are to other women. If they belong to the bourgeoisie, they feel solidarity with men of that class, not with proletarian women; if they are white, their allegiance is to white men, not to Negro women. The proletariat can propose to massacre the ruling class, and a sufficiently fanatical Jew or Negro might dream of getting sole possession of the atomic bomb and making humanity wholly Jewish or black; but woman cannot even dream of exterminating the males. The bond that unites her to her oppressors is not comparable to any other. The division of the sexes is a biological fact, not an event in human history. Male and female stand opposed within a primordial *Mitsein*, and woman has not broken it. The couple is a fundamental unity with its two halves riveted together, and the cleavage of society along the line of sex is impossible. Here is to be found the basic trait of woman: she is the Other in a totality of which the two components are necessary to one another.

One could suppose that this reciprocity might have facilitated the liberation of woman. When Hercules sat at the feet of Omphale and helped with her spinning, his desire for her held him captive; but why did she fail to gain a lasting power? To revenge herself on Jason, Medea killed their children; and this grim legend would seem to suggest that she might have obtained a formidable influence over him through his love for his offspring. In *Lysistrata* Aristophanes gaily depicts a band of women who joined forces to gain social ends through the sexual needs of their men; but this is only a play. In the legend of the Sabine women, the latter soon abandoned their plan of remaining sterile to punish their ravishers. In truth woman has not been socially emancipated through man's need—sexual desire and the desire for offspring—which makes the male dependent for satisfaction upon the female.

Master and slave, also, are united by a reciprocal need, in this case economic, which does not liberate the slave. In the relation of master to slave the master does not make a point of the need that he has for the other; he has in his grasp the power of satisfying this need through his own action; whereas the slave, in his dependent condition, his hope and fear, is quite conscious of the need he has for his master. Even if the need is at bottom equally urgent for both, it always works in favor of the oppressor and against the oppressed. That is why the liberation of the working class, for example, has been slow.

Now, woman has always been man's dependant, if not his slave; the two sexes have never shared the world in equality. And even today woman is heavily handicapped, though her situation is beginning to change. Almost nowhere is her legal status the same as man's, and frequently it is much to her disadvantage. Even when her rights are legally recognized in the abstract, long-standing custom prevents their full expression in the mores. In the economic sphere men and women can almost be said to make up two castes; other things being equal, the former hold the better jobs, get higher wages, and have more opportunity for success than their new competitors. In industry and politics men have a great many more positions and they monopolize the most important posts. In addition to all this, they enjoy a traditional prestige that the education of children tends in every way to support, for the present enshrines the past—and in the past all history has been made by men. At the present time, when women are beginning to take part in the affairs of the world, it is still a world that belongs to men—they have no doubt of it at all and women have scarcely any. To decline to be the Other, to refuse to be a party to the deal—this would be for women to renounce all the advantages conferred upon them by their alliance with the superior caste. Man-the-sovereign will provide woman-the-liege with material protection and will undertake the moral justification of her existence; thus she can evade at once both economic risk and the metaphysical risk of a liberty in which ends and aims must be contrived without assistance. Indeed, along with the ethical urge of each individual to affirm his subjective existence, there is also the temptation to forgo liberty and become a thing. This is an inauspicious road, for he who takes it—passive, lost, ruined becomes henceforth the creature of another's will, frustrated in his transcendence and deprived of every value. But it is an easy road; on it one avoids the strain involved in undertaking an authentic existence. When man makes of woman the Other, he may, then, expect to manifest deep-seated tendencies towards complicity. Thus, woman may fail to lay claim to the status of subject because she lacks definite resources, because she feels the necessary bond that ties her to man regardless of reciprocity, and because she is often very well pleased with her role as the Other.

But it will be asked at once: how did all this begin? It is easy to see that the duality of the sexes, like any duality, gives rise to conflict. And doubtless the winner will assume the status of absolute. But why should man have won from the start? It seems possible that women could have won the victory; or that the outcome of the conflict might never have been decided. How is it that this world has always belonged to the men and that things have begun to change only recently? Is this change a good thing? Will it bring about an equal sharing of the world between men and women?

These questions are not new, and they have often been answered. But the very fact that woman is the Other tends to cast suspicion upon all the justifications that men have ever been able to provide for it. These have all too evidently been dictated by men's interest. A little-known feminist of the seventeenth century, Poulain de la Barre, put it this way: "All that has been written about women by men should be suspect, for the men are at once judge and party to the lawsuit." Everywhere, at all times, the males have displayed their satisfaction in feeling that they are the lords of creation. "Blessed be God ... that He did not make me a woman," say the Jews in their morning prayers, while their wives pray on a note of resignation: "Blessed be the Lord, who created me according to His will." The first among the blessings for which Plato thanked the gods was that he had been created free, not enslaved; the second, a man, not a woman. But the males could not enjoy this privilege fully unless they believed it to be founded on the absolute and the eternal; they sought to make the fact of their supremacy into a right. "Being men, those who have made and compiled the laws have favored their own sex, and jurists have elevated these laws into principles," to quote Poulain de la Barre once more.

Legislators, priests, philosophers, writers, and scientists have striven to show that the subordinate position of woman is willed in heaven and advantageous on earth. The religions invented by men reflect this wish for domination. In the legends of Eve and Pandora men have taken up arms against women. They have made use of philosophy and theology, as the quotations from Aristotle and St Thomas have shown. Since ancient times satirists and moralists have delighted in showing up the weaknesses of women. We are familiar with the savage indictments hurled against women throughout French literature. Montherlant, for example, follows the tradition of Jean de Meung, though with less gusto. This hostility may at times be well founded, often it is gratuitous; but in truth it more or less successfully conceals a desire for self-justification. As Montaigne says, "It is easier to accuse one sex than to excuse the other." Sometimes what is going on is clear enough. For instance, the Roman law limiting the rights of woman cited "the imbecility, the instability of the sex" just when the weakening of family ties seemed to threaten the interests of male heirs. And in the effort to keep the married woman under guardianship, appeal was made in the sixteenth century to the authority of St Augustine, who declared that "woman is a creature neither decisive nor constant," at a time when the single woman was thought capable of managing her property. Montaigne understood clearly how arbitrary and unjust was woman's appointed lot: "Women are not in the wrong when they decline to accept the rules laid down for them, since the men make these rules without consulting them. No wonder intrigue and strife abound." But he did not go so far as to champion their cause.

It was only later, in the eighteenth century, that genuinely democratic men began to view the matter objectively. Diderot, among others, strove to show that woman is, like man, a human being. Later John Stuart Mill came fervently to her defense. But these philosophers displayed unusual impartiality. In the nineteenth century the feminist quarrel became again a quarrel of partisans. One of the consequences of the industrial revolution was the entrance of women into productive labor, and it was just here that the claims of the feminists emerged from the realm of theory and acquired an economic basis, while their opponents became the more aggressive. Although landed property lost power to some extent, the bourgeoisie clung to the old morality that found the guarantee of private property in the solidity of the family. Woman was ordered back into the home the more harshly as her emancipation became a real menace. Even within the working class the men endeavoured to restrain woman's liberation, because they began to see the women as dangerous competitors—the more so because they were accustomed to work for lower wages.

In proving woman's inferiority, the anti-feminists then began to draw not only upon religion, philosophy, and theology, as before, but also upon science—biology, experimental psychology, etc. At most they were willing to grant "equality in difference" to the other sex. That profitable formula is most significant; it is precisely like the "equal but separate" formula of the Jim Crow laws aimed at the North American Negroes. As is well known, this so-called equalitarian segregation has resulted only in the most extreme discrimination. The similarity just noted is in no way due to chance, for whether it is a race, a caste, a class, or a sex that is reduced to a position of inferiority, the methods of justification are the same. "The eternal feminine" corresponds to "the black soul" and to "the Jewish character." True, the Jewish problem is on the whole very different from the other two—to the anti-Semite the Jew is not so much an inferior as he is an enemy for whom there is to be granted no place on earth, for whom annihilation is the fate desired. But there are deep similarities between the situation of woman and that of the Negro. Both are being emancipated today from a like paternalism, and the former master class wishes to "keep them in their place"—that is, the place chosen for them. In both cases the former masters lavish more or less sincere eulogies, either on the virtues of "the good Negro" with his dormant, childish, merry soul—the submissive Negro—or on the merits of the woman who is "truly feminine"—that is, frivolous, infantile, irresponsible the submissive woman. In both cases the dominant class bases its argument on a state of affairs that it has itself created. As George Bernard Shaw puts it, in substance, "The American white relegates the black to the rank of shoeshine boy; and he concludes from this that the black is good for nothing but shining shoes." This vicious circle is met with in all analogous circumstances; when an individual (or a group of individuals) is kept in a situation of inferiority, the fact is that he is inferior. But the significance of the verb *be* must be rightly understood here; it is in bad faith to give it a static value when it really has the dynamic Hegelian sense of "to have become." Yes, women on the whole are today inferior to men; that is, their situation affords them fewer possibilities. The question is: should that state of affairs continue?

Many men hope that it will continue; not all have given up the battle. The conservative bourgeoisie still see in the emancipation of women a menace to their morality and their interests. Some men dread feminine competition. Recently a male student wrote in the Hebdo-Latin: "Every woman student who goes into medicine or law robs us of a job." He never questioned his rights in this world. And economic interests are not the only ones concerned. One of the benefits that oppression confers upon the oppressors is that the most humble among them is made to feel superior, thus, a "poor white" in the South can console himself with the thought that he is not a "dirty nigger"—and the more prosperous whites cleverly exploit this pride.

Similarly, the most mediocre of males feels himself a demigod as compared with women. It was much easier for M. de Montherlant to think himself a hero when he faced women (and women chosen for his purpose) than when he was obliged to act the man among men—something many women have done better than he, for that matter. And in September 1948, in one of his articles in the *Figaro littéraire*, Claude Mauriac—whose great originality is admired by all could write regarding woman: "*We* listen on a tone [*sic*!] of polite indifference ... to the most brilliant among them, well knowing that her wit reflects more or less luminously ideas that come from us." Evidently the speaker referred to is not reflecting the ideas of Mauriac himself, for no one knows of his having any.

It may be that she reflects ideas originating with men, but then, even among men there are those who have been known to appropriate ideas not their own; and one can well ask whether Claude Mauriac might not find more interesting a conversation reflecting Descartes, Marx, or Gide rather than himself. What is really remarkable is that by using the questionable "we" he identifies himself with St Paul, Hegel, Lenin, and Nietzsche, and from the lofty eminence of their grandeur looks down disdainfully upon the bevy of women who make bold to converse with him on a footing of equality. In truth, I know of more than one woman who would refuse to suffer with patience Mauriac's "tone of polite indifference."

I have lingered on this example because the masculine attitude is here displayed with disarming ingenuousness. But men profit in many more subtle ways from the otherness, the alterity of woman. Here is a miraculous balm for those afflicted with an inferiority complex, and indeed no one is more arrogant towards women, more aggressive or scornful, than the man who is anxious about his virility. Those who are not fear-ridden in the presence of their fellow men are much more disposed to recognize a fellow creature in woman, but even to these the myth of Woman, the Other, is precious for many reasons. They cannot be blamed for not cheerfully relinquishing all the benefits they derive from the myth, for they realize what they would lose in relinquishing woman as they fancy her to be, while they fail to realize what they have to gain from the woman of tomorrow. Refusal to pose oneself as the Subject, unique and absolute, requires great self-denial. Furthermore, the vast majority of men make no such claim explicitly. They do not postulate woman as inferior, for today they are too thoroughly imbued with the ideal of democracy not to recognize all human beings as equals.

In the bosom of the family, woman seems in the eyes of childhood and youth to be clothed in the same social dignity as the adult males. Later on, the young man, desiring and loving, experiences the resistance, the independence of the woman desired and loved; in marriage, he respects woman as wife and mother, and in the concrete events of conjugal life she stands there before him as a free being. He can therefore feel that social subordination as between the sexes no longer exists and that on the whole, in spite of differences, woman is an equal. As, however, he observes some points of inferiority—the most important being unfitness for the professions—he attributes these to natural causes. When he is in a co-operative and benevolent relation with woman, his theme is the principle of abstract equality, and he does not base his attitude upon such inequality as may exist. But when he is in conflict with her, the situation is reversed: his theme will be the existing inequality, and he will even take it as justification for denying abstract equality.

So it is that many men will affirm as if in good faith that women are the equals of man and that they have nothing to clamour for, while at the same time they will say that women can never be the equals of man and that their demands are in vain. It is, in point of fact, a difficult matter for man to realize the extreme importance of social discriminations which seem outwardly insignificant but which produce in woman moral and intellectual effects so profound that they appear to spring from her original nature. The most sympathetic of men never fully comprehend woman's concrete situation. And there is no reason to put much trust in the men when they rush to the defense of privileges whose full extent they can hardly measure. We shall not, then, permit ourselves to be intimidated by the number and violence of the attacks launched against women, nor to be entrapped by the self-seeking eulogies bestowed on the "true woman," nor to profit by the enthusiasm for woman's destiny manifested by men who would not for the world have any part of it.

We should consider the arguments of the feminists with no less suspicion, however, for very often their controversial aim deprives them of all real value. If the "woman question" seems trivial, it is because masculine arrogance has made of it a "quarrel"; and when quarrelling one no longer reasons well. People have tirelessly sought to prove that woman is superior, inferior, or equal to man. Some say that, having been created after Adam, she is evidently a secondary being: others say on the contrary that Adam was only a rough draft and that God succeeded in producing the human being in perfection when He created Eve. Woman's brain is smaller; yes, but it is relatively larger. Christ was made a man; yes, but perhaps for his greater humility. Each argument at once suggests its opposite, and both are often fallacious. If we are to gain understanding, we must get out of these ruts; we must discard the vague notions of superiority, inferiority, equality which have hitherto corrupted every discussion of the subject and start afresh.

Very well, but just how shall we pose the question? And, to begin with, who are we to propound it at all? Man is at once judge and party to the case; but so is woman. What we need is an angel neither man nor woman—but where shall we find one? Still, the angel would be poorly qualified to speak, for an angel is ignorant of all the basic facts involved in the problem. With a hermaphrodite we should be no better off, for here the situation is most peculiar; the hermaphrodite is not really the combination of a whole man and a whole woman, but consists of parts of each and thus is neither. It looks to me as if there are, after all, certain women who are best qualified to elucidate the situation of woman. Let us not be misled by the sophism that because Epimenides was a Cretan he was necessarily a liar; it is not a mysterious essence that compels men and women to act in good or in bad faith; it is their situation that inclines them more or less towards the search for truth. Many of today's women, fortunate in the restoration of all the privileges pertaining to the estate of the human being, can afford the luxury of impartiality—we even recognize its necessity. We are no longer like our partisan elders; by and large we have won the game. In recent debates on the status of women the United Nations has persistently maintained that the equality of the sexes is now becoming a reality, and already some of us have never had to sense in our femininity an inconvenience or an obstacle. Many problems appear to us to be more pressing than those which concern us in particular, and this detachment even allows us to hope that our attitude will be objective. Still, we know the feminine world more intimately than do the men because we have our roots in it, we grasp more immediately than do men what it means to a human being to be feminine, and we are more concerned with such knowledge. I have said that there are more pressing problems, but this does not prevent us from seeing some importance in asking how the fact of being women will affect our lives. What opportunities precisely have been given us and what withheld? What fate awaits our younger sisters, and what directions should they take? It is significant that books by women on women are in general animated in our day less by a wish to demand our rights than by an effort towards clarity and understanding. As we emerge from an era of excessive controversy, this book is offered as one attempt among others to confirm that statement.

But it is doubtless impossible to approach any human problem with a mind free from bias. The way in which questions are put, the points of view assumed, presuppose a relativity of interest; all characteristics imply values, and every objective description, so called, implies an ethical background. Rather than attempt to conceal principles more or less definitely implied, it is better to state them openly, at the beginning. This will make it unnecessary to specify on every page in just what sense one uses such words as superior, inferior, better, worse, progress, reaction, and the like. If we survey some of the works on woman, we note that one of the points of view most frequently adopted is that of the public good, the general interest, and one always means by this the benefit of society as one wishes it to be maintained or established. For our part, we hold that the only public good is that which assures the private good of the citizens; we shall pass judgment on institutions according to their effectiveness in giving concrete opportunities to individuals. But we do not confuse the idea of private interest with that of happiness, although that is another common point of view. Are not women of the harem more happy than women voters? Is not the housekeeper happier than the working-woman? It is not too clear just what the word happy really means and still less what true values it may mask. There is no possibility of measuring the happiness of others, and it is always easy to describe as happy the situation in which one wishes to place them.

In particular those who are condemned to stagnation are often pronounced happy on the pretext that happiness consists in being at rest. This notion we reject, for our perspective is that of existentialist ethics. Every subject plays his part as such specifically through exploits or projects that serve as a mode of transcendence; he achieves liberty only through a continual reaching out towards other liberties. There is no justification for present existence other than its expansion into an indefinitely open future. Every time transcendence falls back into immanence, stagnation, there is a degradation of existence into the "*en-sois*" — the brutish life of subjection to given conditions—and of liberty into constraint and contingence. This downfall represents a moral fault if the subject consents to it; if it is inflicted upon him, it spells frustration and oppression. In both cases it is an absolute evil. Every individual concerned to justify his existence feels that his existence involves an undefined need to transcend himself, to engage in freely chosen projects.

Now, what peculiarly signalizes the situation of woman is that she—a free and autonomous being like all human creatures—nevertheless finds herself living in a world where men compel her to assume the status of the Other. They propose to stabilize her as object and to doom her to immanence since her transcendence is to be overshadowed and forever transcended by another ego (conscience) which is essential and sovereign. The drama of woman lies in this conflict between the fundamental aspirations of every subject (ego) —who always regards the self as the essential and the compulsions of a situation in which she is the inessential. How can a human being in woman's situation attain fulfillment? What roads are open to her? Which are blocked? How can independence be recovered in a state of dependency? What circumstances limit woman's liberty and how can they be overcome? These are the fundamental questions on which I would fain throw some light. This means that I am interested in the fortunes of the individual as defined not in terms of happiness but in terms of liberty.

Quite evidently this problem would be without significance if we were to believe that woman's destiny is inevitably determined by physiological, psychological, or economic forces. Hence I shall discuss first of all the light in which woman is viewed by biology, psychoanalysis, and historical materialism. Next I shall try to show exactly how the concept of the "truly feminine" has been fashioned—why woman has been defined as the Other—and what have been the consequences from man's point of view. Then from woman's point of view I shall describe the world in which women must live, and thus we shall be able to envisage the difficulties in their way as, endeavoring to make their escape from the sphere hitherto assigned them, they aspire to full membership in the human race.

## Ⅲ Questions for Further Thinking

1. Please read the introduction and the excerpt, and explain what prompts Simone de Beauvoir to write this book?

2. When Beauvoir says that woman is "the Other," what does she want to convey?

3. Do you think the biological differences between men and women can explain the distinction of social performance between them?

4. Based on De Beauvoir's idea, what is the relationship between men and women? Are they partners or rivals?

5. In real life, people have different expectations of women and men in both social lives and personal development. Pick a few examples and elaborate them.

## Ⅳ Appreciation

Simone de Beauvoir's work *The Second Sex* (1949) is viewed as the Bible of women's education. To many women readers, this book brings them a shocking experience as to who they are. It is the first philosophical book which systematically narrates the history, mythologies, life stages, as well as women's identities in the economic and social institutions. One central idea De Beauvoir wants to convey is that gender is a socially constructed idea rather than a natural quality.

In reviewing the history of gender relationships, De Beauvoir points out that for centuries, women were put into the category of "the Other," in relation to man as "the Self." From ancient mythologies to modern social texts, women and men usually appear as dualities in relation, either in division of opposition or symmetry. As "the Other," women were the object affiliated to men, even though on most occasions, women and men were in reciprocal relationships. It is not easy for men, who are on the side of the beneficiary, to truly understand the disadvantages women experience in their lives. Equally, it is hard for women, who are in a position of being deprived of values, to renounce men for their frustrated existence. Due to this long history of gender duality that masculine arrogance came to be, which in turn, put women in an inferior position.

This is what De Beauvoir termed as "institutionalized gender bias." The gender duality destines women in passive roles, deprives them of their right as equal humans, and constrains them as subordinates to men. If masculinity represents positive qualities, femininity thus is granted the negative features. The result is that women are denied the opportunities to gain intellectual and moral pursuits. As such, the biases towards women are real. Women's lives are considered to be inferior, passive, and trivial.

We are glad to find that after more than half a century, some aspects discussed in *The Second Sex* have been improved. For example, intellectually, women are now generally considered equal with men. However, other problems like the masculine arrogance towards women persist even today, like the masculine arrogance towards women. For many readers, *The Second Sex* can still provide very good explanations to understand why physically, women are more sentimental as well as why socially, they might encounter more obstacles. The proliferation of feminist movements around the world is certainly encouraging to women in their continuous pursuit to become equals to their male counterparts.

## Ⅴ Writing Topic

作为影响西方女性主义第二波浪潮的代表性作品,《第二性》(*The Second Sex*)中所体现的内容是否与当下的女性生存现状有对照性？试讨论和分析中西方女性的生存现状中的进步和改变。

# Unit 2 *A Room of One's Own* by Virginia Woolf

## Ⅰ Introduction to the Author and the Work

Virginia Woolf (1882 –1941) is an English writer whose novels, through their nonlinear approaches to narrative, exert a major influence on the genre of modernism. She was raised in a remarkable household. Her father, Sir Leslie Stephen, was a historian and an author, as well as one of the most prominent figures in the golden age of mountaineering. Woolf's mother had been born in India and later served as a model for several Pre-Raphaelite painters. She was also a nurse and wrote a book on the profession. Both of her parents had been married and widowed before marrying each other.

Woolf wrote pioneering essays on artistic theory, literary history, women's writing, and political power. As a fine stylist, she experimented with several forms of biographical writing, composed painterly short fictions, and sent to her friends and family a lifetime of brilliant letters. Woolf was also a founding member of the intellectual circle known as the Bloomsbury Intellectual Group. Her most famous works include *Mrs. Dalloway* (1925), *To the Lighthouse* (1927), and *A Room of One's Own* (1929).

*A Room of One's Own* is a non-fiction essay first published in 1929. The essay was based on a series of lectures she delivered at the Newnham College and the Girton College, two women's colleges at the University of Cambridge. It employs a fictional narrator to explore women both as writers of and characters in fiction. The essay is generally seen as a feminist text and is noted in its argument for both a literal and figurative space for women writers within a literary tradition dominated by patriarchy.

# Ⅱ *A Room of One's Own* (Excerpt)

## Chapter Three

It was disappointing not to have brought back in the evening some important statement, some authentic fact. Women are poorer than men because—this or that. Perhaps now it would be better to give up seeking for the truth, and receiving on one's head an avalanche of opinion hot as lava, discolored as dishwater. It would be better to draw the curtains, to shut out distractions, to light the lamp, to narrow the enquiry and to ask the historian, who records not opinions but facts, to describe under what conditions women lived, not throughout the ages, but in England, say, in the time of Elizabeth.

For it is a perennial puzzle why no woman wrote a word of that extraordinary literature when every other man, it seemed, was capable of song or sonnet. What were the conditions in which women lived? I asked myself; for fiction, imaginative work that is, is not dropped like a pebble upon the ground, as science may be; fiction is like a spider's web, attached ever so lightly perhaps, but still attached to life at all four corners. Often the attachment is scarcely perceptible; Shakespeare's plays, for instance, seem to hang there complete by themselves. But when the web is pulled askew, hooked up at the edge, torn in the middle, one remembers that these webs are not spun in mid-air by incorporeal creatures, but are the work of suffering human beings, and are attached to grossly material things, like health and money and the houses we live in.

I went, therefore, to the shelf where the histories stand and took down one of the latest, Professor Trevelyan's *History of England*. Once more I looked up Women, found "position of" and turned to the pages indicated. "Wife-beating," I read, "was a recognized right of man, and was practiced without shame by high as well as low ... Similarly ..." The historian goes on, "The daughter who refused to marry the gentleman of her parents' choice was liable to be locked up, beaten and flung about the room, without any shock being inflicted on public opinion.

Marriage was not an affair of personal affection, but of family avarice, particularly in the 'chivalrous' upper classes ... Betrothal often took place while one or both of the parties was in the cradle, and marriage when they were scarcely out of the nurses' charge." That was about 1470, soon after Chaucer's time. The next reference to the position of women is some two hundred years later, in the time of the Stuarts. "It was still the exception for women of the upper and middle class to choose their own husbands, and when the husband had been assigned, he was lord and master, so far at least as law and custom could make him. Yet even so," Professor Trevelyan concludes, "neither Shakespeare's women nor those of authentic seventeenth-century memoirs, like the Verneys and the Hutchinsons, seem wanting in personality and character." Certainly, if we consider it, Cleopatra must have had a way with her; Lady Macbeth, one would suppose, had a will of her own; Rosalind, one might conclude, was an attractive girl. Professor Trevelyan is speaking no more than the truth when he remarks that Shakespeare's women do not seem wanting in personality and character. Not being a historian, one might go even further and say that women have burnt like beacons in all the works of all the poets from the beginning of time—Clytemnestra, Antigone, Cleopatra, Lady Macbeth, Phedre, Cressida, Rosalind, Desdemona, the Duchess of Malfi, among the dramatists; then among the prose writers: Millamant, Clarissa, Becky Sharp, Anna Karenina, Emma Bovary, Madame de Guermantes—the names flock to mind, nor do they recall women "lacking in personality and character." Indeed, if woman had no existence save in the fiction written by men, one would imagine her a person of the utmost importance; very various; heroic and mean; splendid and sordid; infinitely beautiful and hideous in the extreme; as great as a man, some think even greater.[1] But this is woman in fiction. In fact, as Professor Trevelyan pointed out, she was locked up, beaten and flung about the room.

A very queer, composite being thus emerges. Imaginatively she is of the highest importance; practically she is completely insignificant. She pervades poetry from cover to cover; she is all but absent from history. She dominates the lives of kings and conquerors in fiction; in fact she was the slave of any boy whose parents forced a ring upon her finger. Some of the most inspired words, some of the most profound thoughts in literature fall from her lips; in real life she could hardly read, could scarcely spell, and was the property of her husband.

It was certainly an odd monster that one made up by reading the historians first and the poets afterwards a worm winged like an eagle; the spirit of life and beauty in a kitchen chopping up suet. But these monsters, however amusing to the imagination, have no existence in fact. What one must do to bring her to life was to think poetically and prosaically at one and the same moment, thus keeping in touch with fact—that she is Mrs Martin, aged thirty-six, dressed in blue, wearing a black hat and brown shoes; but not losing sight of fiction either—that she is a vessel in which all sorts of spirits and forces are coursing and flashing perpetually. The moment, however, that one tries this method with the Elizabethan woman, one branch of illumination fails; one is held up by the scarcity of facts. One knows nothing detailed, nothing perfectly true and substantial about her. History scarcely mentions her. And I turned to Professor

---

① "It remains a strange and almost inexplicable fact that in Athena's city, where women were kept in almost Oriental suppression as odalisques or drudges, the stage should yet have produced figures like Clytemnestra and Cassandra Atossa and Antigone, Phedre and Medea, and all the other heroines who dominate play after play of the "misogynist" Euripides. But the paradox of this world where in real life a respectable woman could hardly show her face alone in the street, and yet on the stage woman equals or surpasses man, has never been satisfactorily explained. In modern tragedy the same predominance exists. At all events, a very cursory survey of Shakespeare's work (similarly with Webster, though not with Marlowe or Jonson) suffices to reveal how this dominance, this initiative of women, persists from Rosalind to Lady Macbeth. So too in Racine; six of his tragedies bear their heroines' names; and what male characters of his shall we set against Hermione and Andromaque, Berenice and Roxane, Phedre and Athalie? So again with Ibsen; what men shall we match with Solveig and Nora, Heda and Hilda Wangel and Rebecca West?" Qtd. in F. L. Lucas, *Tragedy, Serious Drama in Relation to Aristotle's "Poetics"*. London: Hogarth Press, 1928, pp. 114-115.

Trevelyan again to see what history meant to him. I found by looking at his chapter headings that it meant— "The Manor Court and the Methods of Open-field Agriculture ... The Cistercians and Sheep-farming ... The Crusades ... The University ... The House of Commons ... The Hundred Years' War ... The Wars of the Roses ... The Renaissance Scholars ... The Dissolution of the Monasteries ... Agrarian and Religious Strife ... The Origin of English Sea-power ... The Armada ... " and so on. Occasionally an individual woman is mentioned, an Elizabeth, or a Mary; a queen or a great lady. But by no possible means could middle-class women with nothing but brains and character at their command have taken part in any one of the great movements which, brought together, constitute the historian's view of the past. Nor shall we find her in collection of anecdotes. Aubrey hardly mentions her. She never writes her own life and scarcely keeps a diary; there are only a handful of her letters in existence. She left no plays or poems by which we can judge her. What one wants, I thought—and why does not some brilliant student at Newnham or Girton supply it—is a mass of information: at what age did she marry; how many children had she as a rule; what was her house like, had she a room to herself; did she do the cooking; would she be likely to have a servant? All these facts lie somewhere, presumably, in parish registers and account books; the life of the average Elizabethan woman must be scattered about somewhere, could one collect it and make a book of it. It would be ambitious beyond my daring, I thought, looking about the shelves for books that were not there, to suggest to the students of those famous colleges that they should rewrite history, though I own that it often seems a little queer as it is, unreal, lop-sided; but why should they not add a supplement to history, calling it, of course, by some in conspicuous name so that women might figure there without impropriety? For one often catches a glimpse of them in the lives of the great, whisking away into the back ground, concealing, I sometimes think, a wink, a laugh, perhaps a tear. And, after all, we have lives enough of Jane Austen; it scarcely seems necessary to consider again the influence of the tragedies of Joanna Baillie upon the poetry of Edgar Allan Poe; as for myself, I should not mind if the homes and haunts of Mary Russell Mitford were closed to the public for a century at least. But what I find deplorable, I continued, looking about the bookshelves again, is that nothing is known about women before the eighteenth century. I have no model in my mind to turn about this way and that. Here am I asking why women did not write poetry in the Elizabethan age, and I am not sure how they were educated; whether they were taught to write; whether they had sitting-rooms to themselves; how many women had children before they were twenty-one; what, in short, they did from eight in the morning till eight at night. They had no money evidently; according to Professor Trevelyan they were married whether they liked it or not before they were out of the nursery, at fifteen or sixteen very likely. It would have been extremely odd, even upon this showing, had one of them suddenly written the plays of Shakespeare, I concluded, and I thought of that old gentleman, who is dead now, but was a bishop, I think, who declared that it was impossible for any woman, past, present, or to come, to have the genius of Shakespeare. He wrote to the papers about it. He also told a lady who applied to him for information that cats do not as a matter of fact go to heaven, though they have, he added, souls of a sort. How much thinking those old gentlemen used to save one! How the borders of ignorance shrank back at their approach! Cats do not go to heaven. Women cannot write the plays of Shakespeare.

Be that as it may, I could not help thinking, as I looked at the works of Shakespeare on the shelf, that the bishop was right at least in this; it would have been impossible, completely and entirely, for any woman to have written the plays of Shakespeare in the age of Shakespeare. Let me imagine, since facts are so hard to come by, what would have happened had Shakespeare had a wonderfully gifted sister, called Judith, let us say. Shakespeare himself went, very probably—his mother was an heiress—to the grammar school, where he may have learnt Latin—Ovid, Virgil and Horace—and the elements of grammar and logic. He was, it is well known, a wild boy who poached rabbits, perhaps shot a deer, and had, rather sooner than he should have done, to marry a woman in the neighborhood, who bore him a child rather quicker than was right. That escapade sent him to seek his fortune in London. He had, it seemed, a taste for the theatre; he began by holding horses at the stage door. Very soon he got work in the theatre, became a successful actor, and lived at the hub of the universe, meeting everybody, knowing everybody, practicing his art on the boards, exercising his wits in the streets, and even getting access to the palace of the queen. Meanwhile his extraordinarily gifted sister, let us suppose, remained at home. She was as adventurous, as imaginative, as agog to see the world as he was. But she was not sent to school. She had no chance of learning grammar and logic, let alone of reading Horace and Virgil. She picked up a book now and then, one of her brother's perhaps, and read a few pages. But then her parents came in and told her to mend the stockings or mind the stew and not moon about with books and papers. They would have spoken sharply but kindly, for they were substantial people who knew the conditions of life for a woman and loved their daughter—indeed, more likely than not she was the apple of her father's eye. Perhaps she scribbled some pages up in an apple loft on the sly but was careful to hide them or set fire to them. Soon, however, before she was out of her teens, she was to be betrothed to the son of a neighbouring wool-stapler. She cried out that marriage was hateful to her, and for that she was severely beaten by her father. Then he ceased to scold her. He begged her instead not to hurt him, not to shame him in this matter of her marriage. He would give her a chain of beads or a fine petticoat, he said; and there were tears in his eyes. How could she disobey him? How could she break his heart? The force of her own gift alone drove her to it. She made up a small parcel of her belongings, let herself down by a rope one summer's night and took the road to London. She was not seventeen. The birds that sang in the hedge were not more musical than she was. She had the quickest fancy, a gift like her brother's, for the tune of words. Like him, she had a taste for the theatre. She stood at the stage door; she wanted to act, she said. Men laughed in her face. The manager—a fat, loose-lipped man—guffawed. He bellowed something about poodles dancing and women acting—no woman, he said, could possibly be an actress. He hinted—you can imagine what. She could get no training in her craft. Could she even seek her dinner in a tavern or roam the streets at midnight? Yet her genius was for fiction and lusted to feed abundantly upon the lives of men and women and the study of their ways. At last—for she was very young, oddly like Shakespeare the poet in her face, with the same grey eyes and rounded brows—at last Nick Greene the actor manager took pity on her; she found herself with child by that gentleman and so—who shall measure the heat and violence of the poet's heart when caught and tangled in a woman's body—killed herself one winter's night and lies buried at some cross-roads where the omnibuses now stop outside the Elephant and Castle.

That, more or less, is how the story would run, I think, if a woman in Shakespeare's day had had Shakespeare's genius. But for my part, I agree with the deceased bishop, if such he was—it is unthinkable that any woman in Shakespeare's day should have had Shakespeare's genius. For genius like Shakespeare's is not born among laboring, uneducated, servile people. It was not born in England among the Saxons and the Britons. It is not born today among the working classes. How, then, could it have been born among women whose work began, according to Professor Trevelyan, almost before they were out of the nursery, who were forced to it by their parents and held to it by all the power of law and custom? Yet genius of a sort must have existed among women as it must have existed among the working classes. Now and again an Emily Brontë or a Robert Burns blazes out and proves its presence. But certainly it never got itself on to paper. When, however, one reads of a witch being ducked, of a woman possessed by devils, of a wise woman selling herbs, or even of a very remarkable man who had a mother, then I think we are on the track of a lost novelist, a suppressed poet, of some mute and inglorious Jane Austen, some Emily Brontë who dashed her brains out on the moor or mopped and mowed about the highways crazed with the torture that her gift had put her to. Indeed, I would venture to guess that Anon, who wrote so many poems without singing them, was often a woman. It was a woman Edward Fitzgerald, I think, suggested who made the ballads and the folk-songs, crooning them to her children, beguiling her spinning with them, or the length of the winter's night.

This may be true or it may be false—who can say—but what is true in it, so it seemed to me, reviewing the story of Shakespeare's sister as I had made it, is that any woman born with a great gift in the sixteenth century would certainly have gone crazed, shot herself, or ended her days in some lonely cottage outside the village, half witch, half wizard, feared and mocked at. For it needs little skill in psychology to be sure that a highly gifted girl who had tried to use her gift for poetry would have been so thwarted and hindered by other people, so tortured and pulled asunder by her own contrary instincts, that she must have lost her health and sanity to a certainty. No girl could have walked to London and stood at a stage door and forced her way into the presence of actor—managers without doing herself a violence and suffering an anguish which may have been irrational—for chastity may be a fetish invented by certain societies for unknown reasons—but were none the less inevitable. Chastity had then, it has even now, a religious importance in a woman's life, and has so wrapped itself round with nerves and instincts that to cut it free and bring it to the light of day demands courage of the rarest. To have lived a free life in London in the sixteenth century would have meant for a woman who was poet and playwright a nervous stress and dilemma which might well have killed her. Had she survived, whatever she had written would have been twisted and deformed, issuing from a strained and morbid imagination. And undoubtedly, I thought, looking at the shelf where there are no plays by women, her work would have gone unsigned. That refuge she would have sought certainly. It was the relic of the sense of chastity that dictated anonymity to women even so late as the nineteenth century. Currer Bell, George Eliot, George Sand, all the victims of inner strife as their writings prove, sought ineffectively to veil themselves by using the name of a man. Thus they did homage to the convention, which if not implanted by the other sex was liberally encouraged by them (the chief glory of a woman is not to be talked of, said Pericles, himself a much-talked-of-man) that publicity in women is detestable. Anonymity runs in their blood. The desire to be veiled still possesses them. They are not even now as concerned about the health of their fame as men are, and, speaking generally, will pass a tombstone or a signpost without feeling an irresistible desire to cut their names on it, as Alf, Bert or Chas, must do in obedience to their instinct, which murmurs if it sees a fine woman go by, or even a dog, Ce chien est a moi. And, of course, it may not be a dog, I thought, remembering Parliament Square, the Sieges Allee and other avenues; it may be a piece of land or a man with curly black hair. It is one of the great advantages of being a woman that one can pass even a very fine negress without wishing to make an Englishwoman of her.

That woman, then, who was born with a gift of poetry in the sixteenth century, was an unhappy woman, a woman at strife against herself. All the conditions of her life, all her own instincts, were hostile to the state of mind which is needed to set free whatever is in the brain. But what is the state of mind that is most propitious to the act of creation? I asked. Can one come by any notion of the state that furthers and makes possible that strange activity? Here I opened the volume containing the tragedies of Shakespeare. What was Shakespeare's state of mind, for instance, when he wrote *Lear* and *Antony and Cleopatra*? It was certainly the state of mind most favourable to poetry that there has ever existed. But Shakespeare himself said nothing about it. We only know casually and by chance that he "never blotted a line." Nothing indeed was ever said by the artist himself about his state of mind until the eighteenth century perhaps. Rousseau perhaps began it. At any rate, by the nineteenth century self-consciousness had developed so far that it was the habit for men of letters to describe their minds in confessions and autobiographies. Their lives also were written, and their letters were printed after their deaths. Thus, though we do not know what Shakespeare went through when he wrote *Lear*, we do know what Carlyle went through when he wrote the *French Revolution*; what Flaubert went through when he wrote *Madame Bovary*; what Keats was going through when he tried to write poetry against the coming death and the indifference of the world.

And one gathers from this enormous modern literature of confession and self-analysis that to write a work of genius is almost always a feat of prodigious difficulty. Everything is against the likelihood that it will come from the writer's mind whole and entire. Generally material circumstances are against it. Dogs will bark; people will interrupt; money must be made; health will break down. Further, accentuating all these difficulties and making them harder to bear is the world's notorious indifference. It does not ask people to write poems and novels and histories; it does not need them. It does not care whether Flaubert finds the right word or whether Carlyle scrupulously verifies this or that fact. Naturally, it will not pay for what it does not want. And so the writer, Keats, Flaubert, Carlyle, suffers, especially in the creative years of youth, every form of distraction and discouragement. A curse, a cry of agony, rises from those books of analysis and confession. "Mighty poets in their misery dead"—that is the burden of their song. if anything comes through in spite of all this, it is a miracle, and probably no book is born entire and uncroppled as it was conceived.

But for women, I thought, looking at the empty shelves, these difficulties were infinitely more formidable. In the first place, to have a room of her own, let alone a quiet room or a soundproof room, was out of the question, unless her parents were exceptionally rich or very noble, even up to the beginning of the nineteenth century. Since her pin money, which depended on the goodwill of her father, was only enough to keep her clothed, she was debarred from such alleviations as came even to Keats or Tennyson or Carlyle, all poor men, from a walking tour, a little journey to France, from the separate lodging which, even if it were miserable enough, sheltered them from the claims and tyrannies of their families. Such material difficulties were formidable, but much worse were the immaterial. The indifference of the world which Keats and Flaubert and other men of genius have found so hard to bear was in her case not indifference but hostility. The world did not say to her as it said to them, Write if you choose; it makes no difference to me. The world said with a guffaw, Write? What's the good of your writing? Here the psychologists of Newnham and Girton might come to our help, I thought, looking again at the blank spaces on the shelves. For surely it is time that the effect of discouragement upon the mind of the artist should be measured, as I have seen a dairy company measure the effect of ordinary milk and Grade A milk upon the body of the rat. They set two rats in cages side by side, and of the two one was furtive, timid and small, and the other was glossy, bold and big. Now what food do we feed women as artists upon? I asked, remembering, I suppose, that dinner of prunes and custard. To answer that question I had only to open the evening paper and to read that Lord Birkenhead is of opinion—but really I am not going to trouble to copy out Lord Birkenhead's opinion upon the writing of women. What Dean Inge says I will leave in peace. The Harley Street specialist may be allowed to rouse the echoes of Harley Street with his vociferations without raising a hair on my head. I will quote, however, Mr. Oscar Browning, because Mr. Oscar Browning was a great figure in Cambridge at one time, and used to examine the students at

Girton and Newnham. Mr. Oscar Browning was wont to declare "that the impression left on his mind, after looking over any set of examination papers, was that, irrespective of the marks he might give, the best woman was intellectually the inferior of the worst man." After saying that Mr. Browning went back to his rooms—and it is this sequel that endears him and makes him a human figure of some bulk and majesty—he went back to his rooms and found a stable—boy lying on the sofa—a mere skeleton, his cheeks were cavernous and sallow, his teeth were black, and he did not appear to have the full use of his limbs. "That's Arthur." (said Mr. Browning.) "He's a dear boy really and most high-minded. The two pictures always seem to me to complete each other. And happily in this age of biography the two pictures often do complete each other, so that we are able to interpret the opinions of great men not only by what they say, but by what they do.

But though this is possible now, such opinions coming from the lips of important people must have been formidable enough even fifty years ago. Let us suppose that a father from the highest motives did not wish his daughter to leave home and become writer, painter or scholar. "See what Mr. Oscar Browning says," he would say; and there so was not only Mr. Oscar Browning; there was the *Saturday Review*; there was Mr. Greg—the "essentials of a woman's being," said Mr Greg emphatically, "are that 'THEY ARE SUPPORTED BY, AND THEY MINISTER TO, MEN'"—there was an enormous body of masculine opinion to the effect that nothing could be expected of women intellectually. Even if her father did not read out loud these opinions, any girl could read them for herself; and the reading, even in the nineteenth century, must have lowered her vitality, and told profoundly upon her work. There would always have been that assertion—you cannot do this, you are incapable of doing that—to protest against, to overcome. Probably for a novelist this germ is no longer of much effect; for there have been women novelists of merit. But for painters it must still have some sting in it; and for musicians, I imagine, is even now active and poisonous in the extreme. The woman composer stands where the actress stood in the time of Shakespeare. Nick Greene, I thought, remembering the story I had made about Shakespeare's sister, said that a woman acting put him in mind of a dog dancing. Johnson repeated the phrase two hundred years later of women preaching. And here, I said, opening a book about music, we have the very words used again in this year of grace, 1928, of women who try to write music. "Of Mlle Germaine Tailleferre one can only repeat Dr. Johnson's dictum concerning, a woman preacher, transposed into terms of music. "Sir, a woman's composing is like a dog's walking on his hind legs. It is not done well, but you are surprised to find it done at all."① So accurately does history repeat itself.

Thus, I concluded, shutting Mr. Oscar Browning's life and pushing away the rest, it is fairly evident that even in the nineteenth century a woman was not encouraged to be an artist. On the contrary, she was snubbed, slapped, lectured and exhorted. Her mind must have been strained and her vitality lowered by the need of opposing this, of disproving that. For here again we come within range of that very interesting and obscure masculine complex which has had so much influence upon the woman's movement; that deep-seated desire, not so much that "SHE" shall be inferior as that "HE" shall be superior, which plants him wherever one looks, not only in front of the arts, but barring the way to politics too, even when the risk to himself seems infinitesimal and the suppliant humble and devoted. Even Lady Bessborough, I remembered, with all her passion for politics, must humbly bow herself and write to Lord Granville Leveson-Gower: "... not withstanding all my violence in politics and talking so much on that subject, I perfectly agree with you that no woman has any business to meddle with that or any other serious business, farther than giving her opinion (if she is asked)." And so she goes on to spend her enthusiasm where it meets with no obstacle whatsoever, upon that immensely important subject, Lord Granville's maiden speech in the House of Commons. The spectacle is certainly a strange one, I thought. The history of men's opposition to women's emancipation is more interesting perhaps than the story of that emancipation itself. An amusing book might be made of it if some young student at Girton or Newnham would collect examples and deduce a theory—but she would need thick gloves on her hands, and bars to protect her of solid gold.

---

① Cecil Gray, *A Survey of Contemporary Music*. London: Oxford University Press, p. 246.

But what is amusing now, I recollected, shutting Lady Bessborough, had to be taken in desperate earnest once. Opinions that one now pastes in a book labelled cock-a-doodle-dum and keeps for reading to select audiences on summer nights once drew tears, I can assure you. Among your grandmothers and great—grandmothers there were many that wept their eyes out. Florence Nightingale shrieked aloud in her agony.① Moreover, it is all very well for you, who have got yourselves to college and enjoy sitting-rooms—or is it only bed-sitting-rooms—of your own to say that genius should disregard such opinions; that genius should be above caring what is said of it. Unfortunately, it is precisely the men or women of genius who mind most what is said of them. Remember Keats. Remember the words he had cut on his tombstone. Think of Tennyson; think but I need hardly multiply instances of the undeniable, if very fortunate, fact that it is the nature of the artist to mind excessively what is said about him. Literature is strewn with the wreckage of men who have minded beyond reason the opinions of others.

And this susceptibility of theirs is doubly unfortunate, I thought, returning again to my original enquiry into what state of mind is most propitious for creative work, because the mind of an artist, in order to achieve the prodigious effort of freeing whole and entire the work that is in him, must be incandescent, like Shakespeare's mind, I conjectured, looking at the book which lay open at *Aatony and Cleopatra*. There must be no obstacle in it, no foreign matter unconsumed.

For though we say that we know nothing about Shakespeare's state of mind, even as we say that, we are saying something about Shakespeare's state of mind. The reason perhaps why we know so little of Shakespeare—compared with Donne or Ben Jonson or Milton—is that his grudges and spites and antipathies are hidden from us. We are not held up by some "revelation" which reminds us of the writer. All desire to protest, to preach, to proclaim an injury, to pay off a score, to make the world the witness of some hardship or grievance was fired out of him and consumed. Therefore his poetry flows from him free and unimpeded. If

① See Florence Nightingale, "Cassandra," in R. Strachey, *A Short History of the Women's Movement in Great Britain*. S. L.: s. n.

ever a human being got his work expressed completely, it was Shakespeare. If ever a mind was incandescent, unimpeded, I thought, turning again to the bookcase, it was Shakespeare's mind.

## Ⅲ Questions for Further Thinking

1. Based on your reading, what were the obstacles that stopped women from engaging in creative works, such as writing?

2. According to Virginia Woolf, what were the lives of women like in the sixteenth century?

3. Why was it impossible to have a gifted woman such as an imagined Shakespeare's sister in the sixteenth century?

4. How about women's lives in the nineteenth century? Was there any progress as to women's engagement in creative works?

5. Why does Virginia Woolf claim that "it is necessary to have five hundred pounds a year and a room with a lock on the door if you are to write fiction or poetry"?

## Ⅳ Appreciation

One of the most famous claims made by Virginia Woolf as to how a woman before the nineteenth century could fulfill her dream of writing is that "it is necessary to have five hundred pounds a year and a room with a lock on the door if you are to write fiction or poetry." As a writer and a core figure in Bloomsbury Intellectual Group, Woolf herself was afflicted by the hostile attitude that surrounded her which lasted until her death. In Chapter Three, Woolf illustrated that, from the sixteenth century to the nineteenth century, how the social obstacles stopped gifted women from engaging into creative works. She explained that although the images of women often appeared on pages and in practical life, women in the sixteenth century were in general unable to read and write. A woman of her time usually got married at a very young age and was treated as the property of her husband. She then explained why it was impossible for any woman to have written plays like Shakespeare did, even if she was Shakespeare's sister. Woolf revealed the hostile social convention which stopped the development of women's intellectual activities. She suggested that the denial of women's intelligence might trap a gifted woman "at strife against herself", while the defamation of a woman's moral name in connection with her reading and writing would further discourage her from engaging in any creative works. In a word, the underrepresentation or the lack of woman authors at Woolf's time (or another period) was caused by men's opposition to women's intellectual activities.

## Ⅴ Writing Topic

弗吉尼亚·伍尔夫在文中提到,19世纪末,英国社会对女性从事写作抱有敌视的态度。她举了两个事例:一是奥斯卡·王尔德的言辞,即"the best woman was intellectually the inferior of the worst man";二是女性在智力上低于男性的观点影响了热心参与社会活动的女性,例如,巴萨波尔夫人所说的"no woman has any business to meddle with that or any other serious business, farther than giving her opinion (if she is asked)"。这种观念直到今天还有影响,请举例说明。

# Unit 3 "The Yellow Wallpaper" by Charlotte Perkins Gilman

## Ⅰ Introduction to the Author and the Work

Charlotte Perkins Gilman (1860−1935), is a prominent American, writer of short stories, poetry, non-fiction, and a lecturer for social reform. Her best remembered work is her semi-autobiographical short story, "The Yellow Wallpaper," which she wrote after a severe bout of post-partum depression. She served as a role model for future generations of feminists because of her unconventional concepts.

While she is best known for her fiction, Gilman is also a successful lecturer and intellectual. One of her greatest works of non-fiction, *Women and Economics*, was published in 1898. As a feminist, she called for women to gain economic independence, and the work helped cement her standing as a social theorist. It was even used as a textbook at one time. Other important non-fiction works followed, such as *The Home: Its Work and Influence* (1903) and *Does a Man Support His Wife?* (1915). Along with writing books, Gilman established *The Forerunner*, a magazine that allowed her to express her ideas on women's issues and on social reform.

"The Yellow Wallpaper" is regarded as an important early work of American feminist literature, illustrating attitudes in the 19th century toward women's physical and mental health. Presented in the first person, a woman (Jane) is confined by her physician husband (John) to the upstairs bedroom of a house he has rented for the summer. She is forbidden from working, including writing her diary, so she can recuperate from what he calls a "temporary nervous depression," a diagnosis common to women in that period.

More than merely a narrative of female intellectual oppression or a critique of late 19th century social mores, "The Yellow Wallpaper" documented a practice that was common among the middle and upper class at that time. Known as the "rest cure," women who displayed signs of depression or anxiety were committed to lying in bed for weeks at a time, and allowed no more than 20 minutes of intellectual exertion a day. Believing that intellectual activity would overwhelm the fragile female mind, "rest cure" referred to the prevention of women from thinking, relying on the assumption that the natural state of the female mind was one of emptiness. Seeing as how women were confined to empty rooms with no exercise or stimulation of any kind, the obvious consequence was that women became more anxious, which reinforced the convictions of the doctors and husbands that their wives needed further rest. The "rest cure" was prescribed most commonly to women who had recently given birth. Suffering from what we now know is post-partum depression, women were locked up and kept from seeing their newly born children. Gilman's book, therefore, is not only an American literary classic, but also provides insight into America's social history.

## Ⅱ The Yellow Wallpaper①

It is very seldom that mere ordinary people like John and myself secure ancestral halls for the summer.

A colonial mansion, a hereditary estate, I would say a haunted house, and reach the height of romantic felicity—but that would be asking too much of fate!

Still I will proudly declare that there is something queer about it.

Else, why should it be let so cheaply? And why have stood so long untenanted?

John laughs at me, of course, but one expects that in marriage.

John is practical in the extreme. He has no patience with faith, an intense horror of superstition, and he scoffs openly at any talk of things not to be felt and seen and put down in figures.

John is a physician, and perhaps (I would not say it to a living soul, of

① https://www.owleyes.org/text/yellow-wallpaper/read/yellow-wallpaper#root-422327-1.

course, but this is dead paper and a great relief to my mind), perhaps that is one reason I do not get well faster.

You see he does not believe I am sick!

And what can one do?

If a physician of high standing, and one's own husband, assures friends and relatives that there is really nothing the matter with one but temporary nervous depression—a slight hysterical tendency—what is one to do?

My brother is also a physician, and also of high standing, and he says the same thing.

So I take phosphates or phosphites—whichever it is, and tonics, and journeys, and air, and exercise, and am absolutely forbidden to "work" until I am well again.

Personally, I disagree with their ideas.

Personally, I believe that congenial work, with excitement and change, would do me good.

But what is one to do?

I did write for a while in spite of them; but it does exhaust me a good deal—having to be so sly about it, or else meet with heavy opposition.

I sometimes fancy that in my condition if I had less opposition and more society and stimulus—but John says the very worst thing I can do is to think about my condition, and I confess it always makes me feel bad.

So I will let it alone and talk about the house.

The most beautiful place! It is quite alone, standing well back from the road, quite three miles from the village. It makes me think of English places that you read about, for there are hedges and walls and gates that lock, and lots of separate little houses for the gardeners and people.

There is a delicious garden! I never saw such a garden-large and shady, full of box-bordered paths, and lined with long grape-covered arbors with seats under them.

There were greenhouses, too, but they are all broken now.

There was some legal trouble, I believe, something about the heirs and co-heirs; anyhow, the place has been empty for years.

That spoils my ghostliness, I am afraid, but I don't care—there is something strange about the house—I can feel it.

I even said so to John one moonlight evening, but he said what I felt was a draught, and shut the window.

I get unreasonably angry with John sometimes. I'm sure I never used to be so sensitive. I think it is due to this nervous condition.

But John says if I feel so, I shall neglect proper self-control; so I take pains to control myself—before him, at least, and that makes me very tired.

I don't like our room a bit. I wanted one downstairs that opened on the piazza and had roses all over the window, and such pretty old-fashioned chintz hangings! but John would not hear of it.

He said there was only one window and not room for two beds, and no near room for him if he took another.

He is very careful and loving, and hardly lets me stir without special direction.

I have a schedule prescription for each hour in the day; he takes all care from me, and so I feel basely ungrateful not to value it more.

He said we came here solely on my account, that I was to have perfect rest and all the air I could get. "Your exercise depends on your strength, my dear," said he, "and your food somewhat on your appetite; but air you can absorb all the time." So we took the nursery at the top of the house.

It is a big, airy room, the whole floor nearly, with windows that look all ways, and air and sunshine galore. It was nursery first and then playroom and gymnasium, I should judge; for the windows are barred for little children, and there are rings and things in the walls.

The paint and paper look as if a boys' school had used it. It is stripped off—the paper—in great patches all around the head of my bed, about as far as I can reach, and in a great place on the other side of the room low down. I never saw a worse paper in my life.

One of those sprawling flamboyant patterns committing every artistic sin.

It is dull enough to confuse the eye in following, pronounced enough to constantly irritate and provoke study, and when you follow the lame uncertain curves for a little distance they suddenly commit suicide—plunge off at outrageous angles, destroy themselves in unheard of contradictions.

The color is repellant, almost revolting; a smoldering unclean yellow, strangely faded by the slow-turning sunlight.

It is a dull yet lurid orange in some places, a sickly sulphur tint in others.

No wonder the children hated it! I should hate it myself if I had to live in this room long.

There comes John, and I must put this away—he hates to have me write a word.

• • •

We have been here two weeks, and I haven't felt like writing before, since that first day.

I am sitting by the window now, up in this atrocious nursery, and there is nothing to hinder my writing as much as I please, save lack of strength. John is away all day, and even some nights when his cases are serious.

I am glad my case is not serious!

But these nervous troubles are dreadfully depressing.

John does not know how much I really suffer. He knows there is no reason to suffer, and that satisfies him.

Of course it is only nervousness. It does weigh on me so not to do my duty in any way!

I meant to be such a help to John, such a real rest and comfort, and here I am a comparative burden already!

Nobody would believe what an effort it is to do what little I am able to dress and entertain, and order things.

It is fortunate Mary is so good with the baby. Such a dear baby!

And yet I cannot be with him; it makes me so nervous.

I suppose John never was nervous in his life. He laughs at me so about this wallpaper!

At first he meant to repaper the room, but afterwards he said that I was letting it get the better of me, and that nothing was worse for a nervous patient than to give way to such fancies.

He said that after the wallpaper was changed it would be the heavy bedstead, and then the barred windows, and then that gate at the head of the stairs, and so on.

"You know the place is doing you good," he said, "and really, dear, I don't care to renovate the house just for a three months' rental."

"Then do let us go downstairs," I said, "there are such pretty rooms there."

Then he took me in his arms and called me a blessed little goose, and said he would go down cellar, if I wished, and have it whitewashed into the bargain.

But he is right enough about the beds and windows and things.

It is an airy and comfortable room as anyone need wish, and, of course, I would not be so silly as to make him uncomfortable just for a whim.

I'm really getting quite fond of the big room, all but that horrid paper.

Out of one window I can see the garden, those mysterious deep-shaded arbors, the riotous old-fashioned flowers, and bushes and gnarly trees.

Out of another I get a lovely view of the bay and a little private wharf belonging to the estate. There is a beautiful shaded lane that runs down there from the house. I always fancy I see people walking in these numerous paths and arbors, but John has cautioned me not to give way to fancy in the least. He says that with my imaginative power and habit of storymaking, a nervous weakness like mine is sure to lead to all manner of excited fancies, and that I ought to use my will and good sense to check the tendency. So I try.

I think sometimes that if I were only well enough to write a little it would relieve the press of ideas and rest me.

But I find I get pretty tired when I try.

It is so discouraging not to have any advice and companionship about my work. When I get really well, John says we will ask Cousin Henry and Julia down for a long visit; but he says he would as soon put fireworks in my pillowcase as to let me have those stimulating people about now.

I wish I could get well faster.

But I must not think "about" that. This paper looks to me as if it knew what a vicious influence it had!

There is a recurrent spot where the pattern lolls like a broken neck and two bulbous eyes stare at you upside down.

I get positively angry with the impertinence of it and the ever-lastingness. Up and down and sideways they crawl, and those absurd, unblinking eyes are everywhere. There is one place where two breadths didn't match, and the eyes go all up and down the line, one a little higher than the other.

I never saw so much expression in an inanimate thing before, and we all know how much expression they have! I used to lie awake as a child and get more entertainment and terror out of blank walls and plain furniture than most children could find in a toystore.

I remember what a kindly wink the knobs of our big, old bureau used to have, and there was one chair that always seemed like a strong friend.

I used to feel that if any of the other things looked too fierce I could always hop into that chair and be safe.

The furniture in this room is no worse than inharmonious, however, for we had to bring it all from downstairs. I suppose when this was used as a playroom they had to take the nursery things out, and no wonder! I never saw such ravages as the children have made here.

The wallpaper, as I said before, is torn off in spots, and it sticketh closer than a brother—they must have had perseverance as well as hatred.

Then the floor is scratched and gouged and splintered, the plaster itself is dug out here and there, and this great heavy bed which is all we found in the room, looks as if it had been through the wars.

But I don't mind it a bit—only the paper.

There comes John's sister. Such a dear girl as she is, and so careful of me! I must not let her find me writing.

She is a perfect and enthusiastic housekeeper, and hopes for no better profession. I verily believe she thinks it is the writing which made me sick!

But I can write when she is out, and see her a long way off from these windows.

There is one that commands the road, a lovely shaded winding road, and one that just looks off over the country. A lovely country, too, full of great elms and velvet meadows.

This wallpaper has a kind of sub-pattern in a different shade, a particularly irritating one, for you can only see it in certain lights, and not clearly then.

But in the places where it isn't faded and where the sun is just so—I can see a strange, provoking, formless sort of figure, that seems to skulk about behind that silly and conspicuous front design,

There's sister on the stairs!

• • •

Well, the Fourth of July is over! The people are all gone and I am tired out. John thought it might do me good to see a little company, so we just had mother and Nellie and the children down for a week.

Of course I didn't do a thing. Jennie sees to everything now.

But it tired me all the same.

John says if I don't pick up faster he shall send me to Weir Mitchell in the fall.

But I don't want to go there at all. I had a friend who was in his hands once, and she says he is just like John and my brother, only more so!

Besides, it is such an undertaking to go so far.

I don't feel as if it was worthwhile to turn my hand over for anything, and I'm getting dreadfully fretful and querulous.

I cry at nothing, and cry most of the time.

Of course I don't when John is here, or anybody else, but when I am alone.

And I am alone a good deal just now. John is kept in town very often by serious cases, and Jennie is good and lets me alone when I want her to.

So I walk a little in the garden or down that lovely lane, sit on the porch under the roses, and lie down up here a good deal.

I'm getting really fond of the room in spite of the wallpaper. Perhaps because of the wallpaper.

It dwells in my mind so!

I lie here on this great immovable bed—it is nailed down, I believe—and follow that pattern about by the hour. It is as good as gymnastics, I assure you. I start, we'll say, at the bottom, down in the corner over there where it has not been touched, and I determine for the thousandth time that I will follow that pointless pattern to some sort of a conclusion.

I know a little of the principle of design, and I know this thing was not arranged on any laws of radiation, or alternation, or repetition, or symmetry, or anything else that I ever heard of.

It is repeated, of course, by the breadths, but not otherwise.

Looked at in one way each breadth stands alone, the bloated curves and flourishes—a kind of "debased Romanesque" with delirium tremens—go waddling up and down in isolated columns of fatuity.

But, on the other hand, they connect diagonally, and the sprawling outlines run off in great slanting waves of optic horror, like a lot of wallowing seaweeds in full chase.

The whole thing goes horizontally, too, at least it seems so, and I exhaust myself in trying to distinguish the order of its going in that direction.

They have used a horizontal breadth for a frieze, and that adds wonderfully to the confusion.

There is one end of the room where it is almost intact, and there, when the crosslights fade and the low sun shines directly upon it, I can almost fancy radiation after all—the interminable grotesques seem to form around a common centre and rush off in headlong plunges of equal distraction.

It makes me tired to follow it. I will take a nap I guess.

• • •

I don't know why I should write this.

I don't want to.

I don't feel able.

And I know John would think it absurd. But I must say what I feel and think in some way—it is such a relief!

But the effort is getting to be greater than the relief.

Half the time now I am awfully lazy, and lie down ever so much.

John says I mustn't lose my strength, and has me take cod liver oil and lots of tonics and things, to say nothing of ale and wine and rare meat.

Dear John! He loves me very dearly, and hates to have me sick. I tried to have a real earnest reasonable talk with him the other day, and tell him how I wish he would let me go and make a visit to Cousin Henry and Julia.

But he said I wasn't able to go, nor able to stand it after I got there; and I did not make out a very good case for myself, for I was crying before I had finished.

It is getting to be a great effort for me to think straight. Just this nervous weakness I suppose.

And dear John gathered me up in his arms, and just carried me upstairs and laid me on the bed, and sat by me and read to me till it tired my head.

He said I was his darling and his comfort and all he had, and that I must take care of myself for his sake, and keep well.

He says no one but myself can help me out of it, that I must use my will and self-control and not let any silly fancies run away with me.

There's one comfort, the baby is well and happy, and does not have to occupy this nursery with the horrid wallpaper.

If we had not used it, that blessed child would have! What a fortunate escape! Why, I wouldn't have a child of mine, an impressionable little thing, live in such a room for worlds.

I never thought of it before, but it is lucky that John kept me here after all. I can stand it so much easier than a baby, you see.

Of course I never mention it to them any more—I am too wise—but I keep watch of it all the same.

There are things in that paper that nobody knows but me, or ever will.

Behind that outside pattern the dim shapes get clearer every day.

It is always the same shape, only very numerous.

And it is like a woman stooping down and creeping about behind that pattern. I don't like it a bit. I wonder—I begin to think—I wish John would take me away from here!

• • •

It is so hard to talk with John about my case, because he is so wise, and because he loves me so.

But I tried it last night.

It was moonlight. The moon shines in all around just as the sun does.

I hate to see it sometimes; it creeps so slowly, and always comes in by one window or another.

John was asleep and I hated to waken him, so I kept still and watched the moonlight on that undulating wallpaper till I felt creepy.

The faint figure behind seemed to shake the pattern, just as if she wanted to get out.

I got up softly and went to feel and see if the paper did move, and when I came back John was awake. "What is it, little girl?" he said. "Don't go walking about like that—you'll get cold."

I thought it was a good time to talk, so I told him that I really was not gaining here, and that I wished he would take me away.

"Why, darling!" said he, "our lease will be up in three weeks, and I can't see how to leave before."

"The repairs are not done at home, and I cannot possibly leave town just now. Of course if you were in any danger, I could and would, but you really are better, dear, whether you can see it or not. I am a doctor, dear, and I know. You are gaining flesh and color, your appetite is better, I feel really much easier about you."

"I don't weigh a bit more," said I, "nor as much; and my appetite may be better in the evening when you are here, but it is worse in the morning when you are away!"

"Bless her little heart!" said he with a big hug, "she shall be as sick as she pleases! But now let's improve the shining hours by going to sleep, and talk about it in the morning!?"

"And you won't go away?" I asked gloomily.

"Why, how can I, dear? It is only three weeks more and then we will take a nice little trip of a few days while Jennie is getting the house ready. Really dear you are better!"

"Better in body perhaps—" I began, and stopped short, for he sat up straight and looked at me with such a stern, reproachful look that I could not say another word.

"My darling," said he, "I beg of you, for my sake and for our child's sake, as well as for your own, that you will never for one instant let that idea enter your mind! There is nothing so dangerous, so fascinating, to a temperament like yours. It is a false and foolish fancy. Can you not trust me as a physician when I tell you so?"

So of course I said no more on that score, and we went to sleep before long. He thought I was asleep first, but I wasn't, and lay there for hours trying to decide whether that front pattern and the back pattern really did move together or separately.

• • •

On a pattern like this, by daylight, there is a lack of sequence, a defiance of law, that is a constant irritant to a normal mind.

The color is hideous enough, and unreliable enough, and infuriating enough, but the pattern is torturing.

You think you have mastered it, but just as you get well underway in following, it turns a back-somersault and there you are. It slaps you in the face, knocks you down, and tramples upon you. It is like a bad dream.

The outside pattern is a florid arabesque, reminding one of a fungus. If you can imagine a toadstool in joints, an interminable string of toadstools, budding and sprouting in endless convolutions—why, that is something like it.

That is, sometimes!

There is one marked peculiarity about this paper, a thing nobody seems to notice but myself, and that is that it changes as the light changes.

When the sun shoots in through the east window—I always watch for that first long, straight ray—it changes so quickly that I never can quite believe it.

That is why I watch it always.

By moonlight—the moon shines in all night when there is a moon—I wouldn't know it was the same paper.

At night in any kind of light, in twilight, candlelight, lamplight, and worst of all by moonlight, it becomes bars! The outside pattern I mean, and the woman behind it is as plain as can be.

I didn't realize for a long time what the thing was that showed behind, that dim sub-pattern, but now I am quite sure it is a woman.

By daylight she is subdued, quiet. I fancy it is the pattern that keeps her so still. It is so puzzling. It keeps me quiet by the hour.

I lie down ever so much now. John says it is good for me, and to sleep all I can.

Indeed he started the habit by making me lie down for an hour after each meal.

It is a very bad habit I am convinced, for you see I don't sleep.

And that cultivates deceit, for I don't tell them I'm awake—Oh, no!

The fact is I am getting a little afraid of John.

He seems very queer sometimes, and even Jennie has an inexplicable look.

It strikes me occasionally, just as a scientific hypothesis—that perhaps it is the paper!

I have watched John when he did not know I was looking, and come into the room suddenly on the most innocent excuses, and I've caught him several times looking at the paper! And Jennie too. I caught Jennie with her hand on it once.

She didn't know I was in the room, and when I asked her in a quiet, a very quiet voice, with the most restrained manner possible, what she was doing with the paper—she turned around as if she had been caught stealing, and looked quite angry—asked me why I should frighten her so!

Then she said that the paper stained everything it touched, that she had found yellow smooches on all my clothes and John's, and she wished we would be more careful!

Did not that sound innocent? But I know she was studying that pattern, and I am determined that nobody shall find it out but myself!

• • •

Life is very much more exciting now than it used to be. You see I have something more to expect, to look forward to, to watch. I really do eat better, and am more quiet than I was.

John is so pleased to see me improve! He laughed a little the other day, and said I seemed to be flourishing in spite of my wallpaper.

I turned it off with a laugh. I had no intention of telling him it was because of the wallpaper—he would make fun of me. He might even want to take me away.

I don't want to leave now until I have found it out. There is a week more, and I think that will be enough.

• • •

I'm feeling ever so much better! I don't sleep much at night, for it is so interesting to watch developments; but I sleep a good deal in the daytime.

In the daytime it is tiresome and perplexing.

There are always new shoots on the fungus, and new shades of yellow all over it. I cannot keep count of them, though I have tried conscientiously.

It is the strangest yellow, that wallpaper! It makes me think of all the yellow things I ever saw—not beautiful ones like buttercups, but old foul, bad yellow things.

But there is something else about that paper—the smell! I noticed it the moment we came into the room, but with so much air and sun it was not bad. Now we have had a week of fog and rain, and whether the windows are open or not, the smell is here.

It creeps all over the house.

I find it hovering in the dining-room, skulking in the parlor, hiding in the hall, lying in wait for me on the stairs.

It gets into my hair.

Even when I go to ride, if I turn my head suddenly and surprise it—there is that smell!

Such a peculiar odor, too! I have spent hours in trying to analyze it, to find what it smelled like.

It is not bad—at first, and very gentle, but quite the subtlest, most enduring odor I ever met.

In this damp weather it is awful, I wake up in the night and find it hanging over me.

It used to disturb me at first. I thought seriously of burning the house—to reach the smell.

But now I am used to it. The only thing I can think of that it is like is the color of the paper! A yellow smell.

There is a very funny mark on this wall, low down, near the mopboard. A streak that runs round the room. It goes behind every piece of furniture, except the bed, a long, straight, even smooch, as if it had been rubbed over and over.

I wonder how it was done and who did it, and what they did it for. Round and round and round—round and round and round—it makes me dizzy!

• • •

I really have discovered something at last.

Through watching so much at night, when it changes so, I have finally found out.

The front pattern does move—and no wonder! The woman behind shakes it!

Sometimes I think there are a great many women behind, and sometimes only one, and she crawls around fast, and her crawling shakes it all over.

Then in the very bright spots she keeps still, and in the very shady spots she just takes hold of the bars and shakes them hard.

And she is all the time trying to climb through. But nobody could climb through that pattern—it strangles so; I think that is why it has so many heads.

They get through, and then the pattern strangles them off and turns them upside down, and makes their eyes white!

If those heads were covered or taken off it would not be half so bad.

• • •

I think that woman gets out in the daytime!

And I'll tell you why—privately—I've seen her!

I can see her out of everyone of my windows!

It is the same woman, I know, for she is always creeping, and most women do not creep by daylight.

I see her in that long shaded lane, creeping up and down. I see her in those dark grape arbors, creeping all around the garden.

I see her on that long road under the trees, creeping along, and when a carriage comes she hides under the blackberry vines.

I don't blame her a bit. It must be very humiliating to be caught creeping by daylight!

I always lock the door when I creep by daylight. I can't do it at night, for

I know John would suspect something at once.

And John is so queer now, that I don't want to irritate him. I wish he would take another room! Besides, I don't want anybody to get that woman out at night but myself.

I often wonder if I could see her out of all the windows at once.

But, turn as fast as I can, I can only see out of one at one time.

And though I always see her, she may be able to creep faster than I can turn!

I have watched her sometimes away off in the open country, creeping as fast as a cloud shadow in a high wind.

• • •

If only that top pattern could be gotten off from the under one! I mean to try it, little by little.

I have found out another funny thing, but I shan't tell it this time! It does not do to trust people too much. There are only two more days to get this paper off, and I believe John is beginning to notice. I don't like the look in his eyes.

And I heard him ask Jennie a lot of professional questions about me. She had a very good report to give.

She said I slept a good deal in the daytime.

John knows I don't sleep very well at night, for all I'm so quiet!

He asked me all sorts of questions, too, and pretended to be very loving and kind.

As if I couldn't see through him!

Still, I don't wonder he acts so, sleeping under this paper for three months.

It only interests me, but I feel sure John and Jennie are secretly affected by it.

• • •

Hurrah! This is the last day, but it is enough. John to stay in town over night, and won't be out until this evening.

Jennie wanted to sleep with me—the sly thing! but I told her I should undoubtedly rest better for a night all alone.

That was clever, for really I wasn't alone a bit! As soon as it was moonlight and that poor thing began to crawl and shake the pattern, I got up and ran to help her.

I pulled and she shook, I shook and she pulled, and before morning we had peeled off yards of that paper.

A strip about as high as my head and half around the room.

And then when the sun came and that awful pattern began to laugh at me, I declared I would finish it today!

We go away tomorrow, and they are moving all my furniture down again to leave things as they were before.

Jennie looked at the wall in amazement, but I told her merrily that I did it out of pure spite at the vicious thing.

She laughed and said she wouldn't mind doing it herself, but I must not get tired.

How she betrayed herself that time!

But I am here, and no person touches this paper but me—not alive!

She tried to get me out of the room—it was too patent! But I said it was so quiet and empty and clean now that I believed I would lie down again and sleep all I could; and not to wake me even for dinner—I would call when I woke.

So now she is gone, and the servants are gone, and the things are gone, and there is nothing left but that great bedstead nailed down, with the canvas mattress we found on it.

We shall sleep downstairs tonight, and take the boat home tomorrow.

I quite enjoy the room; now it is bare again.

How those children did tear about here!

This bedstead is fairly gnawed!

But I must get to work.

I have locked the door and thrown the key down into the front path.

I don't want to go out, and I don't want to have anybody come in, till John comes.

I want to astonish him.

I've got a rope up here that even Jennie did not find. If that woman does get out, and tries to get away, I can tie her!

But I forgot I could not reach far without anything to stand on!

This bed will not move!

I tried to lift and push it until I was lame, and then I got so angry I bit off a little piece at one corner—but it hurt my teeth.

Then I peeled off all the paper I could reach standing on the floor. It sticks horribly and the pattern just enjoys it! All those strangled heads and bulbous eyes and waddling fungus growths just shriek with derision!

I am getting angry enough to do something desperate. To jump out of the window would be admirable exercise, but the bars are too strong even to try.

Besides I wouldn't do it. Of course not. I know well enough that a step like that is improper and might be misconstrued.

I don't like to look out of the windows even—there are so many of those creeping women, and they creep so fast.

I wonder if they all come out of that wallpaper as I did?

But I am securely fastened now by my well-hidden rope—you don't get me out in the road there!

I suppose I shall have to get back behind the pattern when it comes night, and that is hard!

It is so pleasant to be out in this great room and creep around as I please!

I don't want to go outside. I won't, even if Jennie asks me to.

For outside you have to creep on the ground, and everything is green instead of yellow.

But here I can creep smoothly on the floor, and my shoulder just fits in that long smooch around the wall, so I cannot lose my way.

Why there's John at the door!

It is no use, young man, you can't open it!

How he does call and pound!

Now he's crying for an axe.

It would be a shame to break down that beautiful door!

"John dear!" said I in the gentlest voice, "the key is down by the front steps, under a plantain leaf!"

That silenced him for a few moments.

Then he said—very quietly indeed, "Open the door, my darling."

"I can't," said I, "the key is down by the front door under a plantain leaf!"

And then I said it again, several times, very gently and slowly, and said it so often that he had to go and see, and he got it of course, and came in. He stopped short by the door.

"What is the matter?" he cried. "For God's sake, what are you doing!"

I kept on creeping just the same, but I looked at him over my shoulder.

"I've got out at last," said I, "in spite of you and Jane! And I've pulled off most of the paper, so you can't put me back!"

Now why should that man have fainted? But he did, and right across my path by the wall, so that I had to creep over him every time!

## Ⅲ Questions for Further Thinking

1. Do you think John loves his wife? How does he respond to his wife's request to leave the house?

2. What is the communicative pattern between John and "I"?

3. The narrator "I" feels that writing "would relieve the press of ideas and rest me." However, she has to hide her act of writing because it has a "vicious" influence. Why is there such a contradiction?

4. One major sign of the narrator's madness is her creeping act. What is the symbolic meaning of "creeping"?

5. The narrator wants to free the woman confined in the wallpaper, but why does she get a rope to tie her to stop her from getting away?

## Ⅳ Appreciation

As a story to actualize Virginia Woolf's criticism on social discouragement of women's intelligence, "The Yellow Wallpaper" depicts how patriarchal social convention pinches a woman gradually into a perplexed mental state until she falls into insanity. Afflicted with post-partum depression, the narrator "I" receives the "rest cure," which was popularly practiced by physicians to treat middle and upper class women in nineteenth century. "I" was required to stay in a room of a big house, isolated from her family members and the newly born baby. "I" was also expected to remain in a state of complete rest without engaging in any intellectual or physical activities.

In the story, the narrator's beloved husband, John, who is a physician, treats his wife as an empty-minded little child. He addresses her as "a little goose" and neglects her opinion because he trusts his scientific judgment more than a woman's emotional need. When the narrator dares to express her dislike for the room and begs to leave, he would pose a fatherly "stern and reproachful look" to silence her into obedience.

The patriarchal pattern of the husband-wife relationship thwarts the narrator's confidence to express herself. At the same time, she is inculcated to believe that intellectual activity is a hazard to health. Pinched both by the patriarchal convention and self-denial, the narrator gives up her self-relieving attempt to keep a journal and falls into wild fantasies. She sees the pattern of the wallpaper as a woman who is barred behind a prison. While the narrator sets the goal to free the woman from the confinement of the wallpaper, which is in fact the reflection of her own liberation, she fancies holding a rope to tie the woman who dares to get away. Consequently, she becomes a woman who splits herself in both revolting and submitting to the patriarchal convention.

The narration carried out in short sentences throughout the story undoubtedly adds a lot weight to the critical power of the story. One important narrative technique adopted in the story is the shift of subjects. In the first half of the story, the sequent shift of the subjective from "John" to "I" suggests how the narrator encounters repeated denial and is reduced to silence. In the latter part of the story, the cross usage of "I," "she" and "we" implies the deranged state of the narrator's mind when she confuses herself with the woman in the wallpaper, and eventually becomes the identity of a mad woman.

## Ⅴ Writing Topic

在《黄色墙纸》("The Yellow Wallpaper")中,由于受到当时社会对女性智力活动的贬低和否定,主人公写作的尝试和欲望逐渐被压制。这一点与弗吉尼亚·伍尔夫在《一间自己的屋子》中的观点相呼应。请结合伍尔夫所介绍的20世纪前社会对女性智力的偏见来理解和分析《黄色墙纸》中主人公内心的冲突、挣扎以及最后的疯癫。

# Part Two

## *Women's Agencies*

# Unit 4 "Cousin Lewis" by Jean Stubbs

## Ⅰ Introduction to the Author and the Work

Jean Stubbs (1926–2012) was born in Lancashire, England. Even as a child, she made up stories and played with her younger brother as a captive audience and a player respectively.

She lived in London for over 20 years, first thriving in city life and later publishing world. Her writings include innumerable short stories for magazines and collections, some of which have been adapted for radio. She also ran seminars and discussion groups at writers' summer schools and was appointed as writer-in-residence for *Avon* for a year.

Her books include three Victorian-set crime novels featuring the charismatic Inspector Lintott, and she also writes some of her fictional works based on historical figures like Henry Ⅷ. In 1975, Jean moved to Cornwall with her husband to live in a small stone cottage on the Lizard Peninsula—a sea change. Once more, Jean's creativity responded to her surroundings. This very different Cornish life inspired a number of books, several set in Cornwall, and the four novels comprising *The Brief Chronicles*, set in industrial-age. Her final novel, *I'm a Stranger Here Myself*, was published in 2004.

"Cousin Lewis" portrays a wife who is bound by societal discipline of being a woman. From her teenage years, she likes to preform male roles of various kinds to express her sense of autonomy. But the habit of cross-dressing herself as a man inspires suspicion from her neighborhood about her motherly role. She is eventually questioned by her husband, accusing her of crossing the traditional disposition of a woman.

## Ⅱ Cousin Lewis[①]

The last time Margery saw Cousin Lewis he was twenty-five and she only thirteen. But time, she felt, was on her side. She hung back, coping with love and puppy fat, and he stood resplendent in his Air Force uniform and talked of bombing raids over Germany in a suitably casual fashion. Outside, beyond the black-out curtains, searchlights picked out clouds and waited for something more important.

"Ah well, back to the circus!" said Cousin Lewis, and pulled his cap peak straight in the hall mirror.

"Best of luck, old chap," said Margery's father.

"Take care of yourself, Lewis," said Margery's mother. "Lovely to see you."

"Will the war last long enough for me to join the R.A.F.?" asked Benny, who was nearly nine.

"Good Lord, I hope not!" said Cousin Lewis. "Give me a kiss, Marjie!"

She put her lips to his cheek, which was cool and brown, and hoped no one would rag her afterwards. And because she was exalted by the kiss and afraid of the ridicule she said something in shocking bad taste.

"What happens if they shoot you down?" she asked.

But Cousin Lewis, having come to terms with that possibility, only laughed.

"I'll be washed up!" he said gaily, and lifted his hand to them in salute.

That was how she remembered him: young and brave, with the war before him and safety behind him. A laugh and a salute and footsteps treading jubilantly into the dark.

A week later his bomber poured from the night sky in one long flame, and seared a field in France. They were all much too worried about his mother to consider Margery, who was only a child and would forget.

She was, thought Benny, as good as a brother—and what greater compliment

① https://www.librarything.com/work/11080204.

could he pay a girl? She climbed trees, cooked potatoes in the hot ash of bonfires, and forgot to wash her neck. But gradually she betrayed him, her breasts rearing shyly beneficial jerseys and dresses, her eyes looking for older boys. She did not marry as soon as they expected, being in her thirties before she met Hugh Jones, and already an aunt twice over.

Margery's father liked Hugh instantly, and they sat smoking identical pipes and discussing farming until midnight.

"Mind you, North Wales is very different from Suffolk," said Hugh defensively, thinking of his stone farmhouse like a fortress on the ridge. "You're very well-groomed down here, compared to Nant Uchaf. Life's easier in the south. But I am not a poor man, and Marjie knows what expect. She isn't a girl to hanker after the bright life, now is she?"

"No-o," said her father, ruminating, "but she does enjoy a binge now and again."

"She can go to Bangor or Caernarvon, Hugh offered. "There's a lot of nice cafes there for morning coffee and afternoon tea and that. I'm not the sort of man who expects a woman to turn into a hermit. Cinemas, there are." He thought. "Dress shops," he said.

"Oh, she hardly ever buys clothes. She's not a great spender. Quite the contrary. Her mother has always had the greatest difficulty in getting her out of slacks and jerseys. She's no highbrow, either. No yearning for the Royal Festival Hall or a night at the Aldwych. Come to think of it," said Margery's father, sucking the stem of his pipe, "I don't know what she *does* do in London. She just walks round, I suppose, and looks up the odd school friend who has a flat in town. Girls' gossip. She was always a reserved child, used to sit in her room for hours, talking to herself. Got a gift for mimicry. We thought she might have wanted to go on the stage at one time, but she's a home bird—isn't she, my love? " as his wife came in.

Margery's mother said, at a tangent, "We've talked the wedding over until we're hoarse, and Margery's having her bath and we're both going to bed. There's a plate of chicken sandwiches on the kitchen table and coffee in the pot and beer in the fridge. Come when you like—only remember the alarm clock's set for five-thirty tomorrow morning!"

"I was telling Hugh that Margery likes a binge in town, now and again, but she's actually a home bird."

"Home bird?" cried Margery's mother, with the fatuous expression of one whose daughter has been a joy to her, "why, you can't drag that girl away from home, I'll be glad to have my kitchen to myself! She can do anything around the house and farm. Anything. Can't she, Ken?"

"Good as a man—and good as a woman, too. I'm surprised—we're both surprised—that she hasn't married earlier. Aren't we, love?"

An expression was born and despatched on the face of Margery's mother, but escaped the notice of both men.

"Oh—she had the good sense to wait until Hugh came along," she said, closing the subject.

"I'm very lucky," said Hugh.

They fastened to agree with him, and to add that their daughter was equally fortunate.

"There's been no other engagement," said her father quickly. "The odd boy-friend, here and there, but none of them seemed to suit her."

"She was wise enough to bide her time," said Margery's mother. "Girls seem to think that the right man comes along like a bar of chocolate, the day they're twenty- one. And that's silly. I always say that if they have a good home and plenty of interests they can wait, and choose well."

"I'm no chicken myself," said Hugh, being thirty-eight. "But with my dad dying when I was twenty, and my mother lingering on all those years, and the farm to pull up after the war—I had to wait too. And I'm glad I did."

"Just remember what I said, about Margery needing a day out now and then, and she'll be a wife in a million," said her father.

The expression hovered for a moment or two, puckering the forehead of Margery's mother, compressing her mouth, and was banished by a smile.

"Oh, you must let wives off the hook occasionally," she said. "We work all the better for a day out."

Margery made a graceful bride, wearing her mother's veil and a satin dress created by Miss Pierce who did all the village fine sewing. Her thin brown face and intent blue eyes looked out from the photograph in her parents' living room. She clasped her husband's arm as though she were drowning, and he stood straight by her side, an able lifesaver. Her letters sounded happy.

She made a couple of expeditions in the first year they were married, and distressed Hugh by refusing to plan ahead.

"I don't mind you going out, love," he said three times over breakfast. "I mind that you didn't give me a bit more warning."

Her long face was obstinate, her eyes remote.

"I simply thought this morning, that I'd like a change," she said, and reminded him of her mother as she sped off on a domestic tangent. "I've put a stew in the oven and I've fed the hens, and you'll be out until this evening. Your sandwiches are ready and I've made a flask of tea. You'll get a drink at the pub—and I must run if I'm to catch that bus."

"But when will you be back?" he cried after her flying headscarf.

She waved, and called something about the bus timetable. He remembered then that she had not even said where she was going. All day he sought comfort in her fathers' advice, whistling up the dog, and saying sorrowfully, "But he never said how sudden she was!"

Margery returned decorously at six o'clock and was serving stew up on his mother's willow-pattern plates when he unlatched the door. He noted with pleasure that she had changed for him, and an air of refreshed serenity was evident in the folds of her dress. After tea she insisted on filling his pipe and sitting on his knee in the rocking-chair.

Soothed, he said, "Did you buy anything?" looking into the bright heart of the coal fire.

"I brought you a jar of Gentleman's Relish to try," she said, teasing, "and if you don't eat it—I shall!"

"Did you go to the pictures?"

"There was nothing I hadn't seen."

"Did you meet anyone we know?"

She shook her head, smiling.

"What have you done, then, all day? Where have you been?"

She was radiant.

"I went to Caernarvon. I looked at the shops, and the sea, and the castle. I was thinking. Can't you guess?"

"No, I can't," he said, too comfortable to be impatient, too loving to be suspicious.

"We're going to have a baby, Hughie!"

In his joy he connected her mysterious absence with a visit to the doctor, and forgot for a long time that their doctor lived only three miles away in the opposite direction to Caernarvon.

The second trip, two months before David was born, occurred in his absence. Foreseeing the probability of an argument, she waited until he began his morning's work, and then left another stew and a message with Mrs. Grffiths who came in to help. This time, it appeared, she visited Bangor, went on to Llandudno, and missed her connection. He was beside himself when the telephone rang and she asked him to come and collect her. All the way he rehearsed accusations, which became dumb at the sight of her woeful face, her swollen body on a bench in the square.

"For God's sake," he cried, as she scrambled into the van, "what possessed you, Marjie?"

"I wanted something for the baby," she said, and her bottom lip trembled. "It was to be a surprise?"

"I was surprised, by Now! You've got three drawerfuls of clothes at home. And what's in that suitcase?"

"Dry-cleaning," she said. "With the winter coming on I might not be able to get out again. And I bought you a Paisley neck scarf. They're all the rage."

"Don't cry then, love," he said, wondering whenever he should wear it, and what clothes she found necessary to clean when they both lived in trousers and sweaters from morning to "Don't cry, love. I didn't know where you were, you see. I didn't know where in God's name to start looking."

Then their son arrived after a long bout in the nearest hospital, and he imagined her safely tethered. But once or twice in David's babyhood she packed a rucksack, put him in his sling, and disappeared unaccountably. She said she had been on the mountains.

"Which mountains?" Hugh asked, aghast to think of those two frail beings at the mercy of height and weather.

"I don't know all their names, yet," she said defensively. "But I showed David our farm from the top of one ridge, and I'm very careful where I go."

When he heard that a second child was expected his pleasure mingled with relief. Now at last she must settle down. Only once did he have to collect her, exhausted by late pregnancy, holding David's small hand and bearing the inevitable rucksack. And this time her condition did not avert his anger, because the child was weeping with cold and tiredness, nor would he unwrap the bribe of a gift.

"You have responsibilities," he cried, "for God's sake put them first. It's not as though you were seventeen."

"What's my age got to do with it," she wept, struggling to push David's heavy limbs into his sleeping-suit.

"Everything," shouted Hugh. "Nobody minds a slip of a girl taking off when she feels like it. But a married woman of your age should have outgrown all that nonsense. And what's in that rucksack, for the love of heaven?"

"Our food and his nappies and bottle," she sobbed, and stuffed it under the stairs cupboard without unpacking it, and said she wanted to go back to Suffolk.

The next day she was weary, white and submissive.

"I know I can't go out like I did," she said, stirring porridge and wiping her eyes. "I'll find some other way of amusing myself."

"What can I do for you, Marjie?" he asked, feeling brutish.

"Nothing," she said, moving away from his hand. "You're very good to me and I'm very lucky. I'll be all right."

"Well, get a telly," he said. "The Thomases have a telly."

"That will be nice for David too. I shall like that."

But he saw he had not plumbed the real depths of her grief. And when their daughter Mair was born, and summer came, he used every opportunity to take them out: sometimes a family day at the seaside, sometimes a working trip in which he left them to picnic while he walked his acres and talked sheep. The children thrived but Margery drooped, in spite of her thanks and her protestations of happiness. Several times she woke him by muttering and crying and turning in her sleep. Once, he tackled the problem of transferring his thoughts to paper without Margery knowing, and wrote to her parents. They drove up the following weekend and took Margery and the children back with them for a holiday. She returned, having spent two days in London, buoyant and transfigured.

Perhaps it's the climate, or the place, Hugh thought. But he could do nothing to alter either, since the farm was his life and Margery had taken on both of them for better or worse, and they loved each other. But as the children grew up and became communicative her interest quickened. She had been a conscientious and tender mother; now she was their amusement center. No games were quite so good as the ones she made up, and the secret games were best of all. The sound of her voice would bring David even from the bam, and she could coax Mair out of a tantrum by whispering in her ear. Invisible strings bound them to their mother, and the strings grew into a web. They loved their father, but could manage without him. The absence of their mother, even though she was only sorting out rubbish in the loft, made them a little fearful.

They had been married six years when their third and last child was born, another boy whom they named Colm. The birth began as it should, in the bed where Hugh was born, and ended in an ambulance ride to Bangor hospital.

"No more now, Hughie lad," said the doctor privately. "Call it a day and be thankful that the ones you've got are sound and hearty. I don't think Margery will grieve, mind you. She's a good mother, but I get the impression she likes them more as they grow up. Not a great one for having a baby round all the time."

Remembering the laughter and flushed faces, the shining eyes, as he came home of an evening, Hugh agreed.

"She's a wonder at amusing them," he said. "I'm the daft one that likes a baby to nurse?" He added, with a dart of jealousy, "Sometimes I think I'm the odd one out, you know!"

"Oh, that's as it should be," said the doctor, getting into his car. "The child belongs to its mother at this age. Your turn will come soon enough. Then she'll be left to fill your stomachs while you show those two boys of yours how to run a farm. And time goes. By now, it goes. Is Mrs. Griffiths still coming in a few mornings a week? That's right, Hughie lad. Give Margery all the rest you can while she feeds this one."

Three-year-old Mair cherished her father and was content to sit in his lap and watch the flames change, and the shadows reach and recede on the white walls, that evening. But David, at five, demanded more sophisticated fare. They had been quietened by the promise of the baby brother, and Mamma home at the end of the week. But a week was a long time to spend with Mrs. Griffiths's admonitions and their father's loving silence.

"I want Cousin Lewis, Dadda!" David cried, and Mair twisted her little brown head round to agree with him.

"Cousin Lewis," she repeated. "Cousin Lewis."

"Who's he?" asked Hugh, in honest bewilderment.

But they could not explain, only say that he made them laugh and told them stories.

"When does he come?" cried Hugh.

They could not cope with the mysteries of time, but said he sometimes came, not every time. All Hugh's old demons became one devil, and he stormed into the maternity ward at Bangor the following afternoon, determined to have this out.

"Who the hell's Cousin Lewis?" he shouted, before Margery could more than smile a welcome.

She flushed from neck to forehead, holding the flowers he had thrust at her in his terror.

"Hush, Hughie," she whispered, humiliated. "Don't shout so, Sister's looking at you!"

Sister's face expressed such a high degree of discontent that Hugh pulled out a chair and sat on it before repeating his question in a lower voice.

"Who is he, eh? Who is he? Is that who you've been meeting all these years? Running off without telling me."

Margery looked puzzled, then relieved, then laughed outright and caught his hand and kissed it.

“You frightened me to death for a minute,” she said. “I couldn’t think. Have the children been talking to you? What did they say?”

“They said they wanted Cousin Lewis because he told them stories and made them laugh, and he only came sometimes.”

“Ah!” Serenity illumined even her maternity nightdress, designed more for practical than ornamental purposes. “It’s only a game,” she said. “My actual Cousin Lewis was killed in the war when I was thirteen, but he always made Benny and me laugh and told us stories. So when they’re fratchy or bored I pretend to be him, to amuse them. “Of course,” she added, “most of the tales I tell them never happened. I make them up by this time, to their level, you know. But we play Cousin Lewis like—oh, Ludo or Snakes and Ladders. That’s all. It’s only play, my love. Only another game.”

He could have wept with thankfulness. Suddenly they all meant so much to him: Margery and David and Mair and now little Colm.

“Oh, God in heaven,” he said on a long breath, “I was so bloody scared!”

“Why, Hughie, Hughie,” she whispered, “you didn’t think I had a fancy man, did you?”

“No, love. I did not.”

“You did!” she said, smiling, “and I’m very flattered. You must be blind, Hughie, if you can’t see that I’m not the type a man looks at twice, I’m just another housewife now, Hughie. Haven’t you seen me lately?”

He stared at the thick brown hair pulled into a plait at the top of her head, at the brown face not so thin these days, at her intent blue gaze and firm round arms, and found her wholly beautiful. But not, he admitted only to his secret male self, the sort to turn anybody’s head.

“The man who didn’t snatch you up and run off with you is a damn fool!” he declared. “And I’d knock him down if he didn’t!”

And then they both laughed together and she put both arms round his neck. Sister looked approvingly in their direction and nodded a stately cap at Hugh as he prepared to leave. But before he went another, and happier, thought occurred to him.

“Why, you’ve settled down, girl!” he cried.

"Oh—the expeditions? Yes, Hughie. I've settled down."

Their farm was isolated. Visitors usually made sure of a welcome before they arrived, and casual callers were infrequent. Therefore David had celebrated his ninth birthday, Mair entered her second year at the local primary school, and Colm reached the chattering stage before Hugh found the first letter stuck in his windscreen. He thought it must be a parking ticket, though he was law-abiding and meticulous almost to the point of obsession. So he drew out the envelope with cold fingers and read it twice before he comprehended the meaning.

"Your wife has a visitor while you're away," read the printed letters.

He crumpled the paper in one big brown hand and stuffed it into a litter-basket. But the words danced in the rain against his windscreen all the way home from market, and loomed from the comers of strange dreams for a week afterwards. He took the message apart in his mind and disproved it a thousand times, without ridding himself of its implications. David and Mair were at school all day, but Colm was still with his mother. She would not, he knew, frighten the child with the presence of another man, would not lay the burden of secrecy on a three-year-old boy. But he began to ask her questions which fretted round the edges of her day.

"Been by yourselves?" he would ask, watching as he lit his pipe.

"Except for Mrs. Griffiths this morning."

"No one this afternoon?"

"Who would there be?" Margery asked amazed. "Unless you count the grocery van, of course?"

"Who drives the van then?"

"Old Bob Williams still."

"Didn't you go out at all?"

"In this rain?" she cried. "We're not ducks, are we, Colm?"

"Not ducks," Colm chattered. "Not duck-duck-duck-ies."

"I just thought you might be feeling lonely."

She shrugged her shoulders, smiling at him.

"If I was frightened of being lonely," she said, "I'd have died of it before now—wouldn't I?"

His pipe held no consolation, nor the fire comfort.

"I can take you out tomorrow," he offered. "I can drop you in Portmadoc and pick you up at five."

"Oh no, Hughie—though it's sweet of you. The children will be home from school before five, and I like to be here when they come in. But if we could go on Saturday..."

"Why Saturday?" he cried, suddenly suspicious, sitting up in his chair.

"Because Colm needs new wellingtons," she said, astonished at him, "and Portmadoc has a better selection than the village."

"Oh, yes. Yes. All right, then. We'll go on Saturday."

The second letter came through the post, three months later.

"*Your wife's friend can't cover all his tracks. I saw him through the window yesterday.*"

"What's wrong?" Margery asked.

Beside himself, he threw the note on her plate, and she set down the teapot before she opened it.

"Well?" he said.

She was very pale as she handed it back.

"Hughie," she said quietly. "I will swear on your mother's bible that no one was here yesterday but me and Colm."

"Then who do they mean?"

"For goodness' sake, don't shout, Hughie! The children."

Three heads turned from one parent to the other. Six pairs of childish eyes noted Margery's pallor and Hugh's shaking hands. Six pairs of childish ears heard fear in her voice and rage in his.

"I want to ask you children something," said Hugh deliberately.

"Hugh Jones!" Margery said, in shocked disbelief.

He waved her to silence and controlled his anger.

"Some nasty-minded..." He began, and then altered his approach and tried to bring it down to the level of their innocence. "Some people say that Mamma has too many visitors," he ended absurdly.

Before he could elaborate the children gave a combined shriek of laughter, so wildly in contrast with his own mood that he could have struck them to the ground.

"Listen to me, listen!" he cried.

But he had started a wave of protest.

"I can't bring even my very best friend Olwen to tea, except in the summer," said David. "Because he can't walk back alone in the dark."

"I can't bring my very best friend Dyllis unless her Dadda is going past in the milk van on his way home," cried Mair.

"And Colm has no school-friends anyway," said Margery quietly.

He looked at her and saw that he had grievously broken some cardinal rule in their relationship. He felt so sick and isolated in that hail of childish reproaches that he shouted "Silence, silence!" And then balled up the letter and flung it into the grate.

The children watched him curiously until Margery spoke, and he noticed how the sound of her voice brought them to attention at once.

"The person who wrote to Daddy thinks that I have too many visitors," she said calmly. "They weren't talking about you. So tell Dadda, all of you, which of my friends comes here."

"On Christmas Day?" Mair asked.

"No, not on Christmas Day because everyone comes then. And Dadda," she said, looking full at him, "is here on Christmas Day."

The children bent to their porridge and considered obediently.

"There's Mrs. Griffiths," said Mair.

"And on a one Wednesday Mrs. Evans comes with Gwyn, and on another one Wednesday we go to Gwyn's house," said Colm, for this was his weekly treat and he could never bear the disappointment of bad weather or measles.

"Does Mrs. Morgan come, now that Olwen is at school with me?" asked David.

"Sometimes she does, but she has another baby now," said Margery.

"She came once on my birthday and brought her baby," said Colin.

"And there's Mrs. Griffiths," said Mair.

"We said Mrs. Griffiths already."

"There are the men on the farm, of course," said Margery in that terrible calm voice. "Do any of them come while Dadda is away, Colm? Do you remember?"

He shook his head and made a road in his porridge and filled it with sugar, unobserved.

Hugh's sick fury dwelled on his few labourers, men mostly in late middle-age who had worked for his father, and seemed hewn from the mountains in which they were reared. He knew he would reject every one of them.

"But we are forgetting someone," said Margery, and he caught himself listening to her voice as the children did, because it said so much more than the words. She was lighthearted now, and funny, and dangerous. "We're forgetting Mamma's best boy-friend—Daffie Richards."

Cooling breakfasts and hurrying clocks were ignored in a whoop of delight, for poor Daffie was half-witted, less than five feet high, had a cleft palate that rendered him unintelligible and a hare-lip to complete his list of disfigurements. Margery lifted one capable hand and hushed them.

"We mustn't laugh at Daffie," she said, penitent. "Tell Dadda, Colm, why we are very kind to poor people like Daffie and don't make fun of them."

"Because it might be us and we're lucky," said Colm obediently, and laughed incredulously.

"So Mamma makes a big fuss over Daffie, doesn't she, Colm?" said Margery, comfortably in control of her own table once more. "And we bring him in and make him sit by the fire and give him cake and tea. I expect other people out in the rain and cold are very jealous when they see Daffie enjoying himself. Now if either of you are to get to school on time Dadda will have to run you down in the van, because the milk lorry will have gone by now."

Nothing had been said which could accuse Hugh, and yet his two elder children accused him with their eyes, and they kissed their mother more affectionately than usual. So he drove in wretched silence to school, and tormented himself all day with the scene at the breakfast table, and wondered who wished him so ill that they taunted his wife for loving-kindness.

"The one in uniform is back again," jeered the note.

"I thought you'd scared him off but he was here again the other day," shrieked another.

"This has been going on for years, you know," whispered a third.

Hugh picked the children up from school that afternoon and drove them into Portmadoc. They gaped at him as he marched them into a teashop.

"I'll cost you, Dadda!" said Mair, always practical.

"I don't care what it costs," said Hugh. "Do you like these cakes?"

"Not blooming half!" said David, and opened his eyes as Hugh ordered a child's dream of tea.

"Now," said Hugh, "I want you to listen carefully, and this is our secret because we don't want to upset Mamma."

They did not want to upset her, and would not. He saw that in the way their faces shut against him and their childish shoulders moved together for protection. He might or might not want to hurt her, but before he did they would be armed in her protection. His secret was nothing to them, except that they might learn from it and so shield her.

"Somebody is trying to make trouble between Mamma and me," he said, and his hands trembled as he pressed delicacies upon them. "Somebody says that a man comes to see her while I am out. They say he wears a uniform."

A curious closed look on their faces terrified him and he shouted, "It's not the truth, is it? Is it?"

"Dadda," Mair whispered, leaning over the table, "you not speak so loud please? The ladies are looking at us."

He passed one hand over his face and started again.

"I'll kill the pair of you if you hide anything!" he whispered fiercely.

Their young eyes were proof against him. They exchanged silent messages.

"It's only a game, Dad," said David. "We couldn't think what you meant for a minute. It's only Mamma being Cousin Lewis."

"She dresses up, like at Christmas, in an old uniform," said Mair, "and tells us stories about Cousin Lewis. She always has done, hasn't she, Davie?"

"And not only Cousin Lewis, either," David joined in. "She does dozens of different people. She once frightened me by being Pew, the blind man in *Treasure*

*Islands*."

"She was the witch, and put us both in the oven in gingerbread people for Hansel and Gretel," cried Mair, her mouth joyful.

They tossed the conversation between them with a skill they had not inherited from their father, and he lost himself gloriously in the explanation.

"Eat up now," he cried, sweating with relief, "and remember—this is our secret. "We won't tell Mamma in case it makes her upset."

"Like she was at breakfast, that other time?" asked David.

"Yes," said Hugh, discomfited. "Yes. Eat up, now. Eat up."

He bought a box of chocolates before they went home, puzzling over the expensive wrappers, clumsy in the smart little shop.

"That damned eagle's got another lamb, Mr. Jones," cried his shepherd.

Hugh stared down in anger at the eyeless toy in the grass, and whistled his dog to come away from it.

"I'll get him," he said, nodding. "I'll get him if I wait a week. John, I'm going home for my gun. When I get back I'll settle behind that wall, and you put a couple of lambs in the field by themselves, and keep well away with the rest of the herd. I'll shoot that bugger if it's the last thing I do."

He was in the farmyard, in his anger, before he heard the man's voice in the kitchen and held his breath to listen. He could not catch what was said and the voice was unknown to him: a pleasant cultured baritone which raised his hackles, roused his temper, and roughened him. Perhaps, he thought, with a leap of heart, it was Margery fooling for the children. Then he remembered that Colm was spending the day at Aunt Morwen's house and the others were at school. Moving quietly to surprise them, he unlatched the door and flung it open in one movement, and slammed it behind him.

The man had just arrived, for he wore a dark blue felt trilby, pulled rakishly down over one eye, and a light grey mackintosh. No uniform. And now Hugh realized how far he and anyone else had been from the truth, with his fears of one man meeting her surreptitiously, at long intervals, over the last ten years. No love affair could flourish on such poor soil, against such odds of circumstance, for such a length of time. There had been many men, met by chance, taken lightly.

And his wife, the stray-running bitch who sought out and drew them, had covered her tracks with little bribes and children's games.

So even as the stranger turned to face him he struck him to the floor, and then lifted his field gun from the rack over the fireplace and covered him.

"I'll kill the bloody pair of you," he said quietly. "Now where is she? Where is she?"

The empty farmhouse echoed "Margery, Margery," and she did not answer. And then he saw that the hand warding him off was Margery's hand, and Margery's voice was weeping with hurt and fear and begging him to stop.

He stood agape as she raised herself to kneeling position, and clasped her bruised face and rocked to and fro in grief. For she had not, in fun, slipped on one of his mackintoshes and crowned it with a hat, she was fully and impeccably clothed in things he had never seen before: suit, shirt, tie, socks. Her shoes were polished, her cuff-links impeccably chosen. Even to his country eyes she seemed smarter as a man than she had ever done as a woman.

"For Chris's sake, Margery, what are you up to?" he whispered.

"Why did you come back?" she cried. "You should be on the mountain!"

"That damned eagle got another lamb," he said stiffly. He could not stop looking at her. He noticed that a three-pointed scarlet handkerchief tucked in her dark-blue breast pocket was the same shade as her tie.

She was still dizzy from the blow and he helped her, with distaste, to her feet. The muzzle of the gun indicated her clothing.

"Where did you get all that stuff?" he asked.

"I've had it for years," she sobbed. "It's out of fashion now. I look a freak walking round these days—like something from an old film. The trousers," she said distractedly, "are too wide in the leg. Men don't wear them like that anymore. And I've seen—lovely ones—in Caernarvon. But they cost too much. I never had that sort of money. Everything else is out of fashion, too."

"You mean you've got some more?"

"Upstairs, in the loft, in a trunk. I've got a trunkful. Evening dress, sports clothes, an old R.A.F. uniform, slacks and sweaters and cravats. It's harmless enough," she added, seeing his face.

"Harmless? With the neighborhood thinking you meet a lot of fancy men? Harmless? What about my children having a mother that dresses up like that?"

She wiped her mouth with her knuckles, where a tooth had cut her lip, and then with a wholly masculine gesture she reached for a handkerchief in her trouser pocket.

"They think it's all a game," she said. "They call me Cousin Lewis."

"How long have you—been this way?" he asked, waving the gun at her outfit.

"I wish you'd stop pointing that thing at me," she said, weary. "Oh, years and years, Hugh. Years and years. It hasn't stopped me from making you happy, has it? It hasn't prevented me from being a good mother. It's my only weakness. I'm all right usually. Then, now and again, I just have to dress up. That's all."

He lowered himself into his armchair and stood the gun carefully against its side.

"All?" he said, at last. "Why—I don't know you. I've never known you."

"Just once in a while," she pleaded. "Once in a while. And I've been careful. Someone must have been watching with binoculars to see me at all."

"No," he shouted, shaking his head from side to side to free himself of her. "No. I don't know you. Oh Christ, I don't know you. I don't know you."

She filled the kettle and set it on the fire, brought out cups and saucers and measured tea into the warmed pot.

"I can't drink with you—like that," he said thickly.

She was upstairs a long time, and he looked about him though the farmhouse was strange and his life an emptiness. When she came down again she had changed, out of deference, into a dress. He accepted his tea and stirred sugar round and round, thinking.

"What are you going to do?" Margery asked.

"I don't know," he said. "I don't know. But I can't—can't touch you again. Not now. I'd feel—I'd not know—who you were. I'd feel—dirty."

"But I'm a woman," she cried. "I love you. We've had children together, lived together, for ten years. It's only the clothes, now and again. I'm quite normal, otherwise. I'm a woman, you. I tell you. I'm a woman."

"Are you?" he said, not out of cruelty but because he no longer knew her.

She wept dreadfully, coughing and sobbing.

"Do your parents know?" he asked.

She shook her head, and said she thought perhaps they had been afraid to find out. It was easier, after all, to set her absences down as a whim.

"Oh my God," he said. "What a burden. Who shall I turn to? Who can I ask?"

"Listen," she said. "I can go to a doctor, a psychiatrist. I can have treatment. We'll be just the same as we always were. I'll have treatment."

"No," he said. "You must go home. I'll manage with the children. You must go home. Mrs. Griffiths will help me."

"I'm not leaving them, too!" she cried. "They love me, and I love them. They were always more mine than yours. If you asked them to choose between us, they wouldn't choose you!"

They had reached a pitch of cruelty that could destroy them now.

"The court wouldn't choose you," he said slowly. "And I should go to court and get it done, legal and proper. Legal and proper."

She was silent, and began to prick sausages, to peel potatoes.

"It's a half-day at school," she said. "They'll be home for dinner. Are you stopping?"

"I couldn't eat it," he said simply. "I don't know what to do. I can't eat."

She drew herself up, embattled but not wholly lost.

"My parents will take us in," she said, with dignity. "And if the court finds out how much those children love and depend on me—and if I promise to have treatment—I'd stand a chance of keeping them. I would."

"Are you telling me that the law would let my sons and my daughter be brought up by a woman who dresses up as a man? Let them get into the way of not knowing one sex from the other?"

"If I had treatment. If they knew."

"This man—they call Cousin Lewis—were you in love with him?"

"Yes," she said, "at thirteen. In love as one never is again, with someone who can never let you down, never be destroyed. At thirteen I was in love with him."

He measured the quality and breadth of the fabric she had woven round him and his children for ten years, and realized its value. He was close on fifty, and had never looked at another woman. He was bound, root and stock, to this heap of wind-driven stones, the wind-driven patch of earth and mountain. And three young lives could be wrecked in their leave-taking. He put his hand on hers, though the touch of her flesh was still unpleasant to him.

"We'll go to a specialist if we have to," he said. "We'll stick it out. For the children, for what we've made together. But I'm promising no miracles, Margery, because I can't. We might be like brother and sister for the rest of our days—not out of spite on my part, but because I couldn't help it."

"I—accept that," she said quietly. "I'll do my best."

"I'm not an educated man," Hugh said tired. "I see life as a simple thing. It's hard for me to know more than that. But I'll try. Only, no more games, Margery. No more games?"

"No," she said. "I promise. Hush now! I can hear the children."

"Then I'll be back at tea-time," he said, and picked up his gun. "I'll have my bread and cheese out there with John, and wait for that eagle."

"It's raining hard," she said. "Wrap up well."

She hesitated, and then put her lips to his hard brown cheek, but he moved away as though her touch burned him. She walked blindly into the scullery, and he, just as blindly, pulled on his mackintosh and drew the hat down over his eyes.

But the children, running round the comer of the farmhouse, freed from school, saw the grey mackintosh and dark blue hat as another extension of their lives, and called out with joy.

"It's Cousin Lewis!" cried Mair, running, bright with wind and rain, to greet him.

## Ⅲ Questions for Further Thinking

1. Do you think Margery's parents know that their daughter has the habit of cross-dressing?

2. When Hugh complains of Margery's unreported expeditions, blaming that "a married woman of your age should have outgrown all that nonsense," what is he referring to?

3. What is the conflict between Hugh and Margery? Why does Hugh want to separate with Margery?

4. What did you learn about the dress code for women in the mid-twentieth century in Britain?

5. Please compare kids' reaction to Margery's cross-dressing and Hugh's fury of it. Do you think that sexuality has anything to do with one's outfit?

## Ⅳ Appreciation

Cross-dressing is the act of dressing in clothes of the opposite sex. Cross-dressing has been used for purposes of disguise, comfort, and self-actualization in modern times and throughout history. Historically, women and girls used it to pass as males in society. Some women have cross-dressed to take up male-dominated or male-exclusive professions, such as Hua Mulan in *Ballad of Mulan*, Portia in *The Merchant of Venice*, and Athena in *The Odyssey*.

In "Cousin Lewis," the protagonist Margery grew up as a tomboy. When she was thirteen years old, her cousin, Lewis, an IRA pilot during World War Ⅱ, whom Margery secretly loved, died in an air fight. Margery carried Lewis's name when she crossed dressing to exercise her life fantasies. After she got married with Hugh and became a mother, she turns cross-dressing as a game to amuse her children. This cross-dressing performance enrages Hugh profusely because he considers her act as a violation of the dressing code of a good woman in the mid-twentieth century Britain. Margery and Hugh thus are on the brink of a divorce.

Compared with the typically submissive women in nineteenth century, the story of Margery illustrates the dilemma which a woman could face to exercise her will in contradiction to social code for a good woman. Although she still performs the wifely duties like many housewives of her time, Margery is still criticized for her habit of cross-dressing. Her husband even goes as far as to deny her female identity because of it. For example, every time when she starts for an expedition, she prepares the stew and has everything well arranged. Even when she is arguing with her husband, who denies her female identity because of her cross-dressing, she performs her role of a housewife in cooking. Her dutiful act as a wife thus forms a strong irony when her female identity is denied simply because of her outfit. In this way, this story also strongly criticizes how gender was prescribed socially only by one's physical features.

## Ⅴ Writing Topic

今天,如果一名居住在城市的普通女性想要外出娱乐,那她对于自己是否可以出门不会过于踌躇。但是,对于 20 世纪中期居住在英国山区的一位母亲而言,外出娱乐可能会是一个问题。请思考,在什么情况下,妻子和母亲的身份会影响女性的娱乐自由?

# Unit 5 "The Office" by Alice Munro

## Ⅰ Introduction to the Author and the Work

Alice Munro (1931–2024) was born in 1931, in Wingham, Ontario, Canada. She attended the University of Western Ontario, where she studied journalism and English, but left the school after only two years when she married her first husband, James Munro (1951–1972). The couple moved to Victoria, Vancouver, British Columbia, where they opened a bookstore. During this time, Munro began publishing her work in various magazines.

Munro's first collection of stories (and first book-length work) was published in 1968 as *Dance of the Happy Shades*. The collection achieved great success in Munro's native country, including her first Governor General's Literary Award. Three years later, she published *Lives of Girls and Women*, a collection of stories that critics deemed a Bildungsroman—a work centering on the main character's moral and psychological development. In October 2013, at the age of 82, Munro was awarded the Nobel Prize in Literature, with the Swedish Academy lauding her as the "master of the contemporary short story."

"The Office" tells a story of how a woman writer, who is frustrated by attempts to find a proper space and time for her writing, decides to rent an office. She finds a suitable room owned by a couple who occupy the apartment. But the landlord keeps interrupting to offer things that she doesn't want—conversation, a chair, a plant, a teapot, tales of himself, gossips about the predecessor tenant. Conscious of her inability to be rude to someone who is being rude to her, she feels annoyed with herself for not being firm.

Gradually, the intrusions get worse. To further control her, the landlord spies on her work through his set notions of what a proper woman should be doing in such a space—or any space. He even hints that she has been using the office for parties and sex and then accuses her of defacing the open bathroom with obscenities scrawled in lipstick. Furious, she firmly rejects his slur by refusing to talk with the landlord. Realizing it's impossible to reason with an insane man, she gives up the office.

## Ⅱ The Office[①]

The solution to my life occurred to me one evening while I was ironing a shirt. It was simple but audacious. I went into the living room where my husband was watching television and I said, "I think I ought to have an office."

It sounded fantastic, even to me. What do I want an office for? I have a house; it is pleasant and roomy and has a view of the sea; it provides appropriate places for eating and sleeping, and having baths and conversations with one's friends. Also I have a garden; there is no lack of space.

No. But here comes the disclosure which is not easy for me: I am a writer. That does not sound right. Too presumptuous, phony, or at least unconvincing. Try again. I write. Is that better? I try to write. That makes it worse. Hypocritical humility. Well then?

It doesn't matter. However I put it, the words create their space of silence, the delicate moment of exposure. But people are kind, the silence is quickly absorbed by the solicitude of friendly voices, crying variously; how wonderful, and good for you, and well, that is intriguing. And what do you write, they inquire with spirit. Fiction, I reply, bearing my humiliation by this time with ease, even a suggestion of flippancy, which was not always mine, and again, again; the perceptible circles of dismay are smoothed out by such ready and tactful voices—which have however exhausted their stock of consolatory phrases, and can say only, "Ah!"

---

① http://uomustansiriyah.edu.iq/media/lectures/8/8_2020_02_29! 04_18_17_PM.pdf (uomustansiriyah.edu.iq).

So this is what I want an office for (I said to my husband): to write in. I was at once aware that it sounded like a finicky requirement, a piece of rare self-indulgence. To write, as everyone knows, you need a typewriter, or at least a pencil, some paper, a table and chair; I have all these things in a corner of my bedroom. But now I want an office as well.

And I was not even sure that I was going to write in it, if we come down to that. Maybe I would sit and stare at the wall; even that prospect was not unpleasant to me. It was really the sound of the word "office" that I liked, its sound of dignity and peace. And purposefulness and importance. But I did not care to mention this to my husband, so I launched instead into a high-flown explanation which went, as I remember, like this:

A house is all right for a man to work in. He brings his work into the house; a place is cleared for it; the house rearranges itself as best it can around him. Everybody recognizes that his work exists. He is not expected to answer the telephone, to find things that are lost, to see why the children are crying, or feed the cat. He can shut his door. Imagine (I said) a mother shutting her door, and the children knowing she is behind it; why, the very thought of it is outrageous to them. A woman who sits staring into space, into a country that is not her husband's or her children's is likewise known to be an offence against nature. So a house is not the same for a woman. She is not someone who walks into the house, to make use of it, and will walk out again. She is the house; there is no separation possible.

(And this is true, though as usual when arguing for something I am afraid I do not deserve, I put it in too emphatic and emotional terms. At certain times, perhaps on long spring evenings, still rainy and sad, with the cold bulbs in bloom and a light too mild for promise drifting over the sea, I have opened the windows and felt the house shrink back into wood and plaster and those humble elements of which is it made, and the life in it subside, leaving me exposed, empty-handed, but feeling a fierce and lawless quiver of freedom, of loneliness too harsh and perfect for me now to bear. Then I know how the rest of the time I am sheltered and encumbered; how insistently I am warmed and bound.)

"Go ahead, if you can find one cheap enough," is all my husband had to say to this. He is not like me, he does not really want explanations. That the heart of another person is a closed book, is something you will hear him say frequently, and without regret.

Even then I did not think it was something that could be accomplished. Perhaps at bottom it seemed to me too improper a wish to be granted. I could almost more easily have wished for a mink coat, for a diamond necklace; these are things women do obtain. The children, learning of my plans, greeted them with the most dashing skepticism and unconcern. Nevertheless I went down to the shopping centre which is two blocks from where I live; there I had noticed for several months, and without thinking how they could pertain to me, a couple of For Rent signs in the upstairs windows of a building that housed a drugstore and a beauty parlour. As I went up the stairs I had a feeling of complete unreality; surely renting was a complicated business, in the case of offices; you did not simply knock on the door of the vacant premises and wait to be admitted; it would have to be done through channels. Also, they would want too much money.

As it turned out, I did not even have to knock. A woman came out of one of the empty offices, dragging a vacuum cleaner, and pushing it with her foot, towards the open door across the hall, which evidently led to an apartment in the rear of the building. She and her husband lived in this apartment; their name was Malley; and it was indeed they who owned the building and rented out the offices. The rooms she had just been vacuuming were, she told me, fitted out for a dentist's office, and so would not interest me, but she would show me the other place. She invited me into her apartment while she put away the vacuum and got her key. Her husband, she said with a sigh I could not interpret, was not at home.

Mrs. Malley was a black-haired, delicate-looking woman, perhaps in her early forties, slatternly but still faintly appealing, with such arbitrary touches of femininity as the thin line of bright lipstick, the pink feather slippers on obviously tender and swollen feet. She had the swaying passivity, the air of exhaustion and muted apprehension; that speaks of a life spent in close attention on a man who is by turns vigorous, crotchety and dependent. How much of this I saw at first; how much decided on later is of course impossible to tell. But I did think that she would have no children, the stress of her life, whatever it was, did not allow it, and in this I was not mistaken.

The room where I waited was evidently a combination living room and office. The first things I noticed were models of ships—galleons, clippers, Queen Marys—sitting on the tables, the window sills, the television. Where there were no ships there were potted plants and a clutter of what are sometimes called "masculine" ornaments—china deer heads, bronze horses, huge ashtrays of heavy, veined, shiny material. On the walls were framed photographs and what might have been diplomas. One photo showed a poodle and a bulldog, dressed in masculine and feminine clothing, and assuming with dismal embarrassment a pose of affection. Written across it was "Old Friends." But the room was really dominated by a portrait, with its own light and a gilded frame; it was of a good-looking, fair-haired man in middle age, sitting behind a desk, wearing a business suit and looking pre-eminently prosperous, rosy and agreeable. Here again, it is probably hindsight on my part that points out that in the portrait there is evident also some uneasiness, some lack of faith the man has in this role, a tendency he has to spread himself too bountifully and insistently, which for all anyone knows may lead to disaster.

Never mind the Malleys. As soon as I saw that office, I wanted it. It was larger than I needed, being divided in such a way that it would be suitable for a doctor's office. (We had a chiropractor in here but he left, says Mrs. Malley in her regretful but uninformative way.) The walls were cold and bare, white with a little grey, to cut the glare for the eyes. Since there were no doctors in evidence, nor had been, as Mrs. Malley freely told me, for some time, I offered twenty-five dollars a month. She said she would have to speak to her husband.

The next time I came my offer was agreed upon, and I met Mr. Malley in the flesh. I explained, as I had already done to his wife, that I did not want to make use of my office during regular business hours, but during the weekends and sometimes in the evening. He asked me what I would use it for, and I told him, not without wondering first whether I ought to say I did stenography.

He absorbed the information with good humor, "Ah, you're a writer." "Well yes. I write."

"Then we'll do our best to see you're comfortable here," he said expansively. "I'm a great man for hobbies myself. All these ship-models, I do them in my spare time; they're a blessing for the nerves. People need an occupation for their nerves. I daresay you're the same."

"Something the same," I said, resolutely agreeable, even relieved that he saw my behaviour in this hazy and tolerant light. At least he did not ask me, as I half-expected, who was looking after the children, and did my husband approve? Ten years, maybe fifteen, had greatly softened, spread and defeated the man in the picture. His hips and thighs had now a startling accumulation of fat, causing him to move with a sigh, a cushiony settling of flesh, a ponderous matriarchal discomfort. His hair and eyes had faded, his features blurred, and the affable, predatory expression had collapsed into one of troubling humility and chronic mistrust. I did not look at him. I had not planned, in taking an office, to take on the responsibility of knowing any more human beings.

• • •

On the weekend I moved in, without the help of my family, who would have been kind. I brought my typewriter and a card table and chair, also a little wooden table on which I set a hot plate, a kettle, a jar of instant coffee, a spoon and a yellow mug. That was all. I brooded with satisfaction on the bareness of my walls, the cheap dignity of my essential furnishings, the remarkable lack of things to dust, wash or polish.

The sight was not so pleasing to Mr. Malley. He knocked on my door soon after I was settled and said that he wanted to explain a few things to me—about unscrewing the light in the outer room, which I would not need, about the radiator and how to work the awning outside the window. He looked around at everything with gloom and mystification and said it was an awfully uncomfortable place for a lady.

"It's perfectly all right for me," I said, not as discouragingly as I would have liked to, because I always have a tendency to placate people whom I dislike for no good reason, or simply do not want to know. I make elaborate offerings of courtesy sometimes, in the foolish hope that they will go away and leave me alone.

"What you want is a nice easy chair to sit in, while you're waiting for inspiration to hit. I've got a chair down in the basement, all kinds of stuff down there since my mother passed on last year. There's a bit of carpet rolled up in a corner down there, it isn't doing anybody any good. We could get this place fixed up so's it'd be a lot more homelike for you."

But really, I said, but really I like it as it is.

"If you wanted to run up some curtains, I'd pay you for the material. Place needs a touch of color; I'm afraid you'll get morbid sitting in here."

Oh, no, I said, and laughed, I'm sure I won't.

"It'd be a different story if you was a man. A woman wants things a bit cosier."

So I got up and went to the window and looked down into the empty Sunday street through the slats of the Venetian blind, to avoid the accusing vulnerability of his fat face and I tried out a cold voice that is to be heard frequently in my thoughts but has great difficulty getting out of my cowardly mouth. "Mr. Malley, please don't bother me about this any more. I said it suits me. I have everything I want. Thanks for showing me about the light."

The effect was devastating enough to shame me. "I certainly wouldn't dream of bothering you," he said, with precision of speech and aloof sadness. "I merely made these suggestions for your comfort. Had I realized I was in your way, I would of left some time ago." When he had gone I felt better, even a little exhilarated at my victory though still ashamed of how easy it had been. I told myself that he would have had to be discouraged sooner or later; it was better to have it over with at the beginning.

The following weekend he knocked on my door. His expression of humility was exaggerated, almost enough so to seem mocking, yet in another sense it was real and I felt unsure of myself.

"I won't take up a minute of your time," he said. "I never meant to be a nuisance. I just wanted to tell you I'm sorry I offended you last time and I apologize. Here's a little present if you will accept."

He was carrying a plant whose name I did not know; it had thick, glossy leaves and grew out of a pot wrapped lavishly in pink and silver foil.

"There," he said, arranging this plant in a corner of my room. "I don't want any bad feelings with you and me. I'll take the blame. And I thought, maybe she won't accept furnishings, but what's the matter with a nice little plant, that'll brighten things up for you."

It was not possible for me, at this moment, to tell him that I did not want a plant. I hate house plants. He told me how to take care of it, how often to water it and so on; I thanked him. There was nothing else I could do, and I had the unpleasant feeling that beneath his offering of apologies and gifts he was well aware of this and in some way gratified by it. He kept on talking, using the words *bad feelings*, *offended*, *apologize*. I tried once to interrupt, with the idea of explaining that I had made provision for an area in my life where good feelings, or bad, did not enter in, that between him and me; in fact, it was not necessary that there be any feelings at all; but this struck me as a hopeless task. How could I confront, in the open, this craving for intimacy? Besides, the plant in its shiny paper had confused me.

"How's the writing progressing?" he said, with an air of putting all our unfortunate differences behind him.

"Oh, about as usual."

"Well if you ever run out of things to write about, I got a barrelful." Pause. "But I guess I'm just eatin' into your time here," he said with a kind of painful buoyancy. This was a test, and I did not pass it. I smiled, my eyes held by that magnificent plant; I said it was all right.

"I was just thinking about the fellow was in here before you, Chiropractor. You could of wrote a book about him."

I assumed a listening position, my hands no longer hovering over the keys. If cowardice and insincerity are big vices of mine, curiosity is certainly another.

"He had a good practice built up here. The only trouble was, he gave more adjustments than was listed in the book of chiropractory. Oh, he was adjusting right and left. I came in here after he moved out, and what do you think I found? Soundproofing! This whole room was soundproofed, to enable him to make his adjustments without disturbing anybody. This very room you're sitting writing your stories in.

"First we knew of it was a lady knocked on my door one day, wanted me to provide her with a passkey to his office. He'd locked his door against her.

"I guess he just got tired of treating her particular case. I guess he figured he'd been knocking away at it long enough. Lady well on in years, you know, and him just a young man. He had a nice young wife too and a couple of the prettiest children you ever would want to see. Filthy some of the things that go on in this world."

It took me some time to realize that he told this story not simply as a piece of gossip, but as something a writer would be particularly interested to hear. Writing and lewdness had a vague delicious connection in his mind. Even this notion, however, seemed so wistful, so infantile, that it struck me as a waste of energy to attack it. I knew now I must avoid hurting him for my own sake, not for his. It had been a great mistake to think that a little roughness would settle things.

• • •

The next present was a teapot. I insisted that I drank only coffee and told him to give it to his wife. He said that tea was better for the nerves and that he had known right away I was a nervous person, like himself. The teapot was covered with gilt and roses and I knew that it was not cheap, in spite of its extreme hideousness. I kept it on my table. I also continued to care for the plant, which thrived obscenely in the corner of my room. I could not decide what else to do. He bought me a wastebasket, a fancy one with Chinese on all eight sides; he got a foam rubber cushion for my chair. I despised myself for submitting to this blackmail. I did not even really pity him; it was just that I could not turn away, I could not turn away from that obsequious hunger. And he knew himself my tolerance was bought, in a way he must have hated me for it.

When he lingered in my office now he told me stories of himself. It occurred to me that he was revealing his life to me in the hope that I would write it down. Of course he had probably revealed it to plenty of people for no particular reason, but in my case there seemed to be a special, even desperate necessity. His life was a series of calamities, as people's lives often are; he had been let down by people he had trusted, refused help by those he had depended on, betrayed by the very friends to whom he had given kindness and material help. Other people, mere strangers and passersby, had taken time to torment him gratuitously, in novel and inventive ways. On occasion, his very life had been threatened. Moreover his wife was a difficulty, her health being poor and her temperament unstable; what was he to do? You see how it is, he said, lifting his hands, but I live. He looked to me to say yes.

I took to coming up the stairs on tiptoe, trying to turn my key without making a noise; this was foolish of course because I could not muffle my typewriter. I actually considered writing in longhand, and wished repeatedly for the evil chiropractor's soundproofing. I told my husband my problem and he said it was not a problem at all. Tell him you're busy, he said. As a matter of fact I did tell him; every time he came to my door, always armed with a little gift or an errand, he asked me how I was and I said that today I was busy. Ah, then, he said, as he eased himself through the door, he would not keep me a minute. And all the time, as I have said, he knew what was going on in my mind, how I weakly longed to be rid of him. He knew but could not afford to care.

• • •

One evening after I had gone home I discovered that I had left at the office a letter I had intended to post, and so I went back to get it. I saw from the street that the light was on in the room where I worked. Then I saw him bending over the card table. Of course, he came in at night and read what I had written! He heard me at the door, and when I came in he was picking up my wastebasket, saying he thought he would just tidy things up for me. He went out at once. I did not say anything, but found myself trembling with anger and gratification. To have found a just cause was a wonder, an unbearable relief.

Next time he came to my door I had locked it on the inside. I knew his step, his chummy cajoling knock. I continued typing loudly, but not uninterruptedly, so he would know I heard. He called my name, as if I was playing a trick; I bit my lips together not to answer. Unreasonably as ever, guilt assailed me but I typed on. That day I saw the earth was dry around the roots of the plant; I let it alone.

I was not prepared for what happened next. I found a note taped to my door, which said that Mr. Malley would be obliged if I would step into his office. I went at once to get it over with. He sat at his desk surrounded by obscure evidences of his authority; he looked at me from a distance, as one who was now compelled to see me in a new and sadly unfavourable light; the embarrassment which he showed seemed not for himself, but me. He started off by saying, with a rather stagey reluctance, that he had known of course when he took me in that I was a writer.

"I didn't let that worry me, though I have heard things about writers and artists and that type of person that didn't strike me as very encouraging. You know the sort of thing I mean."

This was something new; I could not think what it might lead to.

"Now you came to me and said, Mr. Malley, I want a place to write in. I believed you. I gave it to you. I didn't ask any questions. That's the kind of person I am. But you know the more I think about it, well, the more I am inclined to wonder."

"Wonder what?" I said.

"And your own attitude, that hasn't helped to put my mind at ease. Locking yourself in and refusing to answer your door. That's not a normal way for a person to behave. Not if they got nothing to hide. No more than it's normal for a young woman, says she has a husband and kids, to spend her time rattling away on a typewriter."

"But I don't think that—"

He lifted his hand, a forgiving gesture. "Now all I ask is, that you be open and aboveboard with me; I think I deserve that much, and if you are using that office for any other purpose, or at any other times than you let on, and having your friends or whoever they are up to see you—"

"I don't know what you mean."

"And another thing, you claim to be a writer. Well I read quite a bit of material, and I never have seen your name in print. Now maybe you write under some other name?"

"No," I said.

"Well, I don't doubt there are writers whose names I haven't heard," he said genially. "We'll let that pass. Just you give me your word of honor there won't be any more deceptions, or any carryings-on, et cetera, in that office you occupy—"

My anger was delayed somehow, blocked off by a stupid incredulity. I only knew enough to get up and walk down the hall, his voice trailing after me, and lock the door. I thought—I must go. But after I had sat down in my own room, my work in front of me; I thought again how much I liked this room, how well I worked in it, and I decided not to be forced out. After all, I felt, the struggle between us had reached a deadlock. I could refuse to open the door, refuse to look at his notes, refuse to speak to him when we met. My rent was paid in advance and if I left now it was unlikely that I would get any refund. I resolved not to care. I had been taking my manuscript home every night, to prevent his reading it, and now it seemed that even this precaution was beneath me. What did it matter if he read it, any more than if the mice scampered over it in the dark?

Several times after this I found notes on my door. I intended not to read them, but I always did. His accusations grew more specific. He had heard voices in my room. My behavior was disturbing his wife when she tried to take her afternoon nap. (I never came in the afternoons, except on weekends.) He had found a whisky bottle in the garbage.

I wondered a good deal about that chiropractor. It was not comfortable to see how the legends of Mr. Malley's life were built up.

As the notes grew more virulent our personal encounters ceased. Once or twice I saw his stooped, sweatered back disappearing as I came into the hall. Gradually our relationship passed into something that was entirely fantasy. He accused me now, by note, of being intimate with people from *Numéro Cinq*. This was a coffee-house in the neighborhood, which I imagine he invoked for symbolic purposes. I felt that nothing much more would happen now, the notes would go on, their contents becoming possibly more grotesque and so less likely to affect me.

He knocked on my door on a Sunday morning, about eleven o'clock. I had just come in and taken my coat off and put my kettle on the hot plate.

This time it was another face, remote and transfigured, that shone with the cold light of intense joy at discovering the proofs of sin.

"I wonder," he said with emotion, "if you would mind following me down the hall?"

I followed him. The light was on in the washroom. This washroom was mine and no one else used it, but he had not given me a key for it and it was always open. He stopped in front of it, pushed back the door and stood with his eyes cast down, expelling his breath discreetly.

"Now who done that?" he said, in a voice of pure sorrow.

The walls above the toilet and above the washbasin were covered with drawings and comments of the sort you see sometimes in public washrooms on the beach, and in town hall lavatories in the little decaying towns where I grew up. They were done with a lipstick, as they usually are. Someone must have got up here the night before, I thought, possibly some of the gang who always loafed and cruised around the shopping centre on Saturday nights.

"It should have been locked," I said, coolly and firmly as if thus to remove myself from the scene. "It's quite a mess."

"It sure is. It's pretty filthy language, in my book. Maybe it's just a joke to your friends, but it isn't to me. Not to mention the art work. That's a nice thing to see when you open a door on your own premises in the morning."

I said, "I believe lipstick will wash off."

"I'm just glad I didn't have my wife see a thing like this. Upsets a woman that's had a nice bringing up. Now why don't you ask your friends up here to have a party with their pails and brushes? I'd like to have a look at the people with that kind of a sense of humour."

I turned to walk away and he moved heavily in front of me.

"I don't think there's any question how these decorations found their way onto my walls."

"If you're trying to say I had anything to do with it," I said, quite flatly and wearily, "you must be crazy."

"How did they get there then? Whose lavatory is this? Eh, whose?"

"There isn't any key to it. Anybody can come up here and walk in. Maybe some kids off the street came up here and did it last night after I went home; how do I know?"

"It's a shame the way the kids gets blamed for everything, when it's the elders that corrupts them. That's a thing you might do some thinking about, you know. There's laws. Obscenity laws. Applies to this sort of thing and literature too as I believe."

This is the first time I ever remember taking deep breaths, consciously, for purposes of self-control. I really wanted to murder him. I remember how soft and loathsome his face looked, with the eyes almost closed, nostrils extended to the soothing odour righteousness, the odour of triumph. If this stupid thing had not happened, he would never have won. But he had. Perhaps he saw something in my face that unnerved him, even in this victorious moment, for he drew back to the wall, and began to say that actually, as a matter of fact, he had not really felt it was the sort of thing I personally would do, more the sort of thing that perhaps certain friends of mine—I got into my own room, shut the door.

The kettle was making a fearful noise, having almost boiled dry. I snatched it off the hot plate, pulled out the plug and stood for a moment choking on rage. This spasm passed and I did what I had to do. I put my typewriter and paper on the chair and folded the card table. I screwed the top tightly on the instant coffee and put it and the yellow mug and the teaspoon into the bag in which I had brought them; it was still lying folded on the shelf. I wished childishly to take some vengeance on the potted plant, which sat in the corner with the flowery teapot, the wastebasket, the cushion, and—I forgot—a little plastic pencil sharpener behind it.

When I was taking things down to the car Mrs. Malley came. I had seen little of her since that first day. She did not seem upset, but practical and resigned.

"He is lying down," she said. "He is not himself."

She carried the bag with the coffee and the mug in it. She was so still I felt my anger leave me, to be replaced by an absorbing depression.

• • •

I have not yet found another office. I think that I will try again someday, but not yet. I have to wait at least until that picture fades that I see so clearly in my mind, though I never saw it in reality—Mr. Malley with his rags and brushes and a pail of soapy water, scrubbing in his clumsy way, his deliberately clumsy way, at the toilet walls, stooping with difficulty, breathing sorrowfully, arranging in his mind the bizarre but somehow never quite satisfactory narrative of yet another betrayal of trust. While I arrange words, and think it is my right to be rid of him.

## Ⅲ Questions for Further Thinking

1. Why does the narrator want to find an office?

2. Why does the landlord keep interrupting the narrator's work?

3. What kind of room is the office? Why does the landlord propose that the narrator should decorate the office?

4. How does the narrator react to the landlord's "kind offers"?

5. What are the conflicts between the landlord and the narrator? Why does the narrator get annoyed after she rejects the landlord?

6. In your understanding, how does the landlord imagine a woman who assumes her profession as a writer?

## Ⅳ Appreciation

"The Office" is a story in tribute to Virginia Woolf's *A Room of One's Own*. In *A Room of One's Own*, Woolf writes, "It is necessary to have five hundred pounds a year and a room with a lock on the door if you are to write fiction or poetry." After nearly seven decades, this request is replied by Alice Munro. In "The Office," Munro imagines a woman writer—the narrator—who is frustrated by the interruption of children and house chores at home, and goes out to find an office to write. Although her attempt to find refuge at the office is not a successful one, her attempt to shatter off the role of a housewife and become a writer is nonetheless viewed as a tremendous progress for women.

One detail to notice is that the story is a reference to Woolf's writing. The narrator's sudden epiphany, "I think I ought to have an office," alludes to the famous sentence uttered by one of Virginia Woolf's iconic character Mrs. Dalloway, "I think I will buy the flowers myself." The seemingly sudden thought of planning a professional work thus forms a weird contrast with the trivial house chore of ironing the shirt.

Although the act of renting an office is a big leap from her housewife identity, there are naturally bumps and obstacles to self-actualization. In the story, there are several points that foretell upcoming conflicts between the narrator "I" and the landlord, Mr. Malley. The office, where the narrator steps into, hang a photo of Mr. Malley, which imposes a sense of self-importance, foreshadowing the landlord's future defense and reassertion of his male authority. When the narrator brings with her a few items into the office, namely, a typewriter, a table, a plate, a kettle, a jar of instant coffee, a spoon, and a yellow mug, she is creating herself a professional space, thus leaving behind her the household space which has defined her as a housewife. Therefore, there is a tension between a newly self-identified woman writer and a self-conceited misogynistic man concerning the idea of a woman's space.

The conflicts between the narrator and the landlord lie in the idea about women's role and space in domesticity. The landlord finds that his perception of a woman is challenged. When he offers gifts, such as plant, teapot, carpet, and furniture to the narrator, he is unaware that these items suggest household chores which the narrator wants to avoid. When he relates a woman's writing with gossip and sex, he is rejected because his comment suggests a deep-rooted contempt for women's writing. When he goes further to threaten the narrator because she despises his slur, he feels that his male authority is thwarted. Thus, his tricks, from sending small gifts to the bathroom slander, suggests how badly humiliated he is when the set notion that a proper woman should stay in a household, doing house chores, which he adheres to, is not performed by the narrator.

An interesting design of the story is that two opposite images of married couples that represent the changing pattern of the husband-wife relationship existing. The narrator's husband, who, despite not providing any actual help in renting the office, does not stop his wife from doing her writing tasks. In comparison, Mrs. Malley, wife of the landlord, appeared to be a woman who has been resigned to her husband's male authority. Therefore, the conflict between the narrator and the landlord can also be viewed as the tension between women's new gender roles and the gender stereotype men imposes on them. Although, in the end, the narrator gives up the office, her determination to keep her stance as a writer in her polite, rational manner symbolizes the growth of a new generation of woman who is breaking the stereotype of gender roles.

## Ⅴ Writing Topic

在《办公室》("The Office")这个短篇故事中,房东一再忽视主人公婉拒礼物、婉拒聊天等信号,强行给主人公灌输自己的想法。试思考,当下是否也存在这种沟通不对等的情况,并探究男性无视女性真实需求的原因。

# Unit 6 "Rape Fantasies" by Margaret Atwood

## Ⅰ Introduction to the Author and the Work

Margaret Atwood (1939– ) was born in Ottawa, Ontario, Canada. She was best known for her prose fiction and for her feminist perspective. Atwood completed her university studies at the Victoria College of the University of Toronto, and earned a master's degree in English literature from the Radcliffe College (becoming part of the Harvard University in 1999), Cambridge, Massachusetts, in 1962.

In her early poetry collections, *Double Persephone* (1961), *The Circle Game* (1964, revised in 1966), and *The Animals in That Country* (1968), Atwood pondered human behavior, celebrated the natural world, and condemned materialism. Role reversal and new beginning are recurrent themes in her novels, all of them centered on women seeking their relationship to the world and the individuals around them. *The Handmaid's Tale* is constructed around the written record of a woman living in sexual slavery in a repressive Christian theocracy of the future that has seized power in the wake of an ecological upheaval; a TV series based on the novel premiered in 2017 and was co-written by Atwood. The Booker Prize-winning *The Blind Assassin* (2000) is an intricately constructed narrative centering on the memoir of an elderly Canadian woman ostensibly writing in order to dispel confusion about both her sister's suicide and her own role in the posthumous publication of a novel supposedly written by her sister.

Like the title, "Rape Fantasies" revolves around the rape fantasies of a woman named Estella. And the whole novel tells us eight "rape fantasies" through Estella's first-person narrative perspective. The first two stories are shared by Estella's two colleagues. In the women's lunchroom, inspired by the popular magazine, Estella and her colleagues began to discuss their fantasies about rape during the card games. Although her friends romanticized rape fantasies, Estelle broke the trend and made a humorous shift in her fantasies which helped her frustrate the attempt to rape.

## Ⅱ Rape Fantasies[①]

The way they're going on about it in the magazines you'd think it was just invented, and not only that but it's something terrific, like a vaccine for cancer. They put it in capital letters on the front cover whether you were a good enough wife or an endomorph or an ectomorph, remember that? with the scoring upside down on page 73 and then these numbered do-it-yourself dealies, you know? RAPE, TEN THINGS TO DO ABOUT IT, like it was ten new hairdos or something. I mean, what's so new about it?

So at work they all have to talk about it because no matter what magazine you open, there it is, staring you right between the eyes, and they're beginning to have it on the television, too. Personally I'd prefer a June Allyson movie anytime but they don't make them anymore and they don't even have them that much on the *Late Show*. For instance, day before yesterday, that would be Wednesday, thank god it's Friday as they say, we were sitting around in the woman's lunch room—the lunch room, I mean you'd think you could get some peace and quiet in there—and Chrissy closes up the magazine she's been reading and says, "How about it, girls, do you have rape fantasies?"

The four of us were having our game of bridge the way we always do, and I had a bare twelve points counting the singleton with not that much of a bid in anything. So I said one club, hoping Sondra would remember about the one club convention, because the time before when I used that she thought I really meant clubs and she bid us to three, and I had was four little ones with nothing higher than a six, and we went down two and on top of that we were vulnerable. She is not the world's best bridge player. I mean, neither am I but there's a limit.

---

① serichardson. com/Readings/Rape_Fantasies. pdf.

Darlene passed but the damage was done, Sondra's head went round like it was on ball bearings and she said, "What fantasies?"

"Rape fantasies," Chrissy said. She's a receptionist and she looks like one; she's pretty but cool as a cucumber, like she's been painted all over with nail polish, if you know what I mean. Varnished. "It says here all women have rape fantasies."

"For Chrissake, I'm eating an egg sandwich," I said, "and I bid one club and Darlene passed."

"You mean, like some guy jumping you in an alley or something," Sondra said. She was eating her lunch, we all eat our lunches during the game, and she bit into a piece of that celery she always brings and started to chew away on it with this thoughtful expression in her eyes and I knew we might as well pack it in as far as the game was concerned.

"Yeah, sort of like that," Chrissy said. She was blushing a little, you could see it even under her makeup.

"I don't think you should go out alone at night," Darlene said, "you put yourself in a position," and I may have been mistaken but she was looking at me. She's the oldest, she's forty-one though you wouldn't know it and neither does she, but I looked it up in the employees' file. I like to guess a person's age and then look it up to see if I'm right. I let myself have an extra pack of cigarettes if I am, though I'm trying to cut down. I figure it's harmless as long as you don't tell. I mean, not everyone has access to that file, it's more or less confidential. But it's all right if I tell you, I don't expect you'll ever meet her, though you never know, it's a small world. Anyway.

"For heaven's sake, it's only *Toronto*," Greta said. She worked in Detroit for three years and she never lets you forget it, it's like she thinks she's a war hero or something, we should all admire in Windsor the whole time, she just worked in Detroit. Which for me doesn't really count. It's where you sleep, right?"

"Well, do you?" Chrissy said. She was obviously trying to tell us about hers but she wasn't about to go first, she's cautious, that one.

"I certainly don't," Darlene said, and she wrinkled up her nose, like this, and I had to laugh. "I think it's disgusting." She's divorced, I read that in the file too, she never talks about it. It must've been years ago anyway. She got up and went over to the coffee machine and turned her back on us as though she wasn't going to have anything more to do with it.

"Well," Greta said. I could see it was going to be between her and Chrissy. They're both blondes, I don't mean that in a bitchy way but they do try to outdress each other. Greta would like to get out of filing, she'd like to be a receptionist too she could meet more people. You don't meet much of anyone in filing except other people in filing. Me, I don't mind it so much, I have outside interests.

"Well," Greta said, "I sometimes think about, you know my apartment? It's got this little balcony, I like to sit out there in the summer and I have a few plants out there. I never bother that much about locking the door to the balcony, it's one of those sliding glass ones, I'm on the eighteenth floor for heaven's sake, I've got a good view of the lake and the CN Tower and all. But I'm sitting around one night in my housecoat, watching TV with my shoes off, you know how you do, and I see this guy's feet, coming down past the window, and the next thing you know he's standing on the balcony, he's let himself down by a rope with a hook on the end of it from the floor above, that's the nineteenth, and before I can even get up off the chesterfield he's inside the apartment. He's all dressed in black with black gloves on"—I think right away what show she got the black gloves off because I saw the same one—"and then he, well, you know."

"You know what?" Chrissy said, but Greta said, 'And afterwards he tells me that he goes all over the outside of the apartment building like that, from one floor to another, with his rope and his hook ... and then he goes out to the balcony and tosses his rope, and he climbs up it and disappears."

"Just like Tarzan," I said, but nobody laughed.

"Is that all?" Chrissy said. "Don't you ever think about, well, I think about being in the bathtub, with no clothes on ..."

"So who takes a bath in their clothes?" I said, you have to admit it's stupid when you come to think of it, but she just went on, "... with lots of bubbles, what I use is Vitabath, it's more expensive but it's so relaxing, and my hair pinned up, and the door opens and the fellow's standing there ... "

"How'd he get in?" Greta said.

"Oh, I don't know, though a window or something. Well, I can't very well get out of the bathtub, the bathroom's too small and besides he's blocking the doorway, so I just lie there, and he starts to very slowly take his own clothes off, and then he gets into the bathtub with me."

"Don't you scream or anything?" said Darlene. She'd come back with her cup of coffee, she was getting really interested. "I'd scream like bloody murder."

"Who'd hear me?" Chrissy said. "Besides, all the articles say it's better not to resist, that way you don't get hurt."

"Anyway you might get bubbles up your nose," I said, "from the deep breathing," and I swear all four of them looked at me like I was in bad taste, like I'd insulted the Virgin Mary or something. I mean, I don't see what's wrong with a little joke now and then. "Life's too short, right?"

"Listen," I said, "those aren't rape fantasies. I mean, you aren't getting raped, it's just some guy you haven't met formally who happens to be more attractive than Derek Cummins"—he's the Assistant manager, he wears elevator shoes or at any rate they have these thick soles (the bottom supporting member of the shoe) and he has this funny way of talking, we call him Dereck Duck—"and you have a good time. Rape is when they've a knife or something and you don't want to."

"So what about you, Estelle," Chrissy said; she was miffed because I laughed at her fantasy, she thought I was putting her down. Sondra was miffed too, by this time she'd finished her celery and she wanted to tell about hers, but she hadn't got in fast enough.

"All right, let me tell you one," I said. "I'm walking down this dark street at night and this fellow comes up and grabs my arm. Now it so happens that I have a plastic lemon in my purse, you know how it always says you should carry a plastic lemon in your purse? I don't really do it, I tried it once but the darn thing leaked all over my checkbook, but in this fantasy I have one, and I say to him, "You're intending to rape me, right?" and he nods, so I open my purse to get the plastic lemon, and I can't find it! My purse is full of all this junk, Kleenex and cigarettes and my change purse and my lipstick and my driver's license, you know the kind of stuff; so I ask him to hold out his hands, like this, and I pile all this junk into them and down at the bottom there's the plastic lemon, and I can't get the top off. So I hand it to him and he's very obliging, he twists the top off and hands to me, and I squirt him in the eye."

I hope you don't think that's too vicious. Come to think of it, it is a bit mean, especially when he was so polite and all.

"*That* is your rape fantasy?" Chrissy says. "I don't believe it."

"She's a card," Darlene says, she and I are the ones that've been here the longest and she never will forget the time I got drunk at the office party and insisted I was going to dance under the table instead of on top of it, I did a sort of Cossack number but then I hit my head on the bottom of the table—actually it was a desk—when I went to get up, and I knocked myself out cold. She's decided that's the mark of an original mind and she tells everyone new about it and I'm not sure that's fair. Though I did do it.

"I'm being totally honest," I say. I always am and they know it. There's no point in being anything else, is the way I look at it, and sooner or later the truth will come out so you might as well not waste the time, right? "You should hear the one about the Easy-Off Oven Cleaner."

But that was the end of the lunch hour, with one bridge game shot to hell, and the next day we spent most of the time arguing over whether to start a new game or play out the hands we had left over from the day before, so Sondra never did get a chance to tell about her rape fantasy.

It started me thinking though, about my own rape fantasies. Maybe I'm abnormal or something, I mean I have fantasies about handsome strangers coming in through the window too, like Mr. clean, I wish one would, please god somebody without flat feet and big sweat marks on his shirt, and over five feet five, believe me being tall is a handicap though it's getting better, tall guys are starting to like someone whose nose reaches higher than their belly button. But if you're being totally honest you can't count those as rape fantasies. In a real rape fantasy, what you should feel is this anxiety, like when you think about your apartment building catching on fire and whether you should use the elevator or the stairs or maybe just stick your head under a wet towel, and you try to remember everything you've read about what to do but you can't decide.

For instance, I'm walking along this dark street at night and this short, ugly fellow comes up and grabs my arm, and not only is he ugly, you know, with a sort of puffy nothing face, like those fellows you have to talk to in the bank when your account's overdrawn—of course I don't mean they're all like that—but he's absolutely covered in pimples. So he get me pinned against the wall, he's short but he's heavy, and he starts to undo himself and the zipper get stuck. I mean, one of the most significant moments in a girl's life, it's almost like getting married or having a baby or something, and he sticks the zipper.

So I say, kind of disgusted, "Oh, for Chrissake," and he starts to cry. He tells me he's never been able to get anything right in his entire life, and this is the last straw, he's going to go jump off a bridge.

"Look," I say, I feel so sorry for him, in my rape fantasies I always end up feeling sorry for the guy, I mean there has to be something wrong with them, if it was Clint Eastwood it'd be different but worse luck it never is. I was the kind of little girl who buried dead robins, know what I mean? it used to drive my mother nuts, she didn't like me touching them, because of the germs I guess. So I say, "Listen, I know how you feel. You really should do something about those pimples, if you got rid of them you'd be quite good looking, honest; then you wouldn't have to go around doing stuff like this. I had them myself once," I say, to comfort him, but in fact I did, and it ends up I give him the name of my old dermatologist, the one I had in high school, that was back in Leamington, except I used to go to St. Catharine's for the dermatologist. I'm telling you, I was really lonely when I first came here; I thought it was going to be such a big adventure and all, but it's a lot harder to meet people in a city. But I guess it's different for a guy.

Or I'm lying in bed with this terrible cold, my face is all swollen up, my eyes are red and my nose is dripping like a leaky tap, and this fellow comes in through the window and he has a terrible cold too, it's a new kind of flu that's been going around. So he says, "I'd going do rabe (should be rape you) you"—

I hope you don't mind me holding my nose like this but that's the way I imagine it—and he lets out this terrific sneeze, which slows him down a bit, also I'm no object of beauty myself, you'd have to some kind of prevent to want to rape someone with a cold like mine, it'd be like raping a bottle of LePage's mucilage the way my nose is running. He's looking wildly around the room, and I realize it's because he doesn't have a piece of Kleenex! "I'd ride here," I say, and I pass him the Kleenex why he even bothered to get out of bed, you'd think if you were going to go around climbing in windows you'd wait till you were healthier, right? I mean, that takes a certain amount of energy. So I ask him why doesn't he let me fix him a NeoCitran and scotch, that's what I always take, you still have the cold but you don't feel it, so I do and we end up watching the *Late Show* together. I mean, they aren't all sex maniacs, the rest of the time they must lead a normal life. I figure they enjoy watching the late show just like anybody else.

I do have a scarier one though ... where the fellow says he's hearing angel voices that are telling him he's got to kill me, you know, you read about things like that all the time in the papers. In this one I'm not in the apartment where I live now, I'm back in my mother's house in Leamington and the fellow's been hiding in the cellar, he grabs my arm when I go downstairs to get a jar of jam and he's got hold of the axe too, out of the garage, that one is really scary. I mean, what do you say to a nut like that?

So I start to shake but after a minute I get control of myself and I say, is he sure the angel voices have got the right person, because I hear the same angel voices and they've been telling me for some time that I'm going to give birth to the reincarnation of St. Anne who in turn has the Virgin Mary and tight after that comes Jesus Christ and the end of the world, and he wouldn't want to interfere with that, would he? So he gets confused and listens some more, and then he asks for a sign and I show him my vaccination mark, you can see it's sort of an odd-shaped one, it got infected because I scratched the top off, and that does it, he apologizes and climbs out the coal chute again, which I show he got in in the first place, and I say to myself there's some advantage in having been brought up a Catholic even though I haven't been to church since they changed the service into English, it just isn't the same, you might as well be a

Protestant. I must write to Mother and tell her to nail up that coal chute, it always has bothered me. Funny, I couldn't tell you at all what this man looks like but I know exactly what kind of shoes he's wearing, because that's the last I see of him, his shoes going up the coal chute, and they're the old-fashioned kind that lace up the ankles, even though he's young fellow. That's strange, isn't it?

Let me tell you though I really sweat until I see him safely out of there and I go upstairs right away and make myself a cup of tea. I don't think about that one much. My mother always said you shouldn't dwell on unpleasant things and I generally agree with that, I mean, dwelling on them doesn't make them go away. Though not dwelling on them doesn't make them go away either, when you come to think of it.

Sometimes I have these short ones where the fellow grabs my arm but I'm really a Kung-Fu expert, can you believe it , in real life I'm sure it would just be a conk on the head and that's that, like getting your tonsils out, you'd wake up and it would be all over except the sore places , and you'd be lucky if your neck wasn't broken or something, I could never even hit the volleyball in gym and a volleyball is fairly large, you know? —and I just go zap with my fingers into his eyes and that's it, he falls over, or I flip him against a wall or something. But I could never really stick my fingers in anyone's eyes, could you? It would feel like hot jello and I don't even like cold jelly, just thinking about it gives me the creeps. I feel a bit guilty about that one, I mean how would you like walking around knowing someone's been blinded for life because of you?

But maybe it's different for a guy.

The most touching one I have is when the fellow grabs my arm and I say, sad and kind of dignified, "You'd be raping a corpse." That pulls him up short and I explain that I've found out I have leukemia and the doctors have only given me a few months to live. That's why I'm out pacing the streets alone at night, I need to think, you know, come to terms with myself. I don't really have leukemia but in the fantasy I do, I guess I chose that particular disease because a girl in my grade four class died of it, the whole class sent her flowers when she was in hospital. I didn't understand then that she was going to die and

I wanted to have leukemia too so I could get flowers. Kids are funny, aren't they? Well, it turns out that he has leukemia himself, and he only has a few months to live, that's why he's going around raping people, he's very bitter because he's so young and his life is being taken from him before he's really lived it. So we walk along gently under the street lights, it's spring and sort of misty, and we end up going for coffee, we're happy we've found the only other person in the world who can understand what we're going through, it's almost like fate, and after a while we just sort of look at each other and our hands touch, and he comes back with me and moves into my apartment and we spend our last months together before we die, we just sort of don't wake up in the morning, though I've never decided which one of us gets to die first. If it's him I have to go on and fantasize about the funeral, if it's me I don't have to worry about that, so it just about depends on how tired I am at the time. You may not believe this but sometimes I even start crying. I cry at the ends of movies, even the ones that aren't all that sad, so I guess it's the same thing. My mother's like that too.

The funny thing about these fantasies is that the man is always someone I don't know, and the statistics in the magazines, well, most of them anyway, they say it's often someone you do know, at least a little bit, like your boss or something—I mean, it wouldn't be my boss, he's over sixty and I'm sure he couldn't rape his way out of a paper bag, poor old thing, but it might be someone like Dereck Duck, in his elevator shoes, perish the thought—or someone you just met, who invites you up for a drink, it's getting so you can hardly be sociable anymore, and how are you supposed to meet people if you can't trust them even that basic amount? You can't spend your whole life in the filing department or cooped up in your own apartment with all the doors and windows locked and the shades down. I'm not what you would call a drinker but I like to go out now and then for a drink or two in a nice place, even if I am by myself, I'm with Women's Lib on that even though I can't agree with a lot of other things they say. Like here for instance, the waiters all know me and if anyone, you know, bothers me ... I don't know why I'm telling you all this, except I think it helps you get to know a person, especially at first, hearing some of the things they think about. At work they call me the office worry wart, but it isn't much like worrying, it's more like figuring out what you should do in an emergency, like I said before.

Anyway, another thing about it is that there's a lot of conversation, in fact I spend most of my time, in the fantasy that is, wondering what I'm going to say and what he's going to say, I think it would be better if you could get a conversation going. Like, how could a fellow do that to a person he's just had a long conversation with, once you let them know you're human, you have a life too, I don't see how they could go ahead with it, right? I mean, I know it happens but I just don't understand it, that's the part I really don't understand.

## Ⅲ Questions for Further Thinking

1. In the first sentence of the story, "The way they're going on about it in the magazines you'd think it was just invented," who are "they"? What does "it" refers to?

2. In public's perception, what is the power relationship between men and women in the rape event?

3. When people talk about rape, where do people typically imagine a rape to take place?

4. Compare the fantasies made by each woman. Discuss the differences in circumstance, physical environment, the portray of man and woman, as well as strategies involved.

5. Select one of the fantasies which leave you the deepest impression, then analyze the power relationship between the rapist and the woman.

## Ⅳ Appreciation

As the title suggests, "Rape Fantasies" is about the fantasies about rape. Some readers might feel a bit uneasy about the title, because in social norms, the word "rape" connotes deep shame, particularly for women.

People may even speculate on the story as something morally improper. It was particularly so in the 1970s. This is what Margaret Atwood intends to discuss in this story. By entitling the story with a sensitive word "rape," she makes an effort to de-stigmatize the concept and to free women from being morally judged when they were the victims of sexual violence.

This story was published in 1975 during the second wave of feminism, at the time when women were still locked in the conventional idea of being a home bird. The starting paragraph of "Rape Fantasies" reveals how media, like magazines, which were dominated by male editors then, tended to instruct women readers how to respond to rape. This was somewhat ironic because, on most occasions, it was men who raped, while women were the potential victims. It is hypocritical considering that these men are teaching women how to avoid being raped instead of addressing the root issue itself: male rapists. Thus, Atwood designs this story to have women make their say about rape.

The whole story is filled with ironies about gender stereotypes. In it, Atwood challenges male dominance and the false conventional idea that women incapable of discussing intelligent issues through these five women conducting small talks about rape fantasies. The five women represent five different attitudes towards rape. Sondra is silenced by this forbidden topic. Darlene shows her contempt for rape and regards it a disgusting topic. Chrissy and Greta, who are both blondes and are well aware that they could use their beauty as assets to their advantage, glamorize rape as akin to Hollywood romance. In their fantasies, the rapist is brimmed with manly hormones, and is handsomely welcomed. Their responses, unsurprisingly, reflect the internalization of male value in viewing women as merely bodies rather than humans with emotions and minds.

In comparison, the narrator "I" provides a wholly different perspective of rape fantasies. First of all, she de-romanticizes rape by showing its violent nature. Rape is not a romantic sexual experience but a dark situation that provokes fear and anxiety. Secondly, she ironically overthrows the traditional gender stereotype where men are stronger while women are weaker. In each rape event, the rapist, who is physically stronger than the woman, is considered to be less smart, and is either ugly, short, stupid, fanatic, or sick. Their defects offset their physical advantage, so that women who are trapped in the precarious situation can resort to their intelligence to ward off possible harms. One basic strategy the narrator "I" enumerates to avert being raped is communication. The once devalued woman's tittle-tattle now works as a kind of gender privilege which enables women to dissuade the rapist through her communicative power.

## Ⅴ Writing Topic

该篇故事从一开始就点出了20世纪80年代西方媒体(报刊)对女性生活的指导性介入。主人公埃斯塔拉(Estella)的"幻想"无疑是对(男性主导下的)媒体的强烈反讽。当下,媒体从报刊延伸出数字媒体、自媒体等多种形式,但是,媒体对女性生活的强行介入和指导依旧无处不在。请试谈当下媒体对女性形象、审美、言行的潜在影响。

# Part Three

## *Generational Bonds*

# Unit 7 "Two Kinds" by Amy Tan

## Ⅰ Introduction to the Author and the Work

Amy Tan (1952- ) is a Chinese American writer and novelist. She grew up in Northern California, and when her father and older brother both died from brain tumors in 1966, she moved with her mother and younger brother to Europe, where she attended high school in Montreux, Switzerland. She returned to the United States for college. After college, Tan worked as a language development consultant and as a corporate freelance writer. In 1985, she wrote the story "Rules of the Game" for a writing workshop, which formed the early foundation for her first novel, *The Joy Luck Club*. Ever since its publication in 1989, the book explored the relationship between Chinese women and their Chinese American daughters and became the longest-running *The New York Times* bestseller for that year. *The Joy Luck Club* received numerous awards. It has been translated into 25 languages. In 1993, it was made into a major motion picture for which Tan co-wrote the screenplay.

"Two Kinds" begins with a brief passage in which it is made clear that the narrator, Jing-mei Woo, is telling this story from her childhood memory, and she is now in her mid-thirties. It is also a story about Jing-mei's mother and their relationship. When Jing-mei is nine years old, her mother, Suyuan Woo, starts encouraging her to be a "prodigy." While their first several attempts fail (i.e., becoming the first Chinese Shirley Temple), Suyuan is not ready to give up on her daughter. She and Jing-mei start a tension which is typified by Jing-mei's failure in the talent show.

## Ⅱ Two Kinds[①]

My mother believed you could be anything you wanted to be in America. You could open a restaurant. You could work for the government and get good retirement. You could buy a house with almost no money down. You could become rich. You could become instantly famous.

"Of course you can be prodigy, too," my mother told when I was nine. "You can be best anything. What does Auntie Lindo know? Her daughter, she is only best tricky."

America was where all my mother's hopes lay. She had come here in 1949 after losing everything in China: her mother and father, her family home, her first husband, and two daughters, twin baby girls. But she never looked back with regret. There were so many ways for things to get better.

• • •

We didn't immediately pick the right kind of prodigy. At first my mother thought I could be a Chinese Shirley Temple. We'd watch Shirley's old movies on TV as though they were training films. My mother would poke my arm and say, "*Ni kan*" —you watch. And I would see Shirley tapping her feet, or singing a sailor song, or pursing her lips into a very round O while saying, "Oh my goodness."

"*Ni kan*," said my mother as Shirley's eyes flooded with tears. "You already know how. Don't need talent for crying!"

Soon after my mother got this idea about Shirley Temple, she took me to a beauty training school in the Mission district and put me in the hands of a student who could barely hold the scissors without shaking. Instead of getting big fat curls, I emerged with an uneven mass of crinkly black fuzz. My mother dragged me off to the bathroom and tried to wet down my hair.

"You look like Negro Chinese," she lamented, as if I had done this on purpose.

① Two Kinds Amy Tan. pdf (amphi. com).

The instructor of the beauty training school had to lop off these soggy clumps to make my hair even again. "Peter Pan is very popular these days," the instructor assured my mother. I now had hair the length of a boy's, with straight-across bangs that hung at a slant two inches above my eyebrows. I liked the haircut and it made me actually look forward to my future fame.

In fact, in the beginning, I was just as excited as my mother, maybe even more so. I pictured this prodigy part of me as many different images, trying each one on for size. I was a dainty ballerina girl standing by the curtains, waiting to hear the right music that would send me floating on my tiptoes. I was like the Christ child lifted out of the straw manger, crying with holy indignity. I was Cinderella stepping from her pumpkin carriage with sparkly cartoon music filling the air.

In all of my imaginings, I was filled with a sense that I would soon become perfect. My mother and father would adore me. I would be beyond reproach. I would never feel the need to sulk for anything.

But sometimes the prodigy in me became impatient. "If you don't hurry up and get me out of here, I'm disappearing for good," it warned. "And then you'll always be nothing."

• • •

Every night after dinner, my mother and I would sit at the Formica topped kitchen table. She would present new tests, taking her examples from stories of amazing children she had read in *Ripley's Believe It or Not*, or *Good Housekeeping*, *Reader's Digest*, and a dozen other magazines she kept in a pile in our bathroom. My mother got these magazines from people whose houses she cleaned. And since she cleaned many houses each week, we had a great assortment. She would look through them all, searching for stories about remarkable children.

The first night she brought out a story about a three-year-old boy who knew the capitals of all the states and even most of the European countries. A teacher was quoted as saying the little boy could also pronounce the names of the foreign cities correctly.

"What's the capital of Finland?" my mother asked me, looking at the magazine story.

All I knew was the capital of California, because Sacramento was the name of the street we lived on in Chinatown. "Nairobi!" I guessed, saying the most foreign word I could think of. She checked to see if that was possibly one way to pronounce "Helsinki" before showing me the answer.

The tests got harder—multiplying numbers in my head, finding the queen of hearts in a deck of cards, trying to stand on my head without using my hands, predicting the daily temperatures in Los Angeles, New York, and London.

One night I had to look at a page from the Bible for three minutes and then report everything I could remember. "Now Jehoshaphat had riches and honor in abundance and ... that's all I remember, Ma," I said.

And after seeing my mother's disappointed face once again, something inside of me began to die. I hated the tests, the raised hopes and failed expectations. Before going to bed that night, I looked in the mirror above the bathroom sink and when I saw only my face staring back—and that it would always be this ordinary face—I began to cry. Such a sad, ugly girl! I made high-pitched noises like a crazed animal, trying to scratch out the face in the mirror.

And then I saw what seemed to be the prodigy side of me—because I had never seen that face before. I looked at my reflection, blinking so I could see more clearly. The girl staring back at me was angry, powerful. This girl and I were the same. I had new thoughts, willful thoughts, or rather thoughts filled with lots of won'ts. I won't let her change me, I promised myself. I won't be what I'm not.

So now on nights when my mother presented her tests, I performed listlessly, my head propped on one arm. I pretended to be bored. And I was. I got so bored I started counting the bellows of the foghorns out on the bay while my mother drilled me in other areas. The sound was comforting and reminded me of the cow jumping over the moon. And the next day, I played a game with myself, seeing if my mother would give up on me before eight bellows at most. After a while I usually counted only one, maybe two bellows at most. At last she was beginning to give up hope.

• • •

Two or three months had gone by without any mention of my being a prodigy again. And then one day my mother was watching *The Ed Sullivan Show* on TV. The TV was old and the sound kept shorting out. Every time my mother got halfway up from the sofa to adjust the set, the sound would go back on and Ed would be talking. As soon as she sat down, Ed would go silent again. She got up, and the TV broke into loud piano music. She sat down. Silence. Up and down, back and forth, quiet and loud. It was like a stiff embraceless dance between her and the TV set. Finally she stood by the set with her hand on the sound dial.

She seemed entranced by the music, a little frenzied piano piece with this mesmerizing quality, sort of quick passages and then teasing lilting ones before it returned to the quick playful parts.

"*Ni kan*," my mother said, calling me over with hurried hand gestures. "Look here."

I could see why my mother was fascinated by the music. It was being pounded out by a little Chinese girl, about nine years old, with a Peter Pan haircut. The girl had the sauciness of a Shirley Temple. She was proudly modest like a proper Chinese child. And she also did this fancy sweep of a curtsy, so that the fluffy skirt of her white dress cascaded slowly to the floor like petals of a large carnation.

In spite of these warning signs, I wasn't worried. Our family had no piano and we couldn't afford to buy one, let alone reams of sheet music and piano lessons. So I could be generous in my comments when my mother bad-mouthed the little girl on TV.

"Play note right, but doesn't sound good! No singing sound," complained my mother.

"What are you picking on her for?" I said carelessly. "She's pretty good. Maybe she's not the best, but she's trying hard." I knew almost immediately I would be sorry I said that.

"Just like you," she said. "Not the best. Because you not trying." She gave a little huff as she let go of the sound dial and sat down on the sofa.

The little Chinese girl sat down also to play an encore of "Anitra's Dance" by Grieg. I remember the song, because later on I had to learn how to play it.

• • •

Three days after watching *The Ed Sullivan Show*, my mother told me what my schedule would be for piano lessons and piano practice. She had talked to Mr. Chong, who lived on the first floor of our apartment building. Mr. Chong was a retired piano teacher and my mother had traded housecleaning services for weekly lessons and a piano for me to practice on every day, two hours a day, from four until six.

When my mother told me this, I felt as though I had been sent to hell. I whined and then kicked my foot a little when I couldn't stand it anymore.

"Why don't you like me the way I am? I'm *not* a genius! I can't play the piano. And even if I could, I wouldn't go on TV if you paid me a million dollars!" I cried.

My mother slapped me. "Who ask you be genius?" she shouted. "Only ask you be your best. For your sake. You think I want you be genius? Huh! What for! Who ask you!"

"So ungrateful," I heard her mutter in Chinese. "If she had as much talent as she has temper, she would be famous now."

Mr. Chong, whom I secretly nicknamed Old Chong, was very strange, always tapping his fingers to the silent music of an invisible orchestra. He looked ancient in my eyes. He had lost most of the hair on top of his head and he wore thick glasses and had eyes that always looked tired and sleepy. But he must have been younger than I thought, since he lived with his mother and was not yet married.

I met Old Lady Chong once and that was enough. She had this peculiar smell like a baby that had done something in its pants. And her fingers felt like a dead person's, like an old peach I once found in the back of the refrigerator: the skin just slid off the meat when I picked it up.

I soon found out why Old Chong had retired from teaching piano. He was deaf. "Like Beethoven!" he shouted to me. "We're both listening only in our head!" And he would start to conduct his frantic silent sonatas.

Our lessons went like this. He would open the book and point to different things, explaining their purpose: "Key! Treble! Bass! No sharps or flats! So this is C major! Listen now and play after me!"

And then he would play the C scale a few times, a simple chord, and then, as if inspired by an old, unreachable itch, he gradually added more notes and running trills and a pounding bass until the music was really something quite grand.

I would play after him, the simple scale, the simple chord, and then I just played some nonsense that sounded like a cat running up and down on top of garbage cans. Old Chong smiled and applauded and then said, "Very good! But now you must learn to keep time!"

So that's how I discovered that Old Chong's eyes were too slow to keep up with the wrong notes I was playing. He went through the motions in half-time. To help me keep rhythm, he stood behind me, pushing down on my right shoulder for every beat. He balanced pennies on top of my wrists so I would keep them still as I slowly played scales and arpeggios. He had me curve my hand around an apple and keep that shape when playing chords. He marched stiffly to show me how to make each finger dance up and down, staccato like an obedient little soldier.

He taught me all these things, and that was how I also learned I could be lazy and get away with mistakes, lots of mistakes. If I hit the wrong notes because I hadn't practiced enough, I never corrected myself. I just kept playing in rhythm. And Old Chong kept conducting his own private reverie.

So maybe I never really gave myself a fair chance. I did pick up the basics pretty quickly, and I might have become a good pianist at that young age. But I was so determined not to try, not to be anybody different that I learned to play only the most ear-splitting preludes, the most discordant hymns.

Over the next year, I practiced like this, dutifully in my own way. And then one day I heard my mother and her friend Lindo Jong both talking in a loud bragging tone of voice so others could hear. It was after church, and I was leaning against the brick wall wearing a dress with stiff white petticoats. Auntie Lindo's daughter, Waverly, who was about my age, was standing farther down the wall about five feet away. We had grown up together and shared all the closeness of two sisters squabbling over crayons and dolls. In other words, for the most part, we hated each other. I thought she was snotty. Waverly Jong had gained a certain amount of fame as "Chinatown's Littlest Chinese Chess Champion."

"She bring home too many trophy," lamented Auntie Lindo that Sunday. "All day she play chess. All day I have no time do nothing but dust off her winnings." She threw a scolding look at Waverly, who pretended not to see her.

"You lucky you don't have this problem," said Auntie Lindo with a sigh to my mother.

And my mother squared her shoulders and bragged, "Our problem worser than yours. If we ask Jing-mei wash dishes, she hear nothing but music. It's like you can't stop this natural talent."

And right then, I was determined to put a stop to her foolish pride.

• • •

A few weeks later, Old Chong and my mother conspired to have me play in a talent show which would be held in the church hall. By then, my parents had saved up enough to buy me a secondhand piano, a black Wurlitzer spinet with a scarred bench. It was the showpiece of our living room.

For the talent show, I was to play a piece called *Pleading Child* from Schumann's *Scenes from Childhood*. It was a simple, moody piece that sounded more difficult than it was. I was supposed to memorize the whole thing, playing the repeat parts twice to make the piece sound longer. But I dawdled over it, playing a few bars and then cheating, looking up to see what notes followed. I never really listened to what I was playing. I daydreamed about being somewhere else, about being someone else.

The part I liked to practice best was the fancy curtsy: right foot out, touch the rose on the carpet with a pointed foot, sweep to the side, bend left leg, look up and smile.

My parents invited all the couples from the Joy Luck Club to witness my debut. Auntie Lindo and Uncle Tin were there. Waverly and her two older brothers had also come. The first two rows were filled with children both younger and older than I was. The littlest ones got to go first. They recited simple nursery rhymes, squawked out tunes on miniature violins, twirled Hula Hoops in pink ballet tutus, and when they bowed or curtsied, the audience would sigh in unison,

"Awww," and then clap enthusiastically.

When my turn came, I was very confident. I remember my childish excitement. It was as if I knew, without a doubt, that the prodigy side of me really did exist. I had no fear whatsoever, no nervousness. I remember thinking to myself, This is it! This is it! I looked out over the audience, at my mother's blank face, my father's yawn, Auntie Lindo's stiff-lipped smile, Waverly's sulky expression. I had on a white dress layered with sheets of lace, and a pink bow in my Peter Pan haircut. As I sat down I envisioned people jumping to their feet and Ed Sullivan rushing up to introduce me to everyone on TV.

And I started to play. It was so beautiful. I was so caught up in how lovely I looked that at first I didn't worry how I would sound. So it was a surprise to me when I hit the first wrong note and I realized something didn't sound quite right. And then I hit another and another followed that. A chill started at the top of my head and began to trickle down. Yet I couldn't stop playing, as though my hands were bewitched. I kept thinking my fingers would adjust themselves back, like a train switching to the right track. I played this strange jumble through two repeats, the sour notes staying with me all the way to the end.

When I stood up, I discovered my legs were shaking. Maybe I had just been nervous and the audience, like Old Chong, had seen me go through the right motions and had not heard anything wrong at all. I swept my right foot out, went down on my knee, looked up and smiled. The room was quiet, except for Old Chong, who was beaming and shouting, "Bravo! Bravo! Well done!" But then I saw my mother's face, her stricken face. The audience clapped weakly, and as I walked back to my chair, with my whole face quivering as I tried not to cry, I heard a little boy whisper loudly to his mother, "That was awful," and the mother whispered back, "Well, she certainly tried."

And now I realized how many people were in the audience, the whole world it seemed. I was aware of eyes burning into my back. I felt the shame of my mother and father as they sat stiffly throughout the rest of the show.

We could have escaped during intermission. Pride and some strange sense of honor must have anchored my parents to their chairs. And so we watched it all: the eighteen-year-old boy with a fake mustache who did a magic show and juggled flaming hoops while riding a unicycle. The breasted girl with white makeup who sang from *Madama Butterfly* and got an honorable mention. And the eleven-year-old boy who won first prize playing a tricky violin song that sounded like a busy bee.

After the show, the Hsus, the Jongs, and the St. Clairs from the Joy Luck Club came up to my mother and father.

"Lots of talented kids," Auntie Lindo said vaguely, smiling broadly.

"That was somethin' else," said my father, and I wondered if he was referring to me in a humorous way, or whether he even remembered what I had done.

Waverly looked at me and shrugged her shoulders. "You aren't a genius like me," she said matter-of-factly. And if I hadn't felt so bad, I would have pulled her braids and punched her stomach.

But my mother's expression was what devastated me: a quiet, blank look that said she had lost everything. I felt the same way and it seemed as if everybody were now coming up, like gawkers at the scene of an accident, to see what parts were actually missing. When we got on the bus to go home, my father was humming the busy-bee tune and my mother was silent. I kept thinking she wanted to wait until we got home before shouting at me. But when my father unlocked the door to our apartment, my mother walked in and then went to the back, into the bedroom. No accusations. No blame. And in a way, I felt disappointed. I had been waiting for her to start shouting, so I could shout back and cry and blame her for all my misery.

• • •

I assumed my talent-show fiasco meant I never had to play the piano again. But two days later, after school, my mother came out of the kitchen and saw me watching TV.

"Four clock," she reminded me as if it were any other day. I was stunned, as though she were asking me to go through the talent-show torture again. I wedged myself more tightly in front of the TV.

"Turn off TV." She called from the kitchen five minutes later.

I didn't budge. And then I decided I didn't have to do what my mother said anymore. I wasn't her slave. This wasn't China. I had listened to her before and look what happened. She was the stupid one.

She came out from the kitchen and stood in the arched entryway of the living room. "Four clock," she said once again, louder.

"I'm not going to play anymore," I said nonchalantly. "Why should I? I'm not a genius."

She walked over and stood in front of the TV. I saw her chest was heaving up and down in an angry way.

"No!" I said, and I now felt stronger, as if my true self had finally emerged. So this was what had been inside me all along. "No! I won't!" I screamed.

She yanked me by the arm, pulled me off the floor, snapped off the TV. She was frighteningly strong, half pulling, half carrying me toward the piano as I kicked the throw rugs under my feet. She lifted me up and onto the hard bench. I was sobbing by now, looking at her bitterly. Her chest was heaving even more and her mouth was open, smiling crazily as if she were pleased I was crying.

"You want me to be someone that I'm not!" I sobbed. "I'll never be the kind of daughter you want me to be!"

"Only two kinds of daughters," she shouted in Chinese. "Those who are obedient and those who follow their own mind! Only one kind of daughter can live in this house. Obedient daughter!"

"Then I wish I wasn't your daughter. I wish you weren't my mother," I shouted. As I said these things I got scared. It felt like worms and toads and slimy things crawling out of my chest, but it also felt good, as if this awful side of me had surfaced, at last.

"Too late change this," said my mother shrilly.

And I could sense her anger rising to its breaking point. I wanted to see it spill over. And that's when I remembered the babies she had lost in China, the ones we never talked about. "Then I wish I'd never been born!" I shouted. "I wish I were dead! Like them."

It was as if I had said the magic word—Alakazam—and her face went blank, her mouth closed, her arms went slack, and she backed out of the room, stunned, as if she were blowing away like a small brown leaf, thin, brittle, lifeless.

• • •

It was not the only disappointment my mother felt in me. In the years that followed, I failed her so many times, each time asserting my own will, my right to fall short of expectations. I didn't get straight As. I didn't become class president, I didn't get into Stanford. I dropped out of college.

For unlike my mother, I did not believe I could be anything I wanted to be. I could only be me.

And for all those years, we never talked about the disaster at the recital or my terrible accusations afterward at the piano bench. All that remained unchecked, like a betrayal that was now unspeakable. So I never found a way to ask her why she had hoped for something so large that failure was inevitable.

And even worse, I never asked her what frightened me the most: Why had she given up hope?

For after our struggle at the piano, she never mentioned my playing again. The lessons stopped. The lid to the piano was closed, shutting out the dust, my misery, and her dreams.

So she surprised me. A few years ago, she offered to give me the piano, for my thirtieth birthday. I had not played in all those years. I saw the offer as a sign of forgiveness, a tremendous burden removed.

"Are you sure?" I asked shyly. "I mean, won't you and Dad miss it?"

"No, this is your piano," she said firmly. "Always your piano. You only one can play."

"Well, I probably can't play anymore." I said. "It's been years."

"You pick up fast," said my mother, as if she knew this was certain. "You have natural talent. You could be a genius if you want to."

"No I couldn't."

"You just not trying," said my mother. And she was neither angry nor sad. She said it as if to announce a fact that could never be disproved. "Take it." she said.

But I didn't at first. It was enough that she had offered it to me. And after that, every time I saw it in my parents' living room, standing in front of the bay windows, it made me feel proud, as if it were a shiny trophy I had won back.

• • •

Last week I sent a tuner over to my parents' apartment and had the piano reconditioned, for purely sentimental reasons. My mother had died a few months before and I had been getting things in order for my father, a little bit at a time. I put the jewelry in special silk pouches. The sweaters she had knitted in yellow, pink, bright orange—all the colors I hated—I put those in moth-proof boxes. I found some old Chinese silk dresses, the kind with little slits up the sides. I rubbed the old silk against my skin, then wrapped them in tissue and decided to take them home with me.

After I had the piano tuned, I opened the lid and touched the keys. It sounded even richer than I remembered. Really, it was a very good piano. Inside the bench were the same exercise notes with handwritten scales, the same secondhand music books with their covers held together with yellow tape.

I opened up the Schumann book to the dark little piece I had played at the recital. It was on the left-hand side of the page, *Pleading Child*. It looked more difficult than I remembered. I played a few bars, surprised at how easily the notes came back to me.

And for the first time, or so it seemed, I noticed the piece on the right-hand side. It was called *Perfectly Contented*. I tried to play this one as well. It had a lighter melody but the same flowing rhythm and turned out to be quite easy. *Pleading Child* was shorter but slower; *Perfectly Contented* was longer, but faster. And after I played them both a few times, I realized they were two halves of the same song.

## Ⅲ Questions for Further Thinking

1. When Jing-mei's mother tells Jing-mei "you can be best anything," what is she trying to convey to her daughter?

2. When Jing-mei's mother responds to Jing-mei's protest, she says, "Who ask you be genius?" Do you think this justification is contradictory with her previous stimulation that "you can be best anything"?

3. When Jing-mei acts idly in playing the piano, do you believe that she is

simply trying to disappoint her mother?

4. At the end of the story, it mentions another musical piece, *Perfectly Contented*. What is the relationship between this musical piece and the previous one, *Pleading Child*?

5. In this story, generational conflict works together with cultural conflict. Which of the conflicts serves as the foundation? How do they influence each other?

## Ⅳ Appreciation

To many Chinese readers, "Two Kinds" is a story that fits into their knowledge of the mother-daughter relationship. Although the story touches on the cultural conflict between the Chinese immigrants and their American-born children, the adolescent rebellion of Jing-mei against her mother is still likely to strike a chord with many Chinese students.

The way Jing-mei's mother pushes Jing-mei to be the best is a typical example of how a Chinese mother tries to "tiger parenting in educating her kid." However, the value that the Chinese put on education is not the only reason for the generational conflict. Like many immigrants, Jing-mei's mother has adopted the idea of the American Dream to realize one's self-will. It is out of this belief that she tries to instill the idea in her daughter that "you could be anything you wanted to be in America." She believes that if her daughter works hard, she can be her best in life. What she is doing is actually cloaking her tendency to compare Jing-mei to her peers in the language of the American Dream. One catchphrase Jing-mei's mother habitually uses to push Jing-mei is "Ni kan" (meaning "look"), which is usually directed to a popularly known model like Shirley Temple or a trophy child like Jing-mei's best friend, Waverly.

As to Jing-mei, who is stirred up by her mother's encouragement to be the best, she soon realizes that she is only an ordinary girl. To fend off her mother's high expectations and to refuse to become a tool for her mother to win face, she uses small tricks to dodge hard work. One typical example is to cheat her deaf piano teacher by practicing in a disheartened manner. It is not until the talent show that her deception is uncovered. The fiasco in the talent show brings disgrace to Jing-mei's mother, which escalates the conflict between Jing-mei and her mother.

The quarrel between Jing-mei and her mother indicates the meaning of the title "Two Kinds"—two kinds of daughters who are either obedient or strong-minded. The two kinds of daughters respectively refer to the Chinese daughter and American daughter. Jing-mei's mother declares that only the obedient Chinese daughter is allowed to live in the house. To protest, Jing-mei insists on acting at her own will as an American daughter. The generational conflict thus is overtaken by uncompromised cultural conflict.

With harsh remarks to hold up her position, Jing-mei appears to be the indomitable side to win the fight. Years after she grew up, when Jing-mei replays the musical piece that she failed in the recital, she finds another piece on the right page of Schumann book. They are two halves of the same song. Neither of them are very difficult to play. This finding seems to support the idea that her mother is not completely wrong in disciplining her to work hard. By understanding that the two kinds of the daughter are like the two musical pieces, which are two halves of one song, Jing-mei reaches the final appeasement with her mother. Her acceptance of the piano sent by her mother also signifies that Jing-mei inherits some of the Chinese virtues of hard work from her mother.

## Ⅴ Writing Topic

在《两种女儿》("Two Kinds")的节选中，母女的代际冲突由于文化身份的差异而被放大。作为第一代移民，母亲充满中国父母式的对子女的殷切期望。与之对应的是出生在美国的女儿拥有的美国式的个体意识。代际冲突和文化冲突使得母女关系呈现出特别的张力。试谈这种张力的表现方式，以及当下的亲子关系中子女对父母的期望的对抗形式。

# Unit 8 "Who's Irish?" by Gish Jen

## Ⅰ Introduction to the Author and the Work

Gish Jen (1955 – ) is a second-generation Chinese American. Her parents emigrated from China in the 1940s, her mother from Shanghai, and her father from Yixing. Born in Long Island, New York, she grew up in Queens, then Yonkers, then Scarsdale. Her birth name is Lillian, but during her high school years, she acquired the nickname Gish, named for actress Lillian Gish.

She graduated from the Harvard University in 1977 with a BA in English and later attended the Stanford Graduate School of Business (1979 – 1980), but dropped out in favor of the Iowa Writers' Workshop at the University of Iowa, where she earned her MFA in fiction in 1983.

Jen is a member of the American Academy of Arts and Sciences. She has received the Lannan Literary Award for Fiction, the Guggenheim Fellowship, the Radcliffe Fellowship, and the Mildred and Harold Strauss Living Award. She has also delivered "The William E. Massey, Sr. Lectures in the History of American Civilization" at the Harvard University.

Her works include four novels: *Typical American* (1991), *Mona in the Promised Land* (1996), *The Love Wife* (2004), and *World and Town* (2010). She has also written a collection of short fiction, *Who's Irish?* (1999). Her latest publication is her first non-fiction book, entitled *Tiger Writing: Art, Culture, and the Interdependent Self* (2013). Based on the "The William E. Massey, Sr. Lectures in the History of American Civilization" that Jen delivered at Harvard in 2012, *Tiger Writing: Art, Culture and the Interdependent Self* explores East–West differences in self-construction and how these impact art and especially literature.

In "Who's Irish?", the narrator and protagonist, a first-generation Chinese immigrant, babysits for her unruly Chinese and Irish American granddaughter. This story immerses the reader in the grandmother's views and understanding of herself as a Chinese woman in binary opposition to the Irish family that her daughter married into. The story reaches its climax when the grandmother is seen as overstepping her bounds in disciplining the granddaughter and is sent to live with her son-in-law's Irish American mother, Bess.

## Ⅱ Who's Irish?

In China, people say mixed children are supposed to be smart, and definitely my granddaughter Sophie is smart. But Sophie is wild, Sophie is not like my daughter Natalie, or like me. I am work hard my whole life, and fierce besides. My husband always used to say he is afraid of me, and in our restaurant, busboys and cooks all afraid of me too, even the gang members come for protection money, they try to talk to my husband. When I am there, they stay away. If they come by mistake, they pretend they are come to eat. They hide behind the menu, they order a lot of food, they talk about their mothers. Oh, my mother have some arthritis, need to take herbal medicine, they say. Oh, my mother getting old, her hair all white now.

I say, Your mother's hair used to be white, but since she dye it, it become black again. Why don't you go home once in a while and take a look? I tell them, Confucius say a filial son knows what color his mother's hair is.

My daughter is fierce too, she is vice president in the bank now. Her new house is big enough for everybody to have their own room, including me. But Sophie take after Natalie's husband's family, their name is Shea. Irish. I always thought Irish people are like Chinese people, work so hard on the railroad, but now I know why the Chinese beat the Irish. Of course, not all Irish are like the Shea family, of course not. My daughter tell me I should not say Irish this, Irish that.

How do you like it when people say the Chinese this, the Chinese that, she say.

You know, the British call the Irish heathen, just like they call the Chinese, she say.

You think the Opium War was bad, how would you like to live right next door to the British, she say.

And that is that. My daughter have a funny habit when she win an argument, she take a sip of something and look away, so the other person is not embarrassed. So I am not embarrassed. I do not call anybody anything either. I just happen to mention about the Shea family, an interesting fact: four brothers in the family, and not one of them work. The mother, Bess, have a job before she got sick, she was executive secretary in a big company. She is handle everything for a big shot, you would be surprised how complicated her job is, not just type this, type that. Now she is a nice woman with a clean house. But her boys, every one of them is on welfare, or so-called severance pay, or so-called disability pay. Something. They say they cannot find work, this is not the economy of the fifties, but I say, Even the black people doing better these days, some of them live so fancy, you'd be surprised. Why the Shea family have so much trouble? They are white people, they speak English. When I come to this country, I have no money and do not speak English. But my husband and I own our restaurant before he die. Free and clear, no mortgage. Of course, I understand I am just lucky, come from a country where the food is popular all over the world. I understand it is not the Shea family's fault they come from a country where everything is boiled. Still, I say.

She's right, we should broaden our horizons, say one brother, Jim, at Thanksgiving. Forget about the car business. Think about egg rolls.

Pad thai, say another brother, Mike. I'm going to make my fortune in pad thai. It's going to be the new pizza.

I say, You people too picky about what you sell. Selling egg rolls not good enough for you, but at least my husband and I can say, We made it. What can you say? Tell me. What can you say?

Everybody chew their tough turkey.

I especially cannot understand my daughter's husband John, who has no job but cannot take care of Sophie either. Because he is a man, he say, and that's the end of the sentence.

Plain boiled food, plain boiled thinking. Even his name is plain boiled: John. Maybe because I grew up with black bean sauce and hoisin sauce and garlic sauce, I always feel something is missing when my son-in-law talk.

But, okay: so my son-in-law can be man, I am baby-sitter. Six hours a day, same as the old sitter, crazy Amy, who quit. This is not so easy, now that I am sixty-eighty, Chinese age almost seventy. Still, I try. In China, daughter take care of mother. Here it is the other way around. Mother help daughter, mother ask, Anything else I can do? Otherwise daughter complain mother is not supportive. I tell daughter, We do not have this word in Chinese, *supportive*. But my daughter too busy to listen, she has to go to meeting, she has to write memo while her husband go to the gym to be a man. My daughter say otherwise he will be depressed. Seems like all his life he has this trouble, depression.

No one wants to hire someone who is depressed, she say. It is important for him to keep his spirits up.

Beautiful wife, beautiful daughter, beautiful house, oven can clean itself automatically. No money left over, because only one income, but lucky enough, got the baby-sitter for free. If John lived in China, he would be very happy. But he is not happy. Even at the gym things go wrong. One day, he pull a muscle. Another day, weight room too crowded. Always something.

Until finally, hooray, he has a job. Then he feel pressure.

I need to concentrate, he say. I need to focus.

He is going to work for insurance company. Salesman job. A paycheck, he say, and at least he will wear clothes instead of gym shorts. My daughter buy him some special candy bars from the health-food store, they say THINK! on them, and are supposed to help John think.

John is a good-looking boy, you have to say that, especially now that he shave so you can see his face.

I am an old man in a young man's game, say John.

I will need a new suit, say John.

This time I am not going to shoot myself in the foot, say John.

Good, I say.

She means to be supportive, my daughter say. Don't start the send her back to China thing, because we can't.

• • •

Sophie is three years old American age, but already I see her nice Chinese side swallowed up by her wild Shea side. She looks like mostly Chinese. Beautiful black hair, beautiful black eyes. Nose perfect size, not so flat looks like something fell down, not so large looks like some big deal got stuck in wrong face. Everything just right, only her skin is a brown surprise to John's family. So brown, they say. Even John say it. She never goes in the sun, still she is that color, he say. Brown. They say, Nothing the matter with brown. They are just surprised. So brown. Nattie is not that brown, they say. They say, It seems like Sophie should be a color in between Nattie and John. Seems funny, a girl named Sophie Shea be brown. But she is brown, maybe her name should be Sophie Brown. She never go in the sun, still she is that color, they say. Nothing the matter with brown. They are just surprised.

The Shea family talk is like this sometimes, going around and around like a Christmas-tree train.

Maybe John is not her father, I say one day, to stop the train. And sure enough, train wreck. None of the brothers ever say the word brown to me again.

Instead, John's mother Bess, say, I hope you are not offended.

She say, I did my best on those boys. But raising four boys with no father is no picnic.

You have a beautiful family, I say.

I'm getting old, she say.

You deserve a rest, I say. Too many boys make you old.

I never had a daughter, she say. You have a daughter.

I have a daughter, I say. Chinese people don't think a daughter is so great, but you're right. I have a daughter.

I was never against the marriage, you know, she say. I never thought John was marrying down. I always thought Nattie was just as good as white.

I was never against the marriage either, I say. I just wonder if they look at the whole problem.

Of course you pointed out the problem, you are a mother, she say. And now we both have a granddaughter. A little brown granddaughter, she is so precious to me.

I laugh. A little brown granddaughter, I say. To tell you the truth, I don't know how she came out so brown.

We laugh some more. These days Bess need a walker to walk. She take so many pills, she need two glasses of water to get them all down. Her favorite TV show is about bloopers, and she love her bird feeder. All day long, she can watch that bird feeder like a cat.

I can't wait for her to grow up, Bess say. I could use some female company.

Too many boys, I say.

Boys are fine, she say. But they do surround you after a while.

You should take a break, come live with us, I say. Lots of girls at our house.

Be careful what you offer, say Bess with a wink. Where I come from, people mean for you to move in when they say a thing like that.

• • •

Nothing the matter with Sophie's outside, that's the truth. It is inside that she is like not any Chinese girl I ever see. We go to the park, and this is what she does. She stand up in the stroller. She take off all her clothes and throw them in the fountain.

Sophie! I say. Stop!

But she just laugh like a crazy person. Before I take over as baby-sitter, Sophie has that crazy-person sitter, Amy the guitar player. My daughter thought this Amy very creative—another word we do not talk about in China. In China, we talk about whether we have difficulty or no difficulty. We talk about whether life is bitter or not bitter. In America, all day long, people talk about creative. Never mind that I cannot even look at this Amy, with her shirt so short that her belly button showing. This Amy think Sophie should love her body. So when Sophie take off her diaper, Amy laugh. When Sophie run around naked, Amy say she wouldn't want to wear a diaper either. When Sophie go shu-shu in her lap, Amy laugh and say there are no germs in pee. When Sophie take off her shoes, Amy say bare feet is best, even the pediatrician say so. That is why

Sophie now walk around with no shoes like a beggar child. Also why Sophie love to take off her clothes.

Turn around! Say the boys in the park. Let's see that ass!

Of course, Sophie does not understand. Sophie clap her hands, I am the only one to say, NO! This is not a game.

It has nothing to do with John's family, my daughter say. Amy was too permissive, that's all.

But I think if Sophie was not wild inside, she would not take off her shoes and clothes to begin with.

You never take off your clothes when you were little, I say. All my Chinese friends had babies, I Never saw one of them act wild like that.

Look, my daughter say. I have a big presentation tomorrow.

John and my daughter agree Sophie is a problem, but they don't know what to do.

You spank her, she'll stop. I say another day.

But they say, Oh no.

In America, parents not supposed to spank the child.

It gives them low self-esteem, my daughter say. And that lead to problems later, as I happen to know.

My daughter never have big presentation the next day when the subject of spanking come up.

I don't want you to touch Sophie, she say. No spanking, period.

Don't tell me what to do, I say.

I'm not telling you what to say, say my daughter. I'm telling you how I feel.

I am not your servant, I say. Don't you dare talk to me like that.

My daughter have another funny habit when she lose an argument. She spread out all her fingers and look at them, as if she like to make sure they are still there.

My daughter is fierce like me, but she and John think it is better to explain to Sophie that clothes are a good idea. This is not so hard in the cold weather. In the warm weather, it is very hard.

Use your words, my daughter say. That's what we tell Sophie. How about if you set a good example.

As if good example mean anything to Sophie. I am so fierce, the gang members who used to come to the restaurant all afraid of me, but Sophie is not afraid.

I say, Sophie, if you take off your clothes, no snack.

I say, Sophie, if you take off your clothes, no lunch.

I say, Sophie, if you take off your clothes, no park.

Pretty soon we are stay home all day, and by the end of six hours she still did not have one thing to eat. You never saw a child stubborn like that.

I'm hungry! she cry when my daughter come home.

What's the matter, doesn't your grandmother feed you? My daughter laugh.

No! Sophie say. She doesn't feed me anything!

My daughter laugh again. Here you go, she say.

She say to John, Sophie must be growing.

Growing like a weed, I say.

Still Sophie take off her clothes, until one day I spank her. Not too hard, but she cry and cry, and when I tell her if she doesn't put her clothes back on I'll spank her again, she put her clothes back on. Then I tell her she is good girl, and give her some food to eat. The next day we go to the park and, like a nice Chinese girl, she does not take off her clothes.

She stop taking off her clothes, I report. Finally!

How did you do it? my daughter ask.

After twenty-eight years experience with you, I guess I learn something, I say.

It must have been a phase, John say, and his voice is suddenly like an expert.

His voice is like an expert about everything these days, now that he carry a leather briefcase, and wear shiny shoes, and can go shopping for a new car. On the company, he say. The company will pay for it, but he will be able to drive it whenever he want.

A free car, he say. How do you like that.

It's good to see you in the saddle again, my daughter say. Some of your family patterns are scary.

At least I don't drink, he say. He say, And I'm not the only one with scary family patterns.

That's for sure, say my daughter.

• • •

Everyone is happy. Even I am happy, because there is more trouble with Sophie, but now I think I can help her Chinese side fight against her wild side. I teach her to eat food with fork or spoon or chopsticks, she cannot just grab into the middle of a bowl of noodles. I teach her not to play with garbage cans. Sometimes I spank her, but not too often, and not too hard.

Still, there are problems. Sophie like to climb everything. If there is a railing, she is never next to it. Always she is on top of it. Also, Sophie like to hit the mommies of her friends. She learn this from her playground best friend, Sinbad, who is four. Sinbad wear army clothes every day and like to ambush his mommy. He is the one who dug a big hole under the play structure, and foxhole he call it, all by himself. Very hardworking. Now he wait in the foxhole with a shovel full of wet sand. When his mommy come, he throw it right at her.

Oh, it's all right, his mommy say. You can't get rid of war games, it's part of their imaginative play. All the boys go through it.

Also, he like to kick his mommy, and one day he tell Sophie to kick his mommy too.

I wish this story is not true.

Kick her, kick her! Sinbad say.

Sophie kick her. A little kick, as if she just so happened was swinging her little leg and didn't realize that big mommy leg was in the way. Still I spank Sophie and make Sophie say sorry, and what does the mommy say?

Really, it's all right, she say. It didn't hurt.

After that, Sophie learn she can attack mommies in the playground, and some will say, Stop, but others will say, oh, she didn't mean it, especially if they realize Sophie will be punished.

• • •

This is how, one day, bigger trouble come. The bigger trouble start when Sophie hide in the foxhole with that shovel full of sand. She wait, and when I come look for her, she throw it at me. All over my nice clean clothes.

Did you ever see a Chinese girl act this way?

Sophie! I say. Come out of there, say you're sorry.

But she does not come out. Instead, she laugh. Naaah, naahna, naaa-naaa, she say.

I am not exaggerate: millions of children in China, not one act like this.

Sophie! I say. Now! Come out now!

But she know she is in big trouble. She know if she come out, what will happen next. So she does not come out. I am sixty-eight, Chinese age almost seventy, how can I crawl under there to catch her? Impossible. So I yell, yell, yell, and what happen? Nothing. A Chinese mother would help, but American mothers, they look at you, they shake their head, they go home. And, of course, a Chinese child would give up, but not Sophie.

I hate you! she yell. I hate you, Meanie!

Meanie is my new name these days.

Long time this goes on, long long time. The foxhole is deep, you cannot see too much, you don't know where is the bottom. You cannot hear too much either. If she does not yell, you cannot even know she is still there or not. After a while, getting cold out, getting dark out. No one left in the playground, only us.

Sophie, I say. How did you become stubborn like this? I am go home without you now.

I try to use a stick, chase her out of there, and once or twice I hit her, but still she does not come out. So finally I leave. I go outside the gate.

Bye-bye! I say. I'm go home now.

But still she does not come out and does not come out. Now it is dinnertime, the sky is black. I think I should maybe go get help, but how can I leave a little girl by herself in the playground? A bad man could come. A rat could come. I go back in to see what is happen to Sophie. What if she have a shovel and is making a tunnel to escape?

Sophie! I say.

No answer.

Sophie!

I don't know if she is alive. I don't know if she is fall asleep down there. Is she is crying, I cannot hear her.

So I take the stick and poke.

Sophie! I say. I promise I no hit you if you come out, I give you a lollipop.

No answer. By now I worried. What to do, what to do, what to do? I poke some more, even harder, so that I am poking and poking when my daughter and John suddenly appear.

What are you doing? What is going on? Say my daughter.

Put down that stick! say my daughter.

You are crazy! say my daughter.

John wiggle under the structure, into the foxhole, to rescue Sophie.

She fell asleep, say John the expert. She's okay. That is one big hole.

Now Sophie is crying and crying.

Sophia, my daughter say, hugging her. Are you okay, peanut? Are you okay?

She's just scared, say John.

Are you okay? I say too. I don't know what happen, I say.

She's okay, say John. He is not like my daughter, full of questions. He is full of answers until we get home and can see by the lamplight.

Will you look at her? He yell then. What the hell happened?

Bruises all over her brown skin, and a swollen-up eye.

You are crazy! Say my daughter. Look at what you did! You are crazy!

I try very hard, I say.

How could you use a stick! I told you to use your words!

She is hard to handle, I say.

She's three years old! You cannot use a stick! Say my daughter.

She is not like any Chinese girl I ever saw, I say.

I brush some sand off my clothes. Sophie's clothes are dirty too, but at least she has her clothes on.

Has she done this before? Ask my daughter. Has she hit you before?

She hits me all the time, Sophie say, eating ice cream.

Your family, say John.

Believe me, say my daughter.

• • •

A daughter I have, a beautiful daughter. I took care of her when she could not hold her head up. I took care of her before she could argue with me, when she was a little girl with two pigtails, one of them always crooked. I took care of her when we have to escape from China, I took care to her when suddenly we live in a country with cars everywhere, if you are not careful your little girl get run over. When my husband die, I promise him I will keep the family together, even though it was just two of us, hardly a family at all.

But now my daughter take me around to look at apartments. After all, I can cook, I can clean, there's no reason I cannot live by myself, all I need is a telephone. Of course, she is sorry. Sometimes she cry, I am the one to say everything will be okay. She say she have no choice, she doesn't want to end up divorced. I say divorce is terrible, I don't know who invented this terrible idea. Instead of live with a telephone, though, surprise, I come to live with Bess.

Imagine that. Bess make an offer and, sure enough, where she come from, people mean for you to move in when they say things like that. A crazy idea, go to live with someone else's family, but she like to have some female company, not like my daughter, who does not believe in company. These days when my daughter visit, she does not bring Sophie. Bess say we should give Nattie time, we will see Sophie again soon. But seems like my daughter have more presentation than ever before every time she come she have to leave.

I have a family to support, she say, and her voice is heavy, as if soaking wet. I have a young daughter and a depressed husband and no one to turn to.

When she say no one to turn to, she mean me.

These days my beautiful daughter is so tired she can just sit there in a chair and fall asleep. John lost his job again, already, but still they rather hire a baby-sitter than ask me to help, even they can't afford it. Of course, the new baby-sitter is much younger, can run around. I don't know if Sophie these days is wild or not wild. She call me Meanie, but she like to kiss me too, sometimes. I remember that every time I see a child on TV. Sophie like to grab my air, a fistful in each hand and then kiss me smack on the nose. I never see any other child kiss that way.

The satellite TV has so many channels, more channels than I can count, including a Chinese channel from the Mainland and a Chinese channel from Taiwan, but most of the time I watch bloopers with Bess. Also, I watch the bird feeder—so many, many kinds of birds come. The Shea sons hang around all the time, asking when will I go home, but Bess tell them, Get lost.

She's a permanent resident, say Bess. She isn't going anywhere.

Then she wink at me, and switch the channel with the remote control.

Of course, I shouldn't say Irish this, Irish that, especially now I become honorary Irish myself, according to Bess. Me! Who's Irish? I say, and she laugh. All the same, if I could mention one thing about some of the Irish, not all of them of course, I like to mention this: Their talk just stick. I don't know how Bess Shea learn to use her words, but sometimes I hear what she say a long time later. Permanent resident. Not going anywhere. Over and over I hear it, the voice of Bess.

## Ⅲ Questions for Further Thinking

1. Why there are a lot of grammatical errors expressed in Grandma's narration? What does it indicate as to her identity?

2. Please list the differences between these three women, the narrator Grandma, daughter Natalie, and granddaughter Sophie.

3. Why does Grandma complain a lot about the son-in-law John?

4. What kind of marriage relationship do Natalie and John have?

5. What is Natalie's attitude to her mother's way of disciplining Sophie?

6. What is the meaning of the title "Who is Irish"? How can we understand Bess invites Grandma to become the permanent resident of her house?

## Ⅳ Appreciation

"Who's Irish?" is a short story about the generational conflict between a first-generation Chinese American mother, "I," and her second-generation Chinese American daughter Natalie's family. At the same time, this story also talks about the educational differences between Chinese and American cultures by evolving with how to educate the third-generation grandchildren Sophie. The entanglement of two kinds of conflicts within a family illustrates a life of the contemporary Chinese immigrant family.

Gish Jen intentionally preserves much of the language feature in illustrating the strong imprint of Chinese culture in the life of the first-generation Chinese immigrant. Grandma "I" labels herself as fierce (meaning "凶" in Chinese). She was tough in managing the restaurant business. Even when she is 70 years old, she insists that "still I try" to help her daughter raise the granddaughter. Grandma is a typical Chinese American immigrant who is bold, tough, industrious, and determined. Besides the merit, she is a hardened elder. She complains quite a lot about her Irish son-in-law, grumbling things like "Irish this, Irish that."

The assertive Chinese cultural consciousness of Grandma therefore contradicts with the American values acquired by Natalie and her husband John. Grandma mocks at her son-in-law because John is taking government severance pay, even though he is healthy and strong enough to work. Grandma assumes that John is indolent because he does not want to support the family, which, in Chinese culture, is the obligation of the husband. She is particularly disgruntled with the Irish family about their covert discrimination against Asians, fussing about Sophie's brown skin color. The cultural conflicts went into climaxed when Grandma tries hard to discipline Sophie to be an obedient Chinese girl. She forbids Sophie to take off her clothes, kick others, ambush, and throw sand at the parents, because in her mind, a girl should behave in a polite and decent manner. If Sophie disobeys, Grandma would spank her as punishment. Gradually, the small squabble accumulates into a big explosion.

In these cultural and generational conflicts, the reaction from Natalie deserves more attention. As the second-generation of Chinese American daughter, Natalie finds herself with a contradictory self-identification. Although she is equally fierce as her mother and is professionally successful as vice president of the bank, Natalie is not at all confident in her marriage. She dares not blame her husband's idleness, tolerated his sneaky racial discrimination, and endures his dogged inclination to send Grandma back to China. At the same time, Natalie shows distinct American cultural awareness. She welcomes the free nurturing method of Sophie, refuses to punish her kid, and stresses using verbal education on her child rather than simply spanking.

Thus, to compromise both with her mother and her husband, Natalie is in an incompatible in-betweenness. She does not want her mother to leave because she needs her support, but she also has to appease her husband, who refuses to live together with his mother-in-law. Natalie becomes the example of the second-generation Chinese Americans who seems to fit into both cultures, only to find she is compatible with neither.

## Ⅴ Writing Topic

该小说从第一代移民外婆的视角讲述第二代华裔家庭的生活和后代抚养问题,小说中充满了中式思维和西方主流偏见。作为移民后代的女儿娜塔莉(Natalie)处于两种文化的夹缝之中,她既受到美国文化的影响,也受到中国家庭观的影响,在承受族群偏见的同时还要承担中国式家庭性别分工带来的压力。试论以娜塔莉为代表的第二代美国华裔的自我身份认知。

# Unit 9 "Tiny, Smiling Daddy" by Mary Gaitskill

## Ⅰ Introduction to the Author and the Work

Mary Gaitskill (1954 – ) was born in Lexington, Kentucky. She has lived in New York City, Toronto, San Francisco, Marin County, and Pennsylvania, as well as attending the University of Michigan, where she earned her BA in 1981 and won the Hopwood Award. She sold flowers in San Francisco as a runaway teenager. In a conversation with novelist and short story writer Matthew Sharpe for *BOMB Magazine*, Gaitskill said she chose to become a writer at age 18 because she was indignant about things—"it was the typical teenage sense of things are wrong in the world and I must say something." Gaitskill has also recounted (in her essay *Revelation*) becoming a born-again Christian at age 21 but lapsing after six months. Gaitskill has taught at the University of California, Berkeley, the University of Houston, the New York University, The New School, the Brown University, in the MFA program at the Temple University and the Syracuse University. She was the writer-in-residence at the Hobart and William Smith Colleges.

"Tiny, Smiling Daddy" is the first story in Mary Gaitskill's short story collection *Because They Wanted to: Stories* (1998). It opens with the father going to a magazine store, to read an article written by his daughter about him. He hasn't seen his daughter for quite a while because he refuses to accept his daughter's life style. He wonders what his daughter could say about him when father – daughter relationship is so rejecting that one could not tolerate the other's existence at home. He dreads to go and read the words written by his daughter.

## Ⅱ Tiny, Smiling Daddy

The phone rang five times before he got up to answer it. It was his friend Norm. They greeted each other and then Norm, his voice strangely weighted, said, "I saw the issue of *Self* with Kitty in it."

He waited for an explanation. None came, so he said. "What? Issue of *Self*? What's *Self*?"

"Good grief, Stew, I thought for sure you'd of seen it. Now I feel awkward."

"So do I. Do you want to tell me what it is about?"

"My daughter's got a subscription to this magazine, *Self*. And they printed an article that Kitty wrote about fathers and daughters talking to each other, and she, well, she wrote about you. Laurel showed it to me."

"My God."

"It's ridiculous that I'm the one to tell you. I just thought—"

"It was bad?"

"No. No, she didn't say anything bad. I just didn't understand the whole idea of it. And I wondered what you thought."

He got off the phone and walked back into the living room, now fully awake. His daughter, Kitty, was living in South Carolina, working in a used-record store and making animal statuettes, which she sold on commission. She had never written anything that he knew of, yet she'd apparently published an article in a national magazine about him. He lifted his arms and put them on the windowsill; the air from the open window cooled his underarms. Outside, the Starlings' tiny dog marched officiously up and down the pavement, looking for someone to bark at. Maybe she had written an article about how wonderful he was, and she was too shy to show him right away. This was doubtful. Kitty was quiet, but she wasn't shy. She was untactful and she could be aggressive. Uncertainty only made her doubly aggressive.

He turned the edge of one nostril over with his thumb and nervously stroked his nose hairs with one finger. He knew it was a nasty habit, but it soothed him.

When Kitty was a little girl he would do it to make her laugh. "Well," he'd say, "do you think it's time we played with the hairs in our nose?" And she would giggle, holding her hands against her face, eyes sparkling over her knuckles.

Then she was fourteen, and as scornful and rejecting as any girl he had ever thrown a spitball at when he was that age. They didn't get along so well anymore. Once, they were sitting in the rec room watching TV, he on the couch, she on the footstool. There was a Charlie Chan movie on, but he was mostly watching her back and her long, thick brown hair, which she had just washed and was brushing. She dropped her head forward from the neck to let the hair fall between her spread legs and began slowly stroking it with a pink nylon brush.

"Say, don't you think it's time we played with the hairs in our nose?"

No reaction from bent back and hair.

"Who wants to play with the hairs in their nose?"

Nothing.

"Hairs in the nose, hairs in the nose," he sang.

She bolted violently up from the stool. "You are so gross; you disgust me!" She stormed from the room, shoulders in a tailored jacket of indignation.

Sometimes he said it just to see her exasperation, to feel the adorable, futile outrage of her violated girl delicacy.

He wished that his wife would come home with the car so that he could drive to the store and buy a copy of *Self*. His car was being repaired, and he could not walk to the little cluster of stores and parking lots that constituted "town" in this heat. It would take a good twenty minutes, and he would be completely worn out when he got there. He would find the magazine and stand there in the drugstore and read it, and if it was something bad, he might not have the strength to walk back.

He went into the kitchen, opened a beer, and brought it into the living room. His wife had been gone for over an hour, and God knew how much longer she would be. She could spend literally all day driving around the county, doing nothing but buying a jar of honey or a bag of apples. Of course, he could call Kitty, but he'd probably just get her answering machine, and besides, he didn't want to talk to her before he understood the situation. He felt helplessness move through his body the way a swimmer feels a large sea creature pass beneath him. How could she have done this to him? She knew how he dreaded exposure of any kind, she knew the way he guarded himself against strangers, the way he carefully drew all the curtains when twilight approached so that no one could see them walking through the house. She knew how ashamed he had been when, at sixteen, she announced that she was lesbian.

The Starling dog was now across the street, yapping at the heels of a bowlegged old lady in a blue dress who was trying to walk down the sidewalk. "Dammit," he said. He left the window and got the afternoon opera station on the radio. They were in the final act of *La Bobtème*.

He did not remember precisely when it had happened, but Kitty, his beautiful, happy little girl, turned into a glum, weird teenager that other kids picked on. She got skinny and ugly. Her blue eyes, which had been so sensitive and bright, turned filmy, as if the real Kitty had retreated so far from the surface that her eyes existed to shield rather than reflect her. It was as if she deliberately held her beauty away from them, only showing glimpses of it during unavoidable lapses, like the time she sat before the TV, daydreaming and lazily brushing her hair. At moments like this, her dormant charm broke his heart. It also annoyed him. What did she have to retreat from? They had both loved her. When she was little and she couldn't sleep at night, Marsha would sit with her in bed for hours. She praised her stories and her drawings as if she were a genius. When Kitty was seven, she and her mother had special times, during which they went off together and talked about whatever Kitty wanted to talk about.

He tried to compare the sullen, morbid Kitty of sixteen with the slender, self-possessed twenty-eight-year-old lesbian who wrote articles for *Self*. He pictured himself in court, waving a copy of *Self* before a shocked jury. The case would be taken up by the press. He saw the headlines: "Dad Sues Mag-Dyke Daughter Reveals ..." Reveals what? What had Kitty found to say about him that was of interest to the entire country, that she didn't want him to know about?

Anger overrode his helplessness. Kitty could be vicious. He hadn't seen her vicious side in years, but he knew it was there. He remembered the time he'd stood behind the half-open front door when fifteen-year-old Kitty sat hunched on the front steps with one of her few friends, a homely blonde who wore white lipstick and a white leather jacket. He had come to the door to view the weather and say something to the girls, but they were muttering so intently that curiosity got the better of him, and he hung back a moment to listen. "Well, at least your mom's smart," said Kitty. "My mom's not only a bitch, she's stupid."

This after the lullabies and special times! It wasn't just an isolated incident, either; every time he'd come home from work, his wife had something bad to say about Kitty. She hadn't set the table until she had been asked four times. She'd gone to Lois's house instead of coming straight home like she'd been told to do. She'd worn a dress to school that was short enough to show the tops of her panty hose.

By the time Kitty came to dinner, looking as if she'd been doing slave labor all day, he would be mad at her. He couldn't help it. Here was his wife doing her damnedest to raise a family and cook dinner, and here was this awful kid looking ugly, acting mean, and not setting the table. It seemed unreasonable that she should turn out so badly after taking up so much of their time. Her afflicted expression made him angry too. What had anybody ever done to her?

• • •

He sat forward and gently gnawed the insides of his mouth as he listened to the dying girl in *La Bobtème*. He saw his wife's car pull into the driveway. He walked to the back door, almost wringing his hands, and waited for her to come through the door. When she did, he snatched the grocery bag from her arms and said, "Give me the keys." She stood open-mouthed in the stairwell, looking at him with idiotic consternation. "Give me the keys!"

"What is it, Stew? What's happened?"

"I'll tell you when I get back."

He got in the car and became part of it, this panting mobile case propelling him through the incredibly complex and fast-moving world of other people, their houses, their children, their dogs, their lives. He wasn't usually so aware of this unpleasant sense of disconnection between him and everyone else, but he had the feeling that it had been there all along, underneath what he thought about most of the time. It was ironic that it should rear up so visibly at a time when there was in fact a mundane yet invasive and horribly real connection between him and everyone else in Wayne County: the hundreds of copies of *Self* magazine sitting in countless drugstores, bookstores, groceries, and libraries. It was as if there were a tentacle lugged into the side of the car, linking him with the random humans who picked up the magazine, possibly his very neighbors. He stopped at a crowded intersection, feeling like an ant in an enemy swarm.

Kitty had projected herself out of the house and into this swarm very early, ostensibly because life with him and Marsha had been so awful. Well, it had been awful, but because of Kitty, not them. As if it weren't enough to be sullen and dull, she turned into a lesbian. Kids followed her down the street, jeering at her. Somebody dropped her books in a toilet. She got into a fistfight. Their neighbors gave them looks. This reaction seemed only to steel Kitty's grip on her new identity; it made her romanticize herself, like the kid she was. She wrote poems about heroic women warriors, she brought home strange books and magazines, which, among other things, seemed to glorify prostitutes. Marsha looked for them and threw them away. Kitty screamed at her, the tendons leaping out on her slender neck. He punched Kitty and knocked her down. Marsha tried to stop him, and he yelled at her. Kitty jumped up and leapt between them, as if to defend her mother. He grabbed her and shook her, but he could not shake the conviction off her face.

Most of the time, though, they continued as always, eating dinner together, watching TV, making jokes. That was the worst thing; he would look at Kitty and see his daughter, now familiar in her withdrawn sullenness, and feel comfort and affection. Then he would remember that she was a lesbian, and a morass of complication and wrongness would come down between them, making it impossible for him to see her. Then she would just be Kitty again. He hated it.

She ran away at sixteen, and the police found her in the apartment of an eighteen-year-old bodybuilder named Dolores, who had a naked woman tattooed on her sinister bicep. Marsha made them put her in a mental hospital so psychiatrists could observe her, but he hated the psychiatrists—mean, supercilious sons of bitches who delighted in the trick question—so he took her out. She finished school, and they told her if she wanted to leave it was all right with them. She didn't waste any time getting out of the house.

She moved into an apartment near Detroit with a girl named George and took a job at a home for retarded kids. She would appear for visits with a huge bag of laundry every few weeks. She was thin and neurotically muscular, her body having the look of a fighting dog on a leash. She cut her hair like a boy's and wore black sunglasses, black leather half-gloves, and leather belts. The only remnant of her beauty was her erect, martial carriage and her efficient movements; she walked through a room like the commander of a guerrilla force. She would sit at the dining room table with Marsha, drinking tea and having a laconic verbal conversation, her body speaking its precise martial language while the washing machine droned from the utility room, and he wandered in and out, trying to make sense of what she said. Sometimes she would stay into the evening, to eat dinner and watch *All in the Family*. Then Marsha would send her home with a jar of homemade tapioca pudding or a bag of apples and oranges.

One day, instead of a visit they got a letter postmarked San Francisco. She had left George, she said. She listed strange details about her current environment and was vague about how she was supporting herself. He had nightmares about Kitty, with her brave, proudly muscular little body, lost among big fleshy women who danced naked in go-go bars and took drugs with needles, terrible women whom his confused, romantic daughter invested with oppressed heroism and intensely female glamour. He got up at night and stumbled into the bathroom for stomach medicine, the familiar darkness of the house heavy with menacing images that pressed about him, images he saw reflected in his own expression when he turned on the bathroom light over the mirror.

Then one year she came home for Christmas. She came into the house with her luggage and a shopping bag of gifts for them, and he saw that she was beautiful again. It was a beauty that both offended and titillated his senses. Her short, spiky hair was streaked with purple, her dainty mouth was lipsticked, her nose and ears were pierced with amethyst and dangling silver. Her face had opened in thousands of petals. Her eyes shone with quick perception as she put down her bag, and he knew that she had seen him see her beauty. She moved toward him with fluid hips; she embraced him for the first time in years. He felt her live, lithe body against his, and his heart pulsed a message of blood and love. "Merry Christmas, Daddy," she said.

Her voice was husky and coarse; it reeked of knowledge and confidence. Her T-shirt said "Chicks With Balls." She was twenty-two years old.

She stayed for a week, discharging her strange jangling beauty into the house and changing the molecules of its air. She talked about the girls she shared an apartment with, her job at a coffee shop, how Californians were different from Michiganders. She talked about her friends: Lorraine, who was so pretty men fell off their bicycles as they twisted their bodies for a better look at her; Judy, a martial arts expert; and Meredith, who was raising a child with her husband, Angela. She talked of poetry readings, ceramics classes, celebrations of spring.

He realized, as he watched her, that she was now doing things that were as bad as or worse than the things that had made him angry at her five years before, yet they didn't quarrel. It seemed that a large white space existed between him and her, and that it was impossible to enter this space or to argue across it. Besides, she might never come back if he yelled at her.

Instead, he watched her, puzzling at the metamorphosis she had undergone. First she had been a beautiful. Happy child turned homely, snotty, miserable adolescent. From there she had become a martinet girl with the eyes of a stifled pervert. Now she was a vibrant imp, living, it seemed, in a world constructed of topsy-turvy junk pasted with rhinestones. Where had these three different people come from? Not even Marsha, who had spent so much time with her as a child, could trace the genesis of the new Kitty from the old one. Sometimes he bitterly reflected that he and Marsha weren't even real parents anymore, but bereft old people rattling around in a house, connected not to a real child who was going to college, or who at least had some kind of understandable life, but a changeling who was the product of only their most obscure quirks, a being who came from recesses that neither of them suspected they'd had.

• • •

There were only a few cars in the parking lot. He wheeled through it with pointless deliberation before parking near the drugstore. He spent irritating seconds searching for *Self* until he realized that its air-brushed cover girl was grinning right at him. He stormed the table of contents, then headed for the back of the magazine. "Speak Easy" was written sideways across the top of the in round turquoise letters. At the bottom was his daughter's name in a little box. "Kitty Thorne is a ceramic artist living in South Carolina." His hands were trembling.

It was hard for him to rationally ingest the beginning paragraphs, which seemed, incredibly, to be about a phone conversation they'd had some time ago about the emptiness and selfishness of people who have sex but don't get married and have children. A few phrases stood out clearly: "... my father may love me but he doesn't love the way I live." "... even more complicated because I'm gay." "Because it still hurts me."

For reasons he didn't understand, he felt a nervous smile tremble under his skin. He suppressed it.

"This hurt has its roots deep in our relationship, starting, I think, when I was a teenager."

He was horribly aware of being in public, so he paid for the thing and took it out to the car. He drove slowly to another spot in the lot, as far away from the drugstore as possible, picked up the magazine, and began again. She described the "terrible difficulties" between him and her. She recounted, briefly and with hieroglyphic politeness, the fighting, the running away, the return, the tacit reconciliation.

"There is an emotional distance that we have both accepted and chosen to work around, hoping the occasional contact—love, anger, something—will get through."

He put the magazine down and looked out the window. It was near dusk; most of the stores in the little mall were closed. There were only two other cars in the parking lot, and a big, slow, frowning woman with two grocery bags was getting ready to drive one away. He was parked before a weedy piece of land at the edge of the lot. In it were rough, picky weeds spread out like big green tarantulas, young yellow dandelions, frail old dandelions, and bunches of tough blue chickweed. Even in his distress he vaguely appreciated the beauty of the blue weeds against the cool white-and-gray sky. For a moment the sound of insects comforted him. Images of Kitty passed through his memory with terrible speed: her nine-year-old forehead bent over her dish of ice cream, her tiny nightgowned form ran up the stairs, her ringed hand brushed her face, the keys on her belt jiggled as she walked her slow blue-jeaned walk away from the house. Gone, all gone.

The article went on to describe how Kitty hung up the phone feeling frustrated and then listed all the things she could've said to him to let him know how hurt she was, paving the way for "real communication"; it was all in ghastly talk-show language. He was unable to put these words together with the Kitty he had last seen lounging around the house. She was twenty-eight now, and she no longer dyed her hair or wore jewels in her nose. Her demeanor was serious, bookish, almost old-maidish. Once, he'd overheard her saying to Marsha, "So then this Italian girl gives me the once-over and says to Joanne, 'You' ang around with too many Wasp.' And I said, 'I'm white trash.'"

"Speak for yourself," he'd said.

"If the worst occurred and my father was unable to respond to me in kind, I still would have done a good thing. I would have acknowledged my own needs and created the possibility to connect with what therapists call 'the good parent' in myself."

Well, if that was the kind of thing she was going to say to him, he was relieved she hadn't said it. But if she hadn't said it to him, why was she saying it to the rest of the country?

He turned on the radio. It sang: "Try to remember, and if you remember, then follow, follow." He turned it off. The interrupted dream echoed faintly. He closed his eyes. When he was nine or ten, an uncle of his had told him, "Everybody makes his own world. You see what you want to see and hear what you want to hear. You can do it right now. If you blink ten times and then close your eyes real tight, you can see anything you want to see in front of you." He'd tried it, rather halfheartedly, and hadn't seen anything but the vague suggestion of a yellowish-white ball moving creepily through the dark. At the time, he'd thought it was perhaps because he hadn't tried hard enough.

He had told Kitty to do the same thing, or something like it, when she was eight or nine. They were sitting on the back porch in striped lawn chairs, holding hands and watching the fireflies turn off and on.

She closed her eyes for a long time. Then very seriously, she said, "I see big balls of color, like shaggy flowers. They're pink and red and turquoise. I see an island with palm trees and pink rocks. There's dolphins and mermaids swimming in the water around it." He'd been almost awed by her belief in this impossible vision. Then he was sad because she would never see what she wanted to see.

His memory flashed back to his boyhood. He was walking down the middle of the street at dusk, sweating lightly after a basketball game. There were crickets and the muted barks of dogs and the low, affirming mumble of people on their front porches. Securely held by the warm night and its sounds, he felt an exquisite blend of happiness and sorrow that life could contain this perfect moment, and a sadness that he would soon arrive home, walk into bright light, and be on his way into the next day, with its loud noise and alarming possibility. He resolved to hold this evening walk in his mind forever, to imprint in a permanent place all the sensations that occurred to him as he walked by the Oat-landers' house, so that he could always take them out and look at them. He dimly recalled feeling that if he could successfully do that, he could stop time and hold it.

• • •

He knew he had to go home soon. He didn't want to talk about the article with Marsha, but the idea of sitting in the house with her and not talking about it was hard to bear. He imagined the conversation grinding into being, a future conversation with Kitty gestating within it. The conversation was a vast, complex machine like those that occasionally appeared in his dreams; if he could only pull the switch, everything would be all right, but he felt too stupefied by the weight and complexity of the thing to do so. Besides, in this case, everything might not be all right. He put the magazine under his seat and started the car.

Marsha was in her armchair, reading. She looked up, and the expression on her face seemed like the result of internal conflict as complicated and strong as his own, but cross-pulled in different directions, uncomprehending of him and what he knew. In his mind, he withdrew from her so quickly that for a moment the familiar room was fraught with the inexplicable horror of a banal nightmare. Then the ordinariness of the scene threw the extraordinary event of the day into relief, and he felt so angry and bewildered he could've howled.

"Everything all right, Stew?" asked Marsha.

"No, nothing is all right. I'm a tired old man in a shitty world don't want to be in. I go out there, it's like walking on knives. Everything is an attack—the ugliness, the cheapness, the rudeness, everything." He sensed her withdrawing from him into her own world of disgruntlement, her lips drawn together in that look of exasperated perseverance she'd gotten from her mother. Like Kitty, like everyone else, she was leaving him. "I don't have a real daughter, and I don't have a real wife who's here with me, because she's too busy running around on some—"

"We've been through this before. We agreed I could—"

"That was different! That was when we had two cars!" His voice tore through his throat in a jagged whiplash and came out a cracked half scream. "I don't have a car, remember? That means I'm stranded, all alone for hours, and Norm Pisarro can call me up and casually tell me that my lesbian daughter has just betrayed me in a national magazine and what do I think about that?" He wanted to punch the wall until his hand was bloody. He wanted Kitty to see the blood. Marsha's expression broke into soft, openmouthed consternation. The helplessness of it made his anger seem huge and terrible, then impotent and helpless itself. He sat down on the couch and, instead of anger, felt pain.

"What did Kitty do? What happened? What does Norm have—"

"She wrote an article in *Self* magazine about being a lesbian and her problems and something to do with me. I don't know, I could barely read the crap."

Marsha looked down at her nails.

He looked at her and saw the aged beauty of her ivory skin, sagging under the weight of her years and her cockeyed bifocals, the emotional receptivity of her face, the dark down on her upper lip, the childish pearl buttons of her sweater, only the top button done.

"I'm surprised at Norm, that he would call you like that."

"Oh, who the hell knows what he thought." His heart was soothed and slowed by her words, even if they didn't address its real unhappiness.

"Here," she said. "Let me rub your shoulders."

He allowed her to approach him, and they sat sideways on the couch; his weight balanced on the edge by his awkwardly planted legs; she sitting primly on one hip with her legs tightly crossed. The discomfort of the position negated the practical value of the massage, but she welcomed her touch. Marsha had strong, intelligent hands that spoke to his muscles of deep safety and love and the delight of physical life. In her effort, she leaned close, and her sweatered breast touched him, releasing his tension almost against his will. Through half-closed eyes he observed her sneakers on the floor—he could not quite get over this phenomenon of adult women wearing what had been boys' shoes—in the dim light, one toe atop the other as though cuddling, their laces in pretty disorganization.

Poor Kitty. It hadn't really been so bad that she hadn't set the table on time. He couldn't remember why he and Marsha had been so angry over the table. Unless it was Kitty's coldness, her always turning away, her sarcastic voice. But she was a teenager, and that's what teenagers did. Well, it was too bad, but it couldn't be helped now.

He thought of his father. That was too bad too, and nobody was writing articles about that. There had been a distance between them, so great and so absolute that the word "distance" seemed inadequate to describe it. But that was probably because he had known his father only when he was a very young child; if his father had lived longer, perhaps they would've become closer. He could recall his father's face clearly only at the breakfast table, where it appeared silent and still except for lip and jaw motions, comforting in its constancy. His father ate his oatmeal with one hand working the spoon, one elbow on the table, eyes down, sometimes his other hand holding a cold rag to his head, which always hurt with what seemed to be a noble pain, willingly taken on with his duties as a husband and father. He had loved to stare at the big face with its deep lines and long earlobes, its thin lips and loose, loopily chewing jaws. Its almost godlike stillness and expressionlessness filled him with admiration and reassurance, until one day his father slowly looked up from his cereal, met his eyes, and said, "Stop staring at me, you little shit."

In the other memories, his father was a large, heavy body with a vague oblong face. He saw him sleeping in the armchair in the living room, his large, hairy-knuckled hands grazing the floor. He saw him walking up the front walk with the quick, clipped steps that he always used coming home from work, the straight-backed choppy gait that gave the big body an awesome mechanicalness. His shirt was wet under the arms, his head was down, the eyes were abstracted but alert, as though keeping careful watch on the outside world in case something nasty came at him while he attended to the more important business inside.

"The good parent in yourself."

What did the well-meaning idiots who thought of these phrases mean by them? When a father dies, he is gone; there is no tiny, smiling daddy who appears, waving happily, in a secret pocket in your chest. Some kinds of loss are absolute. And no amount of self-realization or self-expression will change that.

As if she had heard him, Marsha urgently pressed her weight into her hands and applied all her strength to relaxing his muscles. Her sweat and scented deodorant filtered through her sweater, which added its muted wooliness to her smell. "All righty!" She rubbed his shoulders and briskly patted him. He reached back and touched her hand in thanks.

Across from where they sat had once been a red chair, and in it had once sat Kitty, gripping her face in her hand, her expression mottled by tears. "And if you ever try to come back here I'm going to spit in your face. I don't care if I'm on my deathbed, I'll still have the energy to spit in your face," he had said.

Marsha's hands lingered on him for a moment. Then she moved and sat away from him on the couch.

## Ⅲ Questions for Further Thinking

1. In this novella, there are quite a few places which indicate the cultural event of the late 1960s as the historical background of the story. Can you find them?

2. If Kitty wrote an article in the local magazine without telling her daddy, what does this suggest about their father-daughter relationship?

3. Please find the descriptions that correspond with Kitty's growth from age eight to twenty-two, then discuss your understanding of her self-transformation.

4. What kind of person is Kitty's dad? Why is it difficult for him to conduct a conversation with his daughter?

5. What kind of impression does Kitty's dad have about his own father? What is the implied meaning when he says "the good parent in yourself"?

## Ⅳ Appreciation

"Tiny, Smiling Daddy" is a heart-rending story of the daughter-father relationship. It describes how an adolescent girl Kitty makes efforts to find her own identity but fails to be accepted by her father. The feeling of being unwanted and rejected pushes Kitty to go on a tougher way to establish her identity.

The generational conflict is revealed from the father's memories. If the story is told from Kitty's narrative, it is prone to be read as a protest from a rebellious girl who lives in strife with her father. Instead, when it is told from the father's perspective, the fatherly emotion of love, which is blended with his incomprehension, helplessness, anger, and even shame of his daughter as a lesbian, become a mirror to reflect the daughter's path of self-exploration. Readers can easily perceive why a father feels mad when his daughter deviates from her parents' expectations and goes on her own way.

For Kitty's father Stew, subconsciously, he refuses to accept his daughter's growth as an independent individual, least of all, a lesbian. Living in a small town throughout his life, Stew does not like to reach out to the neighbors and is unknown of the social events that fundamentally transformed his daughter. He stubbornly clings to his memory of Kitty as the happy little girl of eight years old, thus consequently loses his way when Kitty grew up to possess her own idea and will. Accordingly, the conflicts accumulates and climaxes to the point that he pushes Kitty out from the family so she is forced to defend herself in the unfavorable social environment all alone.

For Kitty, the daughter, her adolescent life is a different picture from her father's recollection. From the time when her self-consciousness starts to sprout at the age of fourteen, Kitty fails to find support from her parents. In her juvenile rebellion against becoming an obedient ignorant girl, Kitty is apparently inspired by the youth culture of the 1960s, which advocates for the youths' free will against authorities of any kind. However, her free self-exploration is not well received by the townspeople who finds it objectionable. As a result, sixteen-year-old Kitty feels that she is despised, excluded, and even ostracized by both her parents and the community. To guard herself from the hostile surroundings, she hardens herself to struggle alone to establish her identity. It is only after years of harsh self-explorative life in California, Kitty starts to find her inner power to accept herself and reconcile with her father.

With the generational conflict as the core subject, this story also implies how Stew was ignored by his own father when he was a kid. Compared with her father's vain yearning of "the good parent in yourself," Kitty goes one step further to write an article to tell that she knows her father might love her. In this way, communication becomes a way to repair the father-daughter relationship.

## Ⅴ Writing Topic

很多人在童年时期都期待拥有守护神一样的父母。但如果父母没有成为这一角色，又不理解孩子的自主选择，就很可能导致亲子关系势同水火。在这种情况下，如何缓解或者消除对立的亲子关系？

# Unit 10 "Able, Baker, Charlie, Dog" by Stephanie Vaughn

## Ⅰ Introduction to the Author and the Work

Stephanie Vaughn (1943- ) was born in Millersburg, Ohio. She spent her childhood moving with her family to various military bases in Ohio, New York, Oklahoma, Texas, the Philippine Islands, and Italy. She received her BA from the Ohio State University, and her MFA from the University of Iowa, and was awarded the Wallace Stegner Fellowship at the Stanford University. Vaughn's stories have appeared in *Antaeus*, *The New Yorker*, *Redbook*, and the O. Henry and Pushcart Prize collections. Her collection of short stories, *Sweet Talk*, was published in 1990. Vaughn currently teaches creative writing and literature at the Cornell University. ①

"Able, Baker, Charlie, Dog" is named in the UK editions as *Sweet Talk* and as *Alfa Bravo Charlie Delta* in Spanish-language editions. It is a series of interconnected stories which feature Gemma, a funny, wise, and sensitive girl raised on American army bases. When the narrator was 12, she lived with her parents and grandmother at Fort Niagara, NY, where her father was the second in command. She recalls various incidents involving the father, including a story he told about two men trapped in a barge above Niagara Falls, and one of whom went insane. That winter, the narrator began menstruating and believed the pain in her developing breasts was cancer. That night she found her parents arguing. She followed her father outside and understood that his career had fallen apart. In the spring, the family moved to Ohio, where the father became a hardware dealer, got obsessed

① Wendy Martin, *More Stories We Tell: The Best Contemporary Short Stories by North American Women*. New York: Pantheon Books, 2004.

with Eskimos and Arctic explorations, and drank a lot. The summer the narrator got her master's degree, he died. The narrator cried at his grave because she had watched him disappear on the river that night, wondering whether he slipped between the floes into the water or not.

## Ⅱ Able, Baker, Charlie, Dog

When I was twelve years old, my father was tall and awesome. I can see him walking across the parade ground behind our quarters. The wind blew snow into the folds of his coat and made the hem swoop around his legs. He did not lower his head; he did not jam his hands into the pockets. He was coming home along a diagonal that would cut the parade ground into perfect triangles, and he was not going to be stopped by any snowstorm. I stood at the kitchen door and watched him through a hole I had rubbed in the steamy glass.

My grandmother and mother fidgeted with pans of food that had been kept warm too long. It was one o'clock on Saturday and he had been expected home at noon.

"You want to know what this chicken looks like?" said my grandmother. "It looks like it died last year."

My mother looked into the pan but didn't say anything.

My grandmother believed my mother should have married a minister, not an Army officer. Once my mother had gone out with a minister, and now he was on the radio every Sunday in Ohio. My grandmother thought my father had misrepresented himself as a religious man. There was a story my mother told about their first date. They went to a restaurant and my father told her that he was going to have twelve sons and name them Peter, James, John, et cetera. "And I thought, twelve sons!" said my mother. "Boy, do I pity your poor wife." My mother had two miscarriages and then she had me. My father named me Gemma, which my grandmother believed was not even a Christian name.

"You want to know what this squash looks like?" said my grandmother.

"It'll be fine," said my mother.

Just then the wind gusted on the parade ground, and my father veered to the left. He stopped and looked up. How is it possible you have caught me off guard, he seemed to ask. Exactly where have I miscalculated the velocities, how have I misjudged the vectors?

"It looks like somebody peed in it," my grandmother said.

• • •

"Keep your voice low," my father told me that day as we ate the ruined squash and chicken. "Keep your voice low and you can win any point."

We were living in Fort Niagara, a little Army post at the juncture of the Niagara River and Lake Ontario. We had been there through the fall and into the winter, as my father, who was second in command, waited for his next promotion. It began to snow in October. The Arctic winds swept across the lake from Canada and shook the windows of our house. Snow drifted across the parade ground, and floes of ice piled up against each other in the river, so that if a person were courageous enough, or foolhardy enough, and also lucky, he could walk the mile across the river to Canada.

"And always speak in sentences," he told me. "You have developed a junior-high habit of speaking in fragments. Learn to come to a full stop when you complete an idea. Use semicolons and periods in your speech."

My mother put down her fork and knife. Her hands were so thin and light they seemed to pass through the table as she dropped them in her lap. "Zachary, perhaps we could save some of the lecture for dessert?" she said.

My grandmother leaned back into her own heaviness. "The poor kid never gets to eat a hot meal," she said. She was referring to the rule that said I could not cut my food or eat while I was speaking or being spoken to. My father used mealtimes to lecture on the mechanics of life, the how-tos of a civilized world. Normally I was receptive to his advice, but that day I was angry with him.

"You know, Dad," I said, "I don't think my friends are going to notice a missing semicolon."

I thought he would give me a fierce look, but instead he winked. "And don't say 'you know,'" he said.

He never said "you know," never spoke in fragments, never slurred his speech, even years later when he had just put away a fifth of Scotch and was trying to describe the Eskimo custom of chewing up the meat before it was given to the elders, who had no teeth. He spoke with such calculation and precision that his sentences hung over us like high vaulted ceilings, or rolled across the table like ornaments sculptured from stone. It was a huge cathedral of a voice, full of volume and complexity.

• • •

He taught me the alphabet. Able, Baker, Charlie, Dog. It was the alphabet the military used to keep b's separate from v's and i's separate from y's. He liked the music of it, the way it sounded on his fine voice. I was four years old and my grandmother had not come to live with us yet. We were stationed in Manila, and living in a house the Army had built on squat stilts to protect us from the insects. There was a typhoon sweeping inland, and we could hear the hoarse sound of metal scraping across the Army's paved street. It was the corrugated roof of the house next door.

"Don't you think it's time we went under the house?" my mother said. She was sitting on a duffel bag that contained our tarps and food rations. The house had a loose plank in the living-room floor, so that if the roof blew away, or the walls caved in, we could escape through the opening and sit in the low space between the reinforced floor and the ground until the military rescue bus came.

My father looked at me and said, "Able, Baker, Charlie, Dog. Can you say it, Gemma?"

I looked up at the dark slope of our own metal roof.

"Can you say it?"

"Able, Baker, Charlie, Dog," I said.

The metal rumbled on the road outside. My mother lifted the plank.

"We will be all right," he said. "Easy, Fox, George, How."

"Anybody want to join me?" said my mother.

"Easy."

"Rachel, please put that plank back."

"Easy, Fox, George, How," I said.

My mother replaced the plank and sat on the floor beside me. The storm grew louder, the rain fell against the roof like handfuls of gravel.

"Item, Jig, King." My father's voice grew lower, fuller. We sat under the sound of it and felt safe. "Love, Mike, Nan."

But then we heard another sound—something that went whap-whap, softly, between the gusts of rain. We tilted our heads toward the shuttered windows.

"Well," said my father, standing up to stretch. "I think we are losing a board or two off the side of the house."

"Where are you going?" said my mother. "Just where do you think you're going?"

He put on his rain slicker and went into the next room. When he returned, he was carrying a bucket of nails and a hammer. "Obviously," he said, "I am going fishing."

• • •

We moved back to the States when I was six, and he taught me how to play Parcheesi, checkers, chess, cribbage, dominoes, and twenty questions. "When you lose," he told me, "don't cry. When you win, don't gloat."

He taught me how to plant tomatoes and load a shotgun shell. He showed me how to gut a dove, turning it inside out as the Europeans do, using the flexible breastbone for a pivot. He read a great many books and never forgot a fact or a technical description. He explained the principles of crop rotation and the flying buttress. He discussed the Defenestration of Prague.

When I was in elementary school, he was sent abroad twice on year—long tours—once to Turkey and once to Greenland, both strategic outposts for America's Early Warning System. I wanted to, but I could not write him letters. His came to me every week, but without the rhythms of his voice the words seemed pale and flat, like the transparent shapes of cells under a microscope. He did not write about his work, because his work was secret. He did not send advice, because that he left to my mother and grandmother in his absence. He wrote about small things—the smooth white rocks he found on a mountainside in Turkey, the first fresh egg he ate in Greenland. When I reread the letters after he died, I was struck by their grace and invention. But when I read them as a child, I looked through the words—"eggs ... shipment ... frozen"—and there was nothing on the other side but the great vacuum of his missing voice.

"I can't think of anything to say," I told my mother the first time she urged me to write to him. He had already been in Turkey for three months. She stood behind me at the heavy library table and smoothed my hair, touched my shoulders. "Tell him about your tap lessons," she said. "Tell him about ballet."

"Dear Dad," I wrote. "I am taking tap lessons. I am also taking ballet." I tried to imagine what he looked like, I tried to put a face before my face, but it was gray and featureless, like the face of a statue worn flat by wind and rain. "And I hope you have a Happy Birthday next month," I concluded, hoping to evade the necessity of writing him again in three weeks.

• • •

The autumn I turned twelve, we moved to Fort Niagara, which was the administrative base for the missile sites strung along the Canadian border between Lake Erie and Lake Ontario. It was a handsome post, full of oak trees, brick buildings, and history. The French had taken the land from the Indians and built the original fort. The British took the fort from the French, and the Americans took it from the British. My father recounted the battles for us as we drove there along the wide sweep of the Niagara River, past apple orchards and thick pastures. My grandmother sat in the back seat and made a note of each red convertible that passed. I was supposed to be counting the white ones. When we drove through the gate and saw the post for the first time—the expanses of clipped grass, the tall trees, the row of Colonial houses overlooking the river—my grandmother put down her tablet and said, "This is some post." She looked at my father admiringly, the first indication she had ever given that he might be a good match for my mother after all. She asked to be taken to the far end of the post, where the Old Fort was. It sat on a point of land at the juncture of the lake and river, and looked appropriately warlike, with its moat and tiny gun windows, but it was surprisingly small—a simple square of yellow stone, a modest French château. "Is this all there is?" I said as my grandmother and I posed for pictures on the drawbridge near two soldiers dressed in Revolutionary War costumes. It was hard to imagine that chunks of a vast continent had been won and lost within the confines of a fortress hardly bigger than Sleeping Beauty's castle at Disneyland. Later, as we drove back along the river, my father said in his aphoristic way, "Sometimes the biggest battles are the smallest ones."

The week after we settled in our quarters, we made the obligatory trip to the Falls. It was a sultry day—Indian summer—and our eyes began to water as we neared the chemical factories that surrounded the city of Niagara Falls. We stopped for iced tea and my father explained how the glaciers had formed the escarpment through which the Falls had cut a deep gorge. Escarpment—that was the term he used, instead of cliff. It skidded along the roof of his mouth and entered the conversation with a soft explosion.

We went to the Niagara Falls Museum and examined the containers people had used successfully to go over the Falls early in the twentieth century, when there was a thousand-dollar prize given to survivors. Two were wooden barrels strapped with metal bands. One was a giant rubber ball reinforced with a steel cage. A fourth was a long steel capsule. On the walls were photographs of each survivor and plaques explaining who had been injured and how. The steel capsule was used by a man who had broken every bone in his body. The plaque said that he was in the hospital for twenty-three weeks and then took his capsule around the world on a speaking tour. One day when he was in New Zealand, he slipped on an orange peel, broke his leg, and died of complications.

We went next to Goat Island and stood on the open bank to watch the leap and dive of the white water. My mother held her handbag close to her breasts. She had a habit of always holding things this way—a stack of dinner plates, the dish towel, some mail she had brought in from the porch; she hunched over slightly, so that her body seemed at once to be protective and protected. "I don't like the river," she said. "I think it wants to hypnotize you." My father put his hands in his pockets to show how at ease he was, and my grandmother went off to buy an ice-cream cone.

At the observation point, we stood at a metal fence and looked into the frothing water at the bottom of the gorge. We watched bits and pieces of rainbows appear and vanish in the sunlight that was refracted off the water through the mist. My father pointed to a black shape in the rapids above the Horseshoe Falls. "That's a river barge," he said. He lowered his voice so that he could be heard under the roar of the water. "A long time ago, there were two men standing on that barge waiting to see whether in the next moment of their lives they would go over."

He told us the story of the barge then—how it had broken loose from a tug near Buffalo and floated downriver, gathering speed. The two men tore at the air, waved and shouted to people on shore, but the barge entered the rapids. They bumped around over the rocks, and the white water rose in the air. One man—"He was the thinking man," said my father—thought they might be able to wedge the barge among the rocks if they allowed the hull to fill with water. They came closer to the Falls—four hundred yards, three hundred—before the barge jerked broadside and stopped. They were there all afternoon and night, listening to the sound of the water pounding into the boulders at the bottom of the gorge. The next morning they were rescued, and one of the men, the thinking man, told the newspapers that he had spent the night playing poker in his head. He played all the hands, and he bluffed himself. He drew to inside straights. If the barge had torn loose from the rocks in the night, he was going to go over the Falls saying, "Five-card draw, jacks or better to open." The other man sat on the barge, his arms clasped around his knees, and watched the mist blow back from the edge of the Falls in the moonlight. He could not speak.

"The scream of the water entered his body," said my father. He paused to let us think about that.

"Well, what does that mean?" my grandmother said at last.

My father rested his arms on the fence and gazed pleasantly at the Falls. "He went insane."

The river fascinated me. I often stood between the yellow curtains of my bedroom and looked down upon it and thought about how deep and swift it was, how black under the glittering surface. The newspaper carried stories about people who jumped over the Falls, fourteen miles upriver from our house. I thought of their bodies pushed along the soft silt of the bottom, tumbling silently, huddled in upon themselves like fetuses—jilted brides, unemployed factory workers, old people who did not want to go to rest homes, teenagers who got bad grades, young women who fell in love with married men. They floated invisibly past my bedroom window, out into the lake.

• • •

That winter, I thought I was going to die. I thought I had cancer of the breasts. My mother had explained to me about menstruation, she had given me a book about the reproductive systems of men and women, but she had not told me about breasts and how they begin as invisible lumps that become tender and sore.

I thought the soreness had begun in a phys. Ed. Class one day in December when I was hit in the chest with a basketball. I didn't worry about it, and it went away by New Year's. In January, I found a pamphlet at the bus stop. I was stamping my feet in the cold, looking down at my boots, when I saw the headline—CANCER: SEVEN WARNING SIGNALS. When I got home, I went into the bathroom and undressed. I examined myself for enlarged moles and small wounds that wouldn't heal. I was systematic. I sat on the edge of the tub with the pamphlet by my side and began with my toenails, looking under the tips of them. I felt my soles, arches, ankles. I worked my way up my body and then I felt the soreness again, around both nipples. At dinner that night I didn't say anything all through the meal. In bed I slept on my back, with my arms stiff against my sides.

The next Saturday was the day my father came home late for lunch. The squash sat on the back of the stove and turned to ocher soup. The chicken fell away from the bones. After lunch he went into the living room and drank Scotch and read a book. When I came down for supper, he was still sitting there, and he told my mother he would eat later. My grandmother, my mother, and I ate silently at the kitchen table. I took a long bath. I scrubbed my chest hard.

I went straight to my bedroom, and after a while my mother came upstairs and said, "What's wrong?"

I didn't say anything.

She stood in front of me with her hands clasped in front of her. She seemed to lean toward her own hands. "But you've been acting, you know"—and here she laughed self-consciously, as she used the forbidden phrase—"you know, you've been acting different. You were so quiet today."

I went to my chest of drawers and took the pamphlet out from under a stack of folded underpants and gave it to her.

"What's this?" she said.

"I think I have Number Four," I said.

She must have known immediately what the problem was, but she didn't smile. She asked me to raise my nightgown and she examined my chest, pressing firmly, as if she were a doctor. I told her about the soreness. "Here?" she said. "And here? What about here, too?" She told me I was beginning to "develop." I knew what she meant, but I wanted her to be precise.

"You're getting breasts," she said.

"But I don't see anything."

"You will."

"You never told me it would hurt."

"Oh, dear. I just forgot. When you're grown up you just forget what it was like."

I asked her whether, just to be safe, I could see a doctor. She said that of course I could, and I felt better, as if I had had a disease and already been cured. As she was leaving the room, I said, "Do you think I need a bra?" She smiled. I went to sleep watching the snow fall past the window. I had my hands cupped over my new breasts.

• • •

When I awoke, I did not recognize the window. The snow had stopped and moonlight slanted through the glass. I could not make out the words, but I heard my father's voice filling up the house. I tiptoed down the back staircase that led to the kitchen and stood in the slice of shadow near the doorjamb. My grandmother was telling my mother to pack her bags. He was a degenerate, she said—she had always seen that in him. My mother said, "Why, Zachary, why are you doing this?"

"Just go pack your bags," my grandmother said. "I'll get the child."

My father said conversationally, tensely, "Do I have to break your arms?"

I leaned into the light. He was holding on to a bottle of Scotch with one hand, and my mother was trying to pull it away with both of hers. He jerked his arm back and forth, so that she was drawn into a little dance, back and forth across the linoleum in front of him.

"The Lord knows the way of righteousness," said my grandmother.

"Please," said my mother. "Please, please."

"And the way of the ungodly shall perish," said my grandmother.

"Whose house is this?" said my father. His voice exploded. He snapped his arm back, trying to take the bottle from my mother in one powerful gesture. It smashed against the wall, and I stepped into the kitchen. The white light from the ceiling fixture burned across the smooth surfaces of the refrigerator, the stove, the white Formica countertops. It was as if an atom had been smashed somewhere and a wave of radiation was rolling through the kitchen. I looked him in the eye and waited for him to speak. I sensed my mother and grandmother on either side of me, in petrified postures. At last, he said, "Well." His voice cracked. The word split in two. "Wel-el." He said it again. His face took on a flatness.

"I am going back to bed," I said. I went up the narrow steps, and he followed me. My mother and grandmother came along behind, whispering. He tucked in the covers, and sat on the edge of the bed, watching me. My mother and grandmother stood stiff against the door. "I am sorry I woke you up," he said finally, and his voice was deep and soothing. The two women watched him go down the hall, and when I heard his steps on the front staircase I rolled over and put my face in the pillow. I heard them turn off the lights and say good-night to me. I heard them go to their bedrooms. I lay there for a long time, listening for a sound downstairs, and then it came—the sound of the front door closing.

I went downstairs and put on my hat, coat, boots. I followed his footsteps in the snow, down the front walk, and across the road to the riverbank. He did not seem surprised to see me next to him. We stood side by side, hands in our pockets, breathing frost into the air. The river was filled from shore to shore with white heaps of ice, which cast blue shadows in the moonlight.

"This is the edge of America," he said, in a tone that seemed to answer a question I had just asked. There was a creak and crunch of ice as two floes below us scraped each other and jammed against the bank.

"You knew all week, didn't you? Your mother and your grandmother didn't know, but I knew that you could be counted on to know."

I hadn't known until just then, but I guessed the unspeakable thing—that his career was falling apart—and I knew. I nodded. Years later, my mother told me what she had learned about the incident, not from him but from another Army wife. He had called a general a son of a bitch. That was all. I never knew what the issue was or whether he had been right or wrong. Whether the defense of the United States of America had been at stake, or merely the pot in a card game. I didn't even know whether he had called the general a son of a bitch to his face or simply been overheard in an unguarded moment. I only knew that he had been given a 7 instead of a 9 on his Efficiency Report and then passed over for promotion. But that night I nodded, not knowing the cause but knowing the consequences, as we stood on the riverbank above the moonlit ice. "I am looking at that thin beautiful line of Canada," he said. "I think I will go for a walk."

"No," I said. I said it again. "No." I wanted to remember later that I had told him not to go.

"How long do you think it would take to go over and back?" he said.

"Two hours."

He rocked back and forth in his boots, looked up at the moon, then down at the river. I did not say anything.

He started down the bank, sideways, taking long, graceful sliding steps, which threw little puffs of snow in the air. He took his hands from his pockets and hopped from the bank to the ice. He tested his weight against the weight of the ice, flexing his knees. I watched him walk a few yards from the shore and then I saw him rise in the air, his long legs scissoring the moonlight, as he crossed from the edge of one floe to the next. He turned and waved to me, one hand making a slow arc.

I could have said anything. I could have said "Come back" or "I love you." Instead, I called after him, "Be sure and write!" The last thing I heard, long after I had lost sight of him far out on the river, was the sound of his laugh splitting the cold air.

• • •

In the spring he resigned his commission and we went back to Ohio. He used his savings to invest in a chain of hardware stores with my uncle. My uncle arranged the contracts with builders and plumbers, and supervised the employees. My father controlled the inventory and handled the books. He had been a logistics officer, and all the skills he might have used in supervising the movement of land, air, and sea cargoes, or in calculating the disposition of several billion dollars' worth of military supplies, were instead brought to bear on the deployment of nuts and bolts, plumbers' joints and nipples, No. 2 pine, contact paper, acrylic paint, caulking guns, and rubber dishpans. He learned a new vocabulary—traffic builders, margins, end-cap displays, perfboard merchandisers, seasonal impulse items—and spoke it with the ostentation and faint amusement of a man who has just mastered a foreign language.

"But what I really want to know, Mr. Jenkins," I heard him tell a man on the telephone one day, "is why you think the Triple Gripper Vegetable Ripper would make a good loss-leader item in mid-winter." He had been in the hardlines industry, as it was called, for six months, and I was making my first visit to his office, and then only because my mother had sent me there on the pretext of taking him a midmorning snack during a busy Saturday. I was reluctant to confront him in his civilian role, afraid I would find him somehow diminished. In fact, although he looked incongruous among the reds, yellows, and blues that the previous owner had used to decorate the office, he sounded much like the man who had taught me to speak in complete sentences.

"Mr. Jenkins, I am not asking for a discourse on coleslaw."

When he hung up, he winked at me and said, "Your father is about to become the emperor of the building—and—housewares trade in Killbuck, Ohio."

I nodded and took a seat in a red-and-blue chair.

Then he looked at his hands spread upon the spotless ink blotter and said, "Of course, you know that I do not give a damn about the Triple Gripper Vegetable Ripper."

I had skipped a grade and entered high school. I saw less and less of him, because I ate dinner early so that I could go to play rehearsals, basketball games, dances. In the evenings he sat in a green chair and smoked cigarettes, drank Scotch, read books—the same kinds of books, year after year. They were all about Eskimos and Arctic explorations—an interest he had developed during his tour in Greenland. Sometimes, when I came in late and was in the kitchen making a snack, I watched him through the doorway. Often he looked away from the book and gazed toward the window. He would strike a match and let it burn to his thumb and fingertip, then wave it out. He would raise the glass but not drink from it. I think he must have imagined himself to be in the Arctic during those moments, a warrior tracking across the ice for bear or seal. Sometimes he was waiting for me to join him. He wanted to tell me about the techniques the Eskimos had developed for survival, the way they stitched up skins to make them watertight vessels. He became obsessive on the subject of meat. The Eskimo diet was nearly all protein. "Eat meat," he said. Two professors at Columbia had tested the value of the Eskimo diet by eating nothing but caribou for a year and claimed they were healthier at the end of the experiment than they had been before.

Later, when I went to college, he developed the habit of calling me long distance when my mother and grandmother had gone to bed and he was alone downstairs with a drink. "Are you getting enough protein?" he asked me once at three in the morning. It was against dorm rules to put through calls after midnight except in cases of emergency, but his deep, commanding voice was so authoritative ("This is Gemma Jackson's father, and I must speak with her immediately") that it was for some time believed on my corridor that the people in my family were either accident-prone or suffering from long terminal illnesses.

• • •

He died the summer I received my master's degree. I had accepted a teaching position at a high school in Chicago, and I went home for a month before school began. He was overweight and short of breath. He drank too much, smoked too many cigarettes. The doctor told him to stop, my mother told him, my grandmother told him.

My grandmother was upstairs watching television and my mother and I were sitting on the front porch. He was asleep in the green chair, with a book in his lap. I left the porch to go to the kitchen to make a sandwich, and as I passed by the chair I heard him say, "Ahhhh. Ahhhhh." I saw his fist rise to his chest. I saw his eyes open and dilate in the lamplight. I knelt beside him.

"Are you okay?" I said. "Are you dreaming?"

We buried him in a small cemetery near the farm where he was born. In the eulogy he was remembered for having survived the first wave of the invasion of Normandy. He was admired for having been the proprietor of a chain of excellent hardware stores.

"He didn't have to do this," my mother said after the funeral. "He did this to himself."

"He was a good man," said my grandmother. "He put a nice roof over our heads. He sent us to Europe twice."

Afterward I went alone to the cemetery. I knelt beside the heaps of wilting flowers—mostly roses and gladiolus, and one wreath of red, white, and blue carnations. Above me, the maple pods spun through the sunlight like wings, and in the distance the corn trumpeted green across the hillsides. I touched the loose black soil at the edge of the flowers. Able, Baker, Charlie, Dog. I could remember the beginning of the alphabet, up through Mike and Nan. I could remember the end. X-ray, Yoke, Zebra. I was his eldest child, and he taught me what he knew. I wept then, but not because he had gone back to Ohio to read about the Eskimos and sell the artifacts of civilized life to homeowners and builders. I wept because when I was twelve years old I had stood on a snowy riverbank as he became a shadow on the ice, and waited to see whether he would slip between the cracking floes into the water.

## Ⅲ Questions for Further Thinking

1. What kind of man is Father Zachary? How does the little girl Gemma think of her dad?

2. What happens the night when Gemma's father gets drunk and lost his temper?

3. When Father Zachary says to Gemma, "You knew all week, didn't you? ...

I knew you could be counted on to know," what is his expectation of Gemma?

4. When Father Zachary resigns and becomes a civilian, how does Gemma view her father?

5. Why does Gemma feel bitterly sad when she reflected on the moment when she accompanied her father walking in the snow at twelve years old?

## Ⅳ Appreciation

"Able, Baker, Charlie, Dog" is another story of the father-daughter relationship. If "Tiny, Smiling Daddy" tells how a father's knowledge of her daughter is frozen in the girl's pleasing age of eight, then it is the opposite version. The story tells how a daughter retains her knowledge of father in a little girl's limited understanding.

At the age of four, Gemma's impression of her father is fixed in her mind—a tall and awesome military senior officer, a desired dad of almost every girl's imagination. Throughout the early years of her growth, this father image is continuously getting fuller and more idealized. He is a calm Dad who taught her alphabet when the typhoon struck, a caring Dad who inventively illustrates small things to a kid, and a knowledgeable Dad who narrates Arctic adventurous stories to a teenager.

Because of his high rank in the military, Gemma's father, Zachary, always stations away from home. Gemma's memory of her father is accumulated by significant life episodes, such as playing chess, the typhoon moment in Manila, along with a family visit to Fort Niagara and the Niagara Falls. In every memory fragment that Gemma remembers, her father takes time to instruct her, particularly on how to speak properly. He requires Gemma to speak in sentences and use the military way to memorize the alphabet, while he himself sets a model for proper speech. Yet, the language expert himself would meet his downfall when he cursed at his superior.

The year when Zachary experienced his fiasco in career promotion in the army, Gemma is experiencing her own critical stage of growth. Her attention has shifted from the admiration of her father to her own life at school and academic pursuit. While she is stepping into the larger world of her own, her father resigns and resumes civilian life as a family warehouse businessman, reminiscing his glory in ruminating the book of Arctic explorations. Moreover, his alcoholic addiction suggests that he is never able to reconcile himself with his blunder in speaking.

Gemma, who was used to looking up at her father as a supreme model, feels uneasy about her father's transformation. Her understanding of her father is paused at those glorious moments when he was in the military service. It is until the sudden death of her father does she start to perceive how hard her father tried to preserve his heroic father image the night when he exploded with temper. Yet, it was such a sorrow for Gemma to realize that at the time when she was twelve, her incomprehension of her father's unruffled act to walk on the ice was something inevitable.

## V Writing Topic

作为一位自我要求完美的父亲,Zachary 知道自己在女儿心目中拥有无尽的光环。这一光环阻止他在家庭关系中坦承自己的情感需求,以至于在职业受挫时他无法面对自己的失误,以致自尊受损,最终黯然离职。从父女关系的角度来看,这种光环给代际沟通和理解带来了障碍。试讨论这一点。

# Part Four

## *Love and Marriage*

# Unit 11 "A Temporary Matter" by Jhumpa Lahiri

## Ⅰ Introduction to the Author and the Work

Jhumpa Lahiri (1967– ) was born in London, England. Her parents immigrated to the United Kingdom from Calcutta, India. Lahiri's father, a university librarian, opted to relocate to the United States for work, eventually settling in South Kingstown, Rhode Island, when she was still a small child. Lahiri went on to attend Barnard College in New York, focusing on English literature. She then joined Boston University, earning three literary master's degrees before receiving her doctorate in Renaissance studies.

Lahiri's first book, a collection of nine stories, *Interpreter of Maladies* (1999), won an array of honors, including the Pulitzer Prize and the PEN/Hemingway Award. In 2003, Lahiri followed up with *The Namesake*, a novel that followed the lives, perspectives, and changing family ties of the Gangulis, an Indian couple in an arranged marriage who relocated to the US. The work was adapted into a 2007 Mira Nair film. Lahiri's 2013 novel, *The Lowland*, was partially inspired by real-world political events.

In "A Temporary Matter," the married couple Shoba and Shukumar had grown increasingly distant over the past few months. Shukumar recalled the event that caused the couple's alienation. Six months ago, Shukumar attended an academic conference in Baltimore. Shoba was pregnant with their child. Her due date was three weeks away. While Shukumar was away, Shoba went into early labor and had to have an emergency C-section (剖宫产). The baby was stillborn. Shukumar regretted the moment he chose to leave. In one electric blackout, Shukumar and Shoba tried to amend their relationship by recalling their past experience of love and marriage. Unfortunately, Shukumar's responses in the "truth and dare" game failed to win back the trust from Shoba.

## Ⅱ A Temporary Matter[①]

The notice informed them that it was a temporary matter: for five days their electricity would be cut off for one hour, beginning at eight p.m. A line had gone down in the last snowstorm, and the repairmen were going to take advantage of the milder evenings to set it right. The work would affect only the houses on the quiet tree-lined street, within walking distance of a row of brick-faced stores and a trolley stop, where Shoba and Shukumar had lived for three years.

"It's good of them to warn us," Shoba conceded after reading the notice aloud, more for her own benefit than Shukumar's. She let the strap of her leather satchel, plump with files, slip from her shoulders, and left it in the hallway as she walked into the kitchen. She wore a navy blue poplin raincoat over gray sweatpants and white sneakers, looking, at thirty-three, like the type of woman she'd once claimed she would never resemble.

She'd come from the gym. Her cranberry lipstick was visible only on the outer reaches of her mouth, and her eyeliner had left charcoal patches beneath her lower lashes. She used to look this way sometimes, Shukumar thought, on mornings after a party or a night at a bar, when she'd been too lazy to wash her face, too eager to collapse into his arms. She dropped a sheaf of mail on the table without a glance. Her eyes were still fixed on the notice in her other hand. "But they should do this sort of thing during the day."

"When I'm here, you mean," Shukumar said. He put a glass lid on a pot of lamb, adjusting it so only the slightest bit of steam could escape. Since January he'd been working at home, trying to complete the final chapters of his dissertation on agrarian revolts in India. "When do the repairs start?"

---

① A-Temporary-Matter. pdf (in-sightforum. com).

"It says March nineteenth. Is today the nineteenth?" Shoba walked over to the framed corkboard that hung on the wall by the fridge, bare except for a calendar of William Morris wallpaper patterns. She looked at it as if for the first time, studying the wallpaper pattern carefully on the top half before allowing her eyes to fall to the numbered grid on the bottom. A friend had sent the calendar in the mail as a Christmas gift, even though Shoba and Shukumar hadn't celebrated Christmas that year.

"Today then," Shoba announced. "You have a dentist appointment next Friday, by the way."

He ran his tongue over the tops of his teeth; he'd forgotten to brush them that morning. It wasn't the first time. He hadn't left the house at all that day, or the day before. The more Shoba stayed out, the more she began putting in extra hours at work and taking on additional projects, the more he wanted to stay in, not even leaving to get the mail, or to buy fruit or wine at the stores by the trolley stop.

Six months ago, in September, Shukumar was at an academic conference in Baltimore when Shoba went into labor, three weeks before her due date. He hadn't wanted to go to the conference, but she had insisted; it was important to make contacts, and he would be entering the job market next year. She told him that she had his number at the hotel, and a copy of his schedule and flight numbers, and she had arranged with her friend Gillian for a ride to the hospital in the event of an emergency. When the cab pulled away that morning for the airport, Shoba stood waving goodbye in her robe, with one arm resting on the mound of her belly as if it were a perfectly natural part of her body.

Each time he thought of that moment, the last moment he saw Shoba pregnant, it was the cab he remembered most, a station wagon, painted red with blue lettering. It was cavernous compared to their own car. Although Shukumar was six feet tall, with hands too big ever to rest comfortably in the pockets of his jeans, he felt dwarfed in the back seat. As the cab sped down Beacon Street, he imagined a day when he and Shoba might need to buy a station wagon of their own, to cart their children back and forth from music lessons and dentist appointments. He imagined himself gripping the wheel, as

Shoba turned around to hand the children juice boxes. Once, these images of parenthood had troubled Shukumar, adding to his anxiety that he was still a student at thirty-five. But that early autumn morning, the trees still heavy with bronze leaves, he welcomed the image for the first time.

A member of the staff had found him somehow among the identical convention rooms and handed him a stiff square of stationery. It was only a telephone number, but Shukumar knew it was the hospital. When he returned to Boston it was over. The baby had been born dead. Shoba was lying on a bed, asleep, in a private room so small there was barely enough space to stand beside her, in a wing of the hospital they hadn't been to on the tour for expectant parents. Her placenta had weakened and she'd had a cesarean, though not quickly enough. The doctor explained that these things happen. He smiled in the kindest way it was possible to smile at people known only professionally. Shoba would be back on her feet in a few weeks. There was nothing to indicate that she would not be able to have children in the future.

These days Shoba was always gone by the time Shukumar woke up. He would open his eyes and see the long black hairs she shed on her pillow and think of her, dressed, sipping her third cup of coffee already, in her office downtown, where she searched for typographical errors in textbooks and marked them, in a code she had once explained to him, with an assortment of colored pencils. She would do the same for his dissertation, she promised, when it was ready. He envied her the specificity of her task, so unlike the elusive nature of his. He was a mediocre student who had a facility for absorbing details without curiosity. Until September he had been diligent if not dedicated, summarizing chapters, outlining arguments on pads of yellow lined paper. But now he would lie in their bed until he grew bored, gazing at his side of the closet which Shoba always left partly open, at the row of the tweed jackets and corduroy trousers he would not have to choose from to teach his classes that semester. After the baby died it was too late to withdraw from his teaching duties. But his adviser had arranged things so that he had the spring semester to himself. Shukumar was in his sixth year of graduate school. "That and the summer should give you a good push," his adviser had said. "You should be able to wrap things up by next September."

But nothing was pushing Shukumar. Instead he thought of how he and Shoba had become experts at avoiding each other in their three-bedroom house, spending as much time on separate floors as possible. He thought of how he no longer looked forward to weekends, when she sat for hours on the sofa with her colored pencils and her files, so that he feared that putting on a record in his own house might be rude. He thought of how long it had been since she looked into his eyes and smiled, or whispered his name on those rare occasions they still reached for each other's bodies before sleeping.

In the beginning he had believed that it would pass, that he and Shoba would get through it all somehow. She was only thirty-three. She was strong, on her feet again. But it wasn't a consolation. It was often nearly lunchtime when Shukumar would finally pull himself out of bed and head downstairs to the coffeepot, pouring out the extra bit Shoba left for him, along with an empty mug, on the countertop.

• • •

Shukumar gathered onion skins in his hands and let them drop into the garbage pail, on top of the ribbons of fat he'd trimmed from the lamb. He ran the water in the sink, soaking the knife and the cutting board, and rubbed a lemon half along his fingertips to get rid of the garlic smell, a trick he'd learned from Shoba. It was seven-thirty. Through the window he saw the sky, like soft black pitch. Uneven banks of snow still lined the sidewalks, though it was warm enough for people to walk about without hats or gloves. Nearly three feet had fallen in the last storm, so that for a week people had to walk single file, in narrow trenches. For a week that was Shukumar's excuse for not leaving the house. But now the trenches were widening, and water drained steadily into grates in the pavement.

"The lamb won't be done by eight," Shukumar said. "We may have to eat in the dark."

"We can light candles," Shoba suggested. She unclipped her hair, coiled neatly at her nape during the days, and pried the sneakers from her feet without untying them. "I'm going to shower before the lights go," she said, heading for the staircase. "I'll be down."

Shukumar moved her satchel and her sneakers to the side of the fridge. She wasn't this way before. She used to put her coat on a hanger, her sneakers in the closet, and she paid bills as soon as they came. But now she treated the house as if it were a hotel. The fact that the yellow chintz armchair in the living room clashed with the blue-and-maroon Turkish carpet no longer bothered her. On the enclosed porch at the back of the house, a crisp white bag still sat on the wicker chaise, filled with lace she had once planned to turn into curtains.

While Shoba showered, Shukumar went into the downstairs bathroom and found a new toothbrush in its box beneath the sink. The cheap, stiff bristles hurt his gums, and he spat some blood into the basin. The spare brush was one of many stored in a metal basket. Shoba had bought them once when they were on sale, in the event that a visitor decided, at the last minute, to spend the night.

It was typical of her. She was the type to prepare for surprises, good and bad. If she found a skirt or a purse she liked she bought two. She kept the bonuses from her job in a separate bank account in her name. It hadn't bothered him. His own mother had fallen to pieces when his father died, abandoning the house he grew up in and moving back to Calcutta, leaving Shukumar to settle it all. He liked that Shoba was different. It astonished him, her capacity to think ahead. When she used to do the shopping, the pantry was always stocked with extra bottles of olive and corn oil, depending on whether they were cooking Italian or Indian. There were endless boxes of pasta in all shapes and colors, zippered sacks of basmati rice, whole sides of lambs and goats from the Muslim butchers at Haymarket, chopped up and frozen in endless plastic bags. Every other Saturday they wound through the maze of stalls Shukumar eventually knew by heart. He watched in disbelief as she bought more food, trailing behind her with canvas bags as she pushed through the crowd, arguing under the morning sun with boys too young to shave but already missing teeth, who twisted up brown paper bags of artichokes, plums, gingerroot, and yams, and dropped them on their scales, and tossed them to Shoba one by one. She didn't mind being jostled, even when she was pregnant. She was tall, and broad-shouldered, with hips that her obstetrician assured her were made for childbearing. During the drive back home, as the car curved along the Charles, they invariably marveled at how much food they'd bought.

It never went to waste. When friends dropped by, Shoba would throw together meals that appeared to have taken half a day to prepare, from things she had frozen and bottled, not cheap things in tins but peppers she had marinated herself with rosemary, and chutneys that she cooked on Sundays, stirring boiling pots of tomatoes and prunes. Her labeled mason jars lined the shelves of the kitchen, in endless sealed pyramids, enough, they'd agreed, to last for their grandchildren to taste. They'd eaten it all by now. Shukumar had been going through their supplies steadily, preparing meals for the two of them, measuring out cupfuls of rice, defrosting bags of meat day after day. He combed through her cookbooks every afternoon, following her penciled instructions to use two teaspoons of ground coriander seeds instead of one, or red lentils instead of yellow. Each of the recipes was dated, telling the first time they had eaten the dish together. April 2, cauliflower with fennel. January 14, chicken with almonds and sultanas. He had no memory of eating those meals, and yet there they were, recorded in her neat proofreader's hand. Shukumar enjoyed cooking now. It was the one thing that made him feel productive. If it weren't for him, he knew, Shoba would eat a bowl of cereal for her dinner.

Tonight, with no lights, they would have to eat together. For months now they'd served themselves from the stove, and he'd taken his plate into his study, letting the meal grow cold on his desk before shoving it into his mouth without pause, while Shoba took her plate to the living room and watched game shows, or proofread files with her arsenal of colored pencils at hand.

At some point in the evening she visited him. When he heard her approach he would put away his novel and begin typing sentences. She would rest her hands on his shoulders and stare with him into the blue glow of the computer screen. "Don't work too hard," she would say after a minute or two, and head off to bed. It was the one time in the day she sought him out, and yet he'd come to dread it. He knew it was something she forced herself to do. She would look around the walls of the room, which they had decorated together last summer with a border of marching ducks and rabbits playing trumpets and drums. By the end of August there was a cherry crib under the window, a white changing table with mint-green knobs, and a rocking chair with checkered cushions. Shukumar had disassembled it all before bringing Shoba back from the hospital, scraping off the rabbits and ducks with a spatula. For some reason the room did not haunt him the way it haunted Shoba. In January, when he stopped working at his carrel in the library, he set up his desk there deliberately, partly because the room soothed him, and partly because it was a place Shoba avoided.

• • •

Shukumar returned to the kitchen and began to open drawers. He tried to locate a candle among the scissors, the eggbeaters and whisks, the mortar and pestle she'd bought in a bazaar in Calcutta, and used to pound garlic cloves and cardamom pods, back when she used to cook. He found a flashlight, but no batteries, and a half-empty box of birthday candles. Shoba had thrown him a surprise birthday party last May. One hundred and twenty people had crammed into the house—all the friends and the friends of friends they now systematically avoided. Bottles of vinho verde had nested in a bed of ice in the bathtub. Shoba was in her fifth month, drinking ginger ale from a martini glass. She had made a vanilla cream cake with custard and spun sugar. All night she kept Shukumar's long fingers linked with hers as they walked among the guests at the party.

Since September their only guest had been Shoba's mother. She came from Arizona and stayed with them for two months after Shoba returned from the hospital. She cooked dinner every night, drove herself to the supermarket, washed their clothes, and put them away. She was a religious woman. She set up a small shrine, a framed picture of a lavender-faced goddess and a plate of marigold petals, on the bedside table in the guest room, and prayed twice a day for healthy grandchildren in the future. She was polite to Shukumar without being friendly. She folded his sweaters with an expertise she had learned from her job in a department store. She replaced a missing button on his winter coat and knitted him a beige and brown scarf, presenting it to him without the least bit of ceremony, as if he had only dropped it and hadn't noticed. She never talked to him about Shoba; once, when he mentioned the baby's death, she looked up from her knitting, and said, "But you weren't even there."

It struck him as odd that there were no real candles in the house. Shoba hadn't prepared for such an ordinary emergency. He looked now for something to put the birthday candles in and settled on the soil of a potted ivy that normally sat on the windowsill over the sink. Even though the plant was inches from the tap, the soil was so dry that he had to water it first before the candles would stand straight. He pushed aside the things on the kitchen table, the piles of mail, the unread library books. He remembered their first meals there, when they were so thrilled to be married, to be living together in the same house at last, that they would just reach for each other foolishly, more eager to make love than to eat. He put down two embroidered place mats, a wedding gift from an uncle in Lucknow, and set out the plates and wineglasses they usually saved for guests. He put the ivy in the middle, the white-edged, star-shaped leaves girded by ten little candles. He switched on the digital clock radio and tuned it to a jazz station.

"What's all this?" Shoba said when she came downstairs. Her hair was wrapped in a thick white towel. She undid the towel and draped it over a chair, allowing her hair, damp and dark, to fall across her back. As she walked absently toward the stove she took out a few tangles with her fingers. She wore a clean pair of sweatpants, a T-shirt, an old flannel robe. Her stomach was flat again, her waist narrow before the flare of her hips, the belt of the robe tied in a floppy knot.

It was nearly eight. Shukumar put the rice on the table and the lentils from the night before into the microwave oven, punching the numbers on the timer.

"You made rogan josh," Shoba observed, looking through the glass lid at the bright paprika stew.

Shukumar took out a piece of lamb, pinching it quickly between his fingers so as not to scald himself. He prodded a larger piece with a serving spoon to make sure the meat slipped easily from the bone. "It's ready," he announced.

The microwave had just beeped when the lights went out, and the music disappeared.

"Perfect timing," Shoba said.

"All I could find were birthday candles." He lit up the ivy, keeping the rest of the candles and a book of matches by his plate.

"It doesn't matter," she said, running a finger along the stem of her wineglass. "It looks lovely."

In the dimness, he knew how she sat, a bit forward in her chair, ankles crossed against the lowest rung, left elbow on the table. During his search for the candles, Shukumar had found a bottle of wine in a crate he had thought was empty. He clamped the bottle between his knees while he turned in the corkscrew. He worried about spilling, and so he picked up the glasses and held them close to his lap while he filled them. They served themselves, stirring the rice with their forks, squinting as they extracted bay leaves and cloves from the stew. Every few minutes Shukumar lit a few more birthday candles and drove them into the soil of the pot.

"It's like India," Shoba said, watching him tend his makeshift candelabra. "Sometimes the current disappears for hours at a stretch. I once had to attend an entire rice ceremony in the dark. The baby just cried and cried. It must have been so hot."

Their baby had never cried, Shukumar considered. Their baby would never have a rice ceremony, even though Shoba had already made the guest list, and decided on which of her three brothers she was going to ask to feed the child its first taste of solid food, at six months if it was a boy, seven if it was a girl.

"Are you hot?" he asked her. He pushed the blazing ivy pot to the other end of the table, closer to the piles of books and mail, making it even more difficult for them to see each other. He was suddenly irritated that he couldn't go upstairs and sit in front of the computer.

"No. It's delicious," she said, tapping her plate with her fork. "It really is."

He refilled the wine in her glass. She thanked him.

They weren't like this before. Now he had to struggle to say something that interested her, something that made her look up from her plate, or from her proofreading files. Eventually he gave up trying to amuse her. He learned not to mind the silences.

"I remember during power failures at my grandmother's house, we all had to say something," Shoba continued. He could barely see her face, but from her tone he knew her eyes were narrowed, as if trying to focus on a distant object. It was a habit of hers.

"Like what?"

"I don't know. A little poem. A joke. A fact about the world. For some reason my relatives always wanted me to tell them the names of my friends in America. I don't know why the information was so interesting to them. The last time I saw my aunt she asked after four girls I went to elementary school with in Tucson. I barely remember them now."

Shukumar hadn't spent as much time in India as Shoba had. His parents, who settled in New Hampshire, used to go back without him. The first time he'd gone as an infant he'd nearly died of amoebic dysentery. His father, a nervous type, was afraid to take him again, in case something were to happen, and left him with his aunt and uncle in Concord. As a teenager he preferred sailing camp or scooping ice cream during the summers to going to Calcutta. It wasn't until after his father died, in his last year of college, that the country began to interest him, and he studied its history from course books as if it were any other subject. He wished now that he had his own childhood story of India.

"Let's do that," she said suddenly.

"Do what?"

"Say something to each other in the dark."

"Like what? I don't know any jokes."

"No, no jokes." She thought for a minute. "How about telling each other something we've never told before."

"I used to play this game in high school," Shukumar recalled. "When I got drunk."

"You're thinking of truth or dare. This is different. Okay, I'll start." She took a sip of wine. "The first time I was alone in your apartment, I looked in your address book to see if you'd written me in. I think we'd known each other two weeks."

"Where was I?"

"You went to answer the telephone in the other room. It was your mother, and I figured it would be a long call. I wanted to know if you'd promoted me from the margins of your newspaper."

"Had I?"

"No. But I didn't give up on you. Now it's your turn."

He couldn't think of anything, but Shoba was waiting for him to speak. She hadn't appeared so determined in months. What was there left to say to her? He thought back to their first meeting, four years earlier at a lecture hall in Cambridge, where a group of Bengali poets were giving a recital. They'd ended up side by side, on folding wooden chairs. Shukumar was soon bored; he was unable to decipher the literary diction, and couldn't join the rest of the audience as they sighed and nodded solemnly after certain phrases. Peering at the newspaper folded in his lap, he studied the temperatures of cities around the world. Ninety-one degrees in Singapore yesterday, fifty-one in Stockholm. When he turned his head to the left, he saw a woman next to him making a grocery list on the back of a folder, and was startled to find that she was beautiful.

"Okay," he said, remembering. "The first time we went out to dinner, to the Portuguese place, I forgot to tip the waiter. I went back the next morning, found out his name, left money with the manager."

"You went all the way back to Somerville just to tip a waiter?"

"I took a cab."

"Why did you forget to tip the waiter?"

The birthday candles had burned out, but he pictured her face clearly in the dark, the wide tilting eyes, the full grape-toned lips, the fall at age two from her high chair still visible as a comma on her chin. Each day, Shukumar noticed, her beauty, which had once overwhelmed him, seemed to fade. The cosmetics that had seemed superfluous were necessary now, not to improve her but to define her somehow.

"By the end of the meal I had a funny feeling that I might marry you," he said, admitting it to himself as well as to her for the first time. "It must have distracted me."

• • •

The next night Shoba came home earlier than usual. There was lamb left over from the evening before, and Shukumar heated it up so that they were able to eat by seven. He'd gone out that day, through the melting snow, and bought a packet of taper candles from the corner store, and batteries to fit the flashlight. He had the candles ready on the countertop, standing in brass holders shaped like lotuses, but they ate under the glow of the copper-shaded ceiling lamp that hung over the table.

When they had finished eating, Shukumar was surprised to see that Shoba was stacking her plate on top of his, and then carrying them over to the sink. He had assumed she would retreat to the living room, behind her barricade of files.

"Don't worry about the dishes," he said, taking them from her hands.

"It seems silly not to," she replied, pouring a drop of detergent onto a sponge. "It's nearly eight o'clock."

His heart quickened. All day Shukumar had looked forward to the lights going out. He thought about what Shoba had said the night before, about looking in his address book. It felt good to remember her as she was then, how bold yet nervous she'd been when they first met, how hopeful. They stood side by side at the sink, their reflections fitting together in the frame of the window. It made him shy, the way he felt the first time they stood together in a mirror. He couldn't recall the last time they'd been photographed. They had stopped attending parties, went nowhere together. The film in his camera still contained pictures of Shoba, in the yard, when she was pregnant.

After finishing the dishes, they leaned against the counter, drying their hands on either end of a towel. At eight o'clock the house went black. Shukumar lit the wicks of the candles, impressed by their long, steady flames.

"Let's sit outside," Shoba said. "I think it's warm still."

They each took a candle and sat down on the steps. It seemed strange to be sitting outside with patches of snow still on the ground. But everyone was out of their houses tonight, the air fresh enough to make people restless. Screen doors opened and closed. A small parade of neighbors passed by with flashlights.

"We're going to the bookstore to browse," a silver-haired man called out.

He was walking with his wife, a thin woman in a windbreaker, and holding a dog on a leash. They were the Bradfords, and they had tucked a sympathy card into Shoba and Shukumar's mailbox back in September. "I hear they've got their power."

"They'd better," Shukumar said. "Or you'll be browsing in the dark."

The woman laughed, slipping her arm through the crook of her husband's elbow. "Want to join us?"

"No thanks," Shoba and Shukumar called out together. It surprised Shukumar that his words matched hers.

He wondered what Shoba would tell him in the dark. The worst possibilities had already run through his head. That she'd had an affair. That she didn't respect him for being thirty-five and still a student. That she blamed him for being in Baltimore the way her mother did. But he knew those things weren't true. She'd been faithful, as had he. She believed in him. It was she who had insisted he go to Baltimore. What didn't they know about each other? He knew she curled her fingers tightly when she slept, that her body twitched during bad dreams. He knew it was honeydew she favored over cantaloupe. He knew that when they returned from the hospital the first thing she did when she walked into the house was pick out objects of theirs and toss them into a pile in the hallway: books from the shelves, plants from the windowsills, paintings from walls, photos from tables, pots and pans that hung from the hooks over the stove. Shukumar had stepped out of her way, watching as she moved methodically from room to room. When she was satisfied, she stood there staring at the pile she'd made, her lips drawn back in such distaste that Shukumar had thought she would spit. Then she'd started to cry.

He began to feel cold as he sat there on the steps. He felt that he needed her to talk first, in order to reciprocate.

"That time when your mother came to visit us," she said finally. "When I said one night that I had to stay late at work, I went out with Gillian and had a martini."

He looked at her profile, the slender nose, the slightly masculine set of her jaw. He remembered that night well; eating with his mother, tired from teaching two classes back to back, wishing Shoba were there to say more of the right things because he came up with only the wrong ones. It had been twelve years since his father had died, and his mother had come to spend two weeks with him and Shoba, so they could honor his father's memory together. Each night his mother cooked something his father had liked, but she was too upset to eat the dishes herself, and her eyes would well up as Shoba stroked her hand. "It's so touching," Shoba had said to him at the time. Now he pictured Shoba with Gillian, in a bar with striped velvet sofas, the one they used to go to after the movies, making sure she got her extra olive, asking Gillian for a cigarette. He imagined her complaining, and Gillian sympathizing about visits from in-laws. It was Gillian who had driven Shoba to the hospital.

"Your turn," she said, stopping his thoughts.

At the end of their street Shukumar heard sounds of a drill and the electricians shouting over it. He looked at the darkened facades of the houses lining the street. Candles glowed in the windows of one. In spite of the warmth, smoke rose from the chimney.

"I cheated on my Oriental Civilization exam in college," he said. "It was my last semester, my last set of exams. My father had died a few months before. I could see the blue book of the guy next to me. He was an American guy, a maniac. He knew Urdu and Sanskrit. I couldn't remember if the verse we had to identify was an example of a ghazal or not. I looked at his answer and copied it down."

It had happened over fifteen years ago. He felt relief now, having told her.

She turned to him, looking not at his face, but at his shoes—old moccasins he wore as if they were slippers, the leather at the back permanently flattened. He wondered if it bothered her, what he'd said. She took his hand and pressed it. "You didn't have to tell me why you did it," she said, moving closer to him.

They sat together until nine o'clock, when the lights came on. They heard some people across the street clapping from their porch, and televisions being turned on. The Bradfords walked back down the street, eating ice cream cones and waving. Shoba and Shukumar waved back. Then they stood up, his hand still in hers, and went inside.

• • •

Somehow, without saying anything, it had turned into this. Into an exchange of confessions—the little ways they'd hurt or disappointed each other, and themselves. The following day Shukumar thought for hours about what to say to her. He was torn between admitting that he once ripped out a photo of a woman in one of the fashion magazines she used to subscribe to and carried it in his books for a week, or saying that he really hadn't lost the sweater-vest she bought him for their third wedding anniversary but had exchanged it for cash at Filene's, and that he had gotten drunk alone in the middle of the day at a hotel bar. For their first anniversary, Shoba had cooked a ten-course dinner just for him. The vest depressed him. "My wife gave me a sweater-vest for our anniversary," he complained to the bartender, his head heavy with cognac. "What do you expect?" the bartender had replied. "You're married."

As for the picture of the woman, he didn't know why he'd ripped it out. She wasn't as pretty as Shoba. She wore a white sequined dress, and had a sullen face and lean, mannish legs. Her bare arms were raised, her fists around her head, as if she were about to punch herself in the ears. It was an advertisement for stockings. Shoba had been pregnant at the time, her stomach suddenly immense, to the point where Shukumar no longer wanted to touch her. The first time he saw the picture he was lying in bed next to her, watching her as she read. When he noticed the magazine in the recycling pile he found the woman and tore out the page as carefully as he could. For about a week he allowed himself a glimpse each day. He felt an intense desire for the woman, but it was a desire that turned to disgust after a minute or two. It was the closest he'd come to infidelity.

He told Shoba about the sweater on the third night, the picture on the fourth. She said nothing as he spoke, expressed no protest or reproach. She simply listened, and then she took his hand, pressing it as she had before. On the third night, she told him that once after a lecture they'd attended, she let him speak to the chairman of his department without telling him that he had a dab of pâté on his chin. She'd been irritated with him for some reason, and so she'd let him go on and on, about securing his fellowship for the following semester, without putting a finger to her own chin as a signal. The fourth night, she said that she never liked the one poem he'd ever published in his life, in a literary magazine in Utah. He'd written the poem after meeting Shoba. She added that she found the poem sentimental.

Something happened when the house was dark. They were able to talk to each other again. The third night after supper they'd sat together on the sofa, and once it was dark he began kissing her awkwardly on her forehead and her face, and though it was dark he closed his eyes, and knew that she did, too. The fourth night they walked carefully upstairs, to bed, feeling together for the final step with their feet before the landing, and making love with a desperation they had forgotten. She wept without sound, and whispered his name, and traced his eyebrows with her finger in the dark. As he made love to her he wondered what he would say to her the next night, and what she would say, the thought of it exciting him. "Hold me," he said, "hold me in your arms," By the time the lights came back on downstairs, they'd fallen asleep.

• • •

The morning of the fifth night Shukumar found another notice from the electric company in the mailbox. The line had been repaired ahead of schedule, it said. He was disappointed. He had planned on making shrimp malai for Shoba, but when he arrived at the store he didn't feel like cooking anymore. It wasn't the same, he thought, knowing that the lights wouldn't go out. In the store the shrimp looked gray and thin. The coconut milk tin was dusty and overpriced. Still, he bought them, along with a beeswax candle and two bottles of wine.

She came home at seven-thirty. "I suppose this is the end of our game," he said when he saw her reading the notice.

She looked at him. "You can still light candles if you want." She hadn't been to the gym tonight. She wore a suit beneath the raincoat. Her makeup had been retouched recently.

When she went upstairs to change, Shukumar poured himself some wine and put on a record, a Thelonius Monk album he knew she liked.

When she came downstairs they ate together. She didn't thank him or compliment him. They simply ate in a darkened room, in the glow of a beeswax candle. They had survived a difficult time. They finished off the shrimp. They finished off the first bottle of wine and moved on to the second. They sat together until the candle had nearly burned away. She shifted in her chair, and Shukumar thought that she was about to say something. But instead she blew out the candle, stood up, turned on the light switch, and sat down again.

"Shouldn't we keep the lights off?" Shukumar asked.

She set her plate aside and clasped her hands on the table. "I want you to see my face when I tell you this," she said gently.

His heart began to pound. The day she told him she was pregnant, she had used the very same words, saying them in the same gentle way, turning off the basketball game he'd been watching on television. He hadn't been prepared then. Now he was.

Only he didn't want her to be pregnant again. He didn't want to have to pretend to be happy.

"I've been looking for an apartment and I've found one," she said, narrowing her eyes on something; it seemed, behind his left shoulder. It was nobody's fault, she continued. They'd been through enough. She needed some time alone. She had money saved up for a security deposit. The apartment was on Beacon Hill, so she could walk to work. She had signed the lease that night before coming home.

She wouldn't look at him, but he stared at her. It was obvious that she'd rehearsed the lines. All this time she'd been looking for an apartment, testing the water pressure, asking a Realtor if heat and hot water were included in the rent. It sickened Shukumar, knowing that she had spent these past evenings preparing for a life without him. He was relieved and yet he was sickened. This was what she'd been trying to tell him for the past four evenings. This was the point of her game.

Now it was his turn to speak. There was something he'd sworn he would never tell her, and for six months he had done his best to block it from his mind. Before the ultrasound she had asked the doctor not to tell her the sex of their child, and Shukumar had agreed. She had wanted it to be a surprise.

Later, those few times they talked about what had happened, she said at least they'd been spared that knowledge. In a way she almost took pride in her decision, for it enabled her to seek refuge in a mystery. He knew that she assumed it was a mystery for him, too. He'd arrived too late from Baltimore—when it was all over and she was lying on the hospital bed. But he hadn't. He'd arrived early enough to see their baby, and to hold him before they cremated him. At first he had recoiled at the suggestion, but the doctor said holding the baby might help him with the process of grieving. Shoba was asleep. The baby had been cleaned off, his bulbous lids shut tight to the world.

"Our baby was a boy," he said. "His skin was more red than brown. He had black hair on his head. He weighed almost five pounds. His fingers were curled shut, just like yours in the night."

Shoba looked at him now, her face contorted with sorrow. He had cheated on a college exam, ripped a picture of a woman out of a magazine. He had returned a sweater and got drunk in the middle of the day instead. These were the things he had told her. He had held his son, who had known life only within her, against his chest in a darkened room in an unknown wing of the hospital. He had held him until a nurse knocked and took him away, and he promised himself that day that he would never tell Shoba, because he still loved her then, and it was the one thing in her life that she had wanted to be a surprise.

Shukumar stood up and stacked his plate on top of hers. He carried the plates to the sink, but instead of running the tap he looked out the window. Outside the evening was still warm, and the Bradfords were walking arm in arm. As he watched the couple the room went dark, and he spun around. Shoba had turned the lights off. She came back to the table and sat down, and after a moment Shukumar joined her. They wept together, for the things they now knew.

## Ⅲ Questions for Further Thinking

1. What is the cause for the cold war between Shukumar and Shoba in their marriage?

2. In the marriage between Shukumar and Shoba, who do you think devotes more love than the other?

3. When Shukumar is hesitant about attending the academic conference, it is Shoba who persuades him to go; when the baby is aborted, Shukumar is blamed for being away. Do you think it is Shukumar's fault for not being present at the hospital?

4. In the game of "truth and dare," what are the focuses of the confession made by Shukumar and Shoba?

5. At the end of the story, why does Shukumar choose to tell Shoba the secret that their baby was a boy?

## Ⅳ Appreciation

This is a story about the love crisis for a young Indian American couple, Shukumar and Shoba. Shukumar is a 35-years-old doctorate candidate, who is bogged down in writing his dissertation and is anxious about his new identity of becoming a father. Shoba is three years younger than Shukumar, expecting her baby in her meticulous plan of life. The sudden miscarriage brings their marriage life into a state of stagnancy. After coming back from the hospital, Shoba is no longer devoted to her marriage. She lingers out at her work, and is reluctant to face Shukumar who shields himself at home behind his dissertation. Shukumar attributes Shoba's change to her sadness of losing the baby. He thinks it is a temporary matter that will be overcome with time.

It is not hard to see that Shoba's idea of her marriage relationship is deeply influence by the traditional Indian culture. She performs the role of a devoted wife in a willing manner. On the other hand, Shukumar seems contented to be the one being taken care of. He is accustomed to receiving birthday gifts, being pampered with big parties, and being arranged in marriage life. When Shoba is about to go into labor, he fails to make his own judgment and misses the chance to carry out the duty of a caring and loving husband. Everything suggests that Shukumar is the habitual receiver rather than the provider in their relationship. It is only after he takes over the household chores, cooks with the recipes dated in the cookbooks, and eats up the food stocked in the refrigerator, does Shukumar notice how much efforts Shoba had devoted to their relationship.

Unfortunately, hindsight does not haul Shukumar out from his inertia as a passive husband in their relationship. When Shoba proposes to play the "truth and dare" game during the blackout and offered the last chance to test his love for her, Shukumar fails because his confessions are all self-centered. Disappointed, Shoba gives up the mending effort and is determined to start a new life. Unsurprisingly, Shukumar feels hurt. When Shoba says she is going to move out, he blurts out that he had held the dead baby in the hospital and the baby was a boy. Shukumar's final confession completely destroyed their remaining affection. The hampered communication that had been conducted as a remedy for their trauma announced the ending of their love.

## Ⅴ Writing Topic

在这个作品中,Shukumar 和 Shoba 深爱对方。但是他们因 Shoba 的流产而产生嫌隙,陷入冷战。在面对失去孩子的创伤时,两人各自的疗愈方式与婚姻关系的破裂不无关系。尝试对不同性别处理危机事件的方式及差异进行讨论。

# Unit 12 "The Littoral Zone" by Andrea Barrett

## Ⅰ Introduction to the Author and the Work

Andrea Barrett (1954– ) was born in Boston in 1954. She began her studies in the sciences, and her writing conveyed her enthusiasm for history, science, and literature. Barrett had written four novels, *Lucid Stars* (1988), *Secret Harmonies* (1989), *The Middle Kingdom* (1991), and *The Forms of Water* (1993). She won the National Book Award for her first collection of short stories, *Ship Fever*, in 1996. Later, she had published a novel, *The Voyage of the Narwhal* (1998), and more short fiction in *Servants of the Map* (2002). Her body of work has taken on a life of its own as readers discover intertextual connections among her many characters.

"The Littoral Zone" centers on Jonathan and Ruby, teachers of zoology and botany who met fifteen years earlier while doing summer research on an island off New Hampshire. The story is about the inexplicable puzzle of mutual attraction and how to sustain this passion. At the time of the story, Jonathan and Ruby are near fifty and their children cannot imagine them young and strong and wrung by passion.

The title of the story refers to the space between high and low watermarks where organisms struggle to adapt to the daily rhythm of immersion and exposure. By referring to the rise of the tide as the passion of love, it also suggests the ebbing moment of the loving relationship.

## Ⅱ The Littoral Zone[①]

When they met, fifteen years ago, Jonathan had a job teaching botany at a small college near Albany, and Ruby was teaching invertebrate zoology at a college in the Berkshires. Both of them, along with an ornithologist, an ichthyologist, and an oceanographer, had agreed to spend three weeks of their summer break at a marine biology research station on an island off the New Hampshire coast. They had spouses, children, mortgages, bills; they went, they later told each other, because the pay was too good to refuse. Two-thirds of the way through the course, they agreed that the pay was not enough.

How they reached that first agreement is a story they've repeated to each other again and again and told, separately, to their closest friends. Ruby thinks they had this conversation on the second Friday of the course, after Frank Kenary's slide show on the abyssal fish and before Carol Dagliesh's lecture on the courting behavior of herring gulls. Jonathan maintains that they had it earlier—that Wednesday, maybe, when they were still recovering from Gunnar Erickson's trawling expedition. The days before they became so aware of each other have blurred in their minds, but they agree that their first real conversation took place on the afternoon devoted to the littoral zone.

The tide was all the way out. The students were clumped on the rocky, pitted apron between the water and the ledges, peering into the tidal pools and listing the species they found. Gunnar was in the equipment room, repairing one of the sampling claws. Frank was setting up dissections in the tiny lab; Carol had gone back to the mainland on the supply boat, hoping to replace the camera one of the students had dropped. And so the two of them, Jonathan and Ruby, were left alone for a little while.

They both remember the granite ledge where they sat, and the raucous quarrels of the nesting gulls. They agree that Ruby was scratching furiously at

---

① https://www.researchgate.net/publication/286140379_The_Littoral_Zone.

her calves and that Jonathan said, "Take it easy, okay? You'll draw blood."

Her calves were slim and tan, Jonathan remembers. Covered with blotches and scrapes.

I folded my fingers, Ruby remembers. Then I blushed. My throat felt sunburned.

Ruby said, "I know, it's so embarrassing. But all this salt on my poison ivy—God, what I wouldn't give for a bath! They never told me there wouldn't be any water here ..."

Jonathan gestured at the ocean surrounding them and then they started laughing. Hysteria, they have told each other since. They were so tired by then, twelve days into the course, and so dirty and overworked and strained by pretending to the students that these things didn't matter, that neither of them could understand that they were also lonely. Their shared laughter felt like pure relief.

"No water?" Jonathan said. "I haven't been dry since we got here. My clothes are damp, my sneakers are damp, my hair never dries ..."

His hair was beautiful, Ruby remembers. Thick, a little too long. Part blond and part brown.

"I know," she said. "But you know what I mean. I didn't realize they'd have to bring our drinking water over on a boat."

"Or that they'd expect us to wash in the ocean," Jonathan said. Her forearms were dusted with salt, he remembers. The down along them sparkled in the sun.

"And those cots," Ruby said. "Does yours have a sag in it like a hammock?"

"Like a slingshot," Jonathan said.

For half an hour they sat on their ledge and compared their bubbling patches of poison ivy and the barnacle wounds that scored their hands and feet. Nothing healed out here, they told each other. Everything got infected. When one of the students called, "Look what I found!" Jonathan rose and held his hand out to Ruby. She took it easily and hauled herself up and they walked down to the water together. Jonathan's hand was thick and blunt-fingered, with nails bitten down so far that the skin around them was raw. Odd, Ruby remembers thinking. Those bitten stumps attached to such a good-looking man.

• • •

They have always agreed that the worst moment, for each of them, was when they stepped from the boat to the dock on the final day of the course and saw their families waiting in the parking lot. Jonathan's wife had their four-year-old daughter balanced on her shoulders. Their two older children were leaning perilously over the guardrails and shrieking at the sight of him. Jessie had turned nine in Jonathan's absence, and Jonathan can't think of her eager face without remembering the starfish he brought as his sole, guilty gift.

Ruby's husband had parked their car just a few yards from Jonathan's family. Her sons were wearing baseball caps, and what Ruby remembers is the way the yellow linings lit their faces. For a minute she saw the children squealing near her sons as faceless, inconsequential; Jonathan later told her that her children had been similarly blurred for him. Then Jonathan said, "That's my family, there," and Ruby said, "That's mine, right next to yours," and all the faces leapt into focus for both of them.

Nothing that was to come—not the days in court, nor the days they moved, nor the losses of jobs and homes—would ever seem so awful to them as that moment when they first saw their families standing there, unaware and hopeful. Deceitfully, treacherously, Ruby and Jonathan separated and walked to the people awaiting them. They didn't introduce each other to their spouses. They didn't look at each other—although, they later admitted, they cast covert looks at each other's families. They thought they were invisible, that no one could see what had happened between them. They thought their families would not remember how they had stepped off the boat and stood, for an instant, together.

On that boat, sitting dumb and miserable in the litter of nets and equipment, they had each pretended to be resigned to going home. Each foresaw (or so they later told each other) the hysterical phone calls and the frenzied, secret meetings. Neither foresaw how much the sight of each other's family would hurt. "Sweetie," Jonathan remembers Ruby's husband saying. "You've lost so much weight." Ruby remembers staring over her husband's shoulder and watching Jessie butt her head like a dog under Jonathan's hand.

• • •

For the first twelve days on the island, Jonathan and Ruby were so busy that they hardly noticed each other. For the next few days, after their conversation on the ledge, they sat near each other during faculty lectures and student presentations. These were held in the library, a ramshackle building separated from the bunkhouse and the dining hall by a stretch of wild roses and poison ivy.

Jonathan had talked about algae in there, holding up samples of Fucus and Hilden brandtia. Ruby had talked about the littoral zone, that space between high and low watermarks where organisms struggled to adapt to the daily rhythm of immersion and exposure. They had drawn on the blackboard in colored chalk while the students, itchy and hot and tired, scratched their arms and legs and feigned attention.

Neither of them, they admitted much later, had focused fully on the other's lecture. "It was before," Ruby has said ruefully. "I didn't know that I was going to want to have listened." And Jonathan has laughed and confessed that he was studying the shells and skulls on the walls while Ruby was drawing on the board.

The library was exceedingly hot, they agreed, and the chairs remarkably uncomfortable; the only good spot was the sofa in front of the fireplace. That was the spot they commandeered on the evening after their first conversation, when dinner led to a walk and then the walk led them into the library a few minutes before the scheduled lecture.

Erika Moorhead, Ruby remembers. Talking about the tensile strength of byssus threads.

Walter Schank, Jonathan remembers. Something to do with hydrozoans.

They both remember feeling comfortable for the first time since their arrival. And for the next few days—three by Ruby's accounting; four by Jonathan's—one of them came early for every lecture and saved a seat on the sofa for the other.

They giggled at Frank Kenary's slides, which he'd arranged like a creepy fashion show: abyssal fish sporting varied blobs of luminescent flesh. When Gunnar talked for two hours about subduction zones and the calcium carbonate cycle, they amused themselves exchanging doodles. They can't remember, now, whether Gunnar's endless lecture came before Carol Dagliesh's filmstrip on the herring gulls, or which of the students tipped over the dissecting scope and sent the dish of copepods to their deaths. But both of them remember those days and nights as being almost purely happy. They swam in that odd, indefinite zone where they were more than friends, not yet lovers, still able to deny to themselves that they were headed where they were headed.

Ruby made the first phone call, a week after they left the island. At eleven o'clock on a Sunday night, she told her husband she'd left something in her office that she needed to prepare the next day's class. She drove to campus, unlocked her door, picked up the phone and called Jonathan at his house. One of his children—Jessie, she thinks—answered the phone. Ruby remembers how, even through the turmoil of her emotions, she'd been shocked at the idea of a child staying up so late.

There was a horrible moment while Jessie went to find her father; another when Jonathan, hearing Ruby's voice, said, "Wait, hang on, I'll just be a minute," and then negotiated Jessie into bed. Ruby waited, dreading his anger, knowing she'd been wrong to call him at home. But Jonathan, when he finally returned, said, "Ruby. You got my letter."

"What letter?" she asked. He wrote to tell me good-bye, she remembers thinking.

"My letter," he said. "I wrote you, I have to see you. I can't stand this."

Ruby released the breath she hadn't known she was holding.

"You didn't get it?" he said. "You just called?" It wasn't only me, he remembers thinking. She feels it too.

"I had to hear your voice," she said.

Ruby called, but Jonathan wrote. And so when Jonathan's youngest daughter, Cora, later fell in love and confided in Ruby, and then asked her, "Was it like this with you two? Who started it—you or Dad?" all Ruby could say was, "It happened to both of us."

• • •

Sometimes, when Ruby and Jonathan sit on the patio looking out at the hills above Palmyra, they will turn and see their children watching them through the kitchen window. Before the children went off to college, the house bulged with them on weekends and holidays and seemed empty in between; Jonathan's wife had custody of Jessie and Gordon and Cora, and Ruby's husband took her sons,

Mickey and Ryan, when he remarried. Now that the children are old enough to come and go as they please, the house is silent almost all the time.

Jessie is twenty-four, and Gordon is twenty-two; Mickey is twenty-one, and Cora and Ryan are both nineteen. When they visit Jonathan and Ruby they spend an unhealthy amount of time talking about their past. In their conversations they seem to split their lives into three epochs: the years when what they think of as their real families were whole; the years right after Jonathan and Ruby met, when their parents were coming and going, fighting and making up, separating and divorcing; and the years since Jonathan and Ruby's marriage, when they were forced into a reconstituted family. Which epoch they decide to explore depends on who's visiting and who's getting along with whom.

"But we were happy," Mickey may say to Ruby, if he and Ryan are visiting and Jonathan's children are absent. "We were, we were fine."

"It wasn't like you and Mom ever fought," Cora may say to Jonathan, if Ruby's sons aren't around. "You could have worked it out if you'd tried."

When they are all together, they tend to avoid the first two epochs and to talk about their first strained weekends and holidays together. They've learned to tolerate each other, despite their forced introductions; Cora and Ryan, whose birthdays are less than three months apart, seem especially close. Ruby and Jonathan know that much of what draws their youngest children together is shared speculation about what happened on that island.

They look old to their children, they know. Both of them are nearing fifty. Jonathan has grown quite heavy and has lost much of his hair; Ruby's fine-boned figure has gone gaunt and stringy. They know their children can't imagine them young and strong and wrung by passion. The children can't think—can't stand to think—about what happened on the island, but they can't stop themselves from asking questions.

"Did you have other girlfriends?" Cora asks Jonathan. "Were you so unhappy with Mom?"

"Did you know him before?" Ryan asks Ruby. "Did you go there to be with him?"

"We met there," Jonathan and Ruby say. "We had never seen each other before. We fell in love." That is all they will say, they never give details, they say "yes" or "no" to the easy questions and evade the hard ones. They worry that even the little they offer may be too much.

• • •

Jonathan and Ruby tell each other the stories of their talk by the tidal pool, their walks and meals, the sagging sofa, the moment in the parking lot, and the evening Ruby made her call. They tell these to console themselves when their children chide them or when, alone in the house, they sit quietly near each other and struggle to conceal their disappointments.

Of course they have expected some of these. Mickey and Gordon have both had trouble in school, and Jessie has grown much too close to her mother; neither Jonathan nor Ruby has found jobs as good as the ones they lost, and their new home in Palmyra still doesn't feel quite like home. But all they have lost in order to be together would seem bearable had they continued to feel the way they felt on the island.

They're sensible people, and very well-mannered; they remind themselves that they were young then and are middle-aged now, and that their fierce attraction would naturally ebb with time. Neither likes to think about how much of the thrill of their early days together came from the obstacles they had to overcome. Some days, when Ruby pulls into the driveway still thinking about her last class and catches sight of Jonathan out in the garden, she can't believe the heavyset figure pruning shrubs so meticulously is the man for whom she fought such battles. Jonathan, who often wakes very early, sometimes stares at Ruby's sleeping face and thinks how much more gracefully his ex-wife is aging.

They never reproach each other. When the tension builds in the house and the silence becomes overwhelming, one or the other will say, "Do you remember ...?" And then launch into one of the myths on which they have founded their lives. But there is one story they never tell each other, because they can't bear to talk about what they have lost. This is the one about the evening that has shaped their life together.

Jonathan's hand on Ruby's back, Ruby's hand on Jonathan's thigh, a shirt unbuttoned, a belt undone. They never mention this moment, or the moments that followed it, because that would mean discussing who seduced whom, and any resolution of that would mean assigning blame. Guilt they can handle; they've been living with guilt for fifteen years. But blame? It would be more than either of them could bear, to know the exact moment when one of them precipitated all that has happened to them. The most either of them has ever said is, "How could we have known?"

But the night in the library is what they both think about, when they lie silently next to each other and listen to the wind. It must be summer for them to think about it; the children must be with their other parents and the rain must be falling on the cedar shingles overhead. A candle must be burning on the mantel above the bed and the maple branches outside their window must be tossing against each other. Then they think of the story they know so well and never say out loud.

There was a huge storm three nights before they left the island, the tail end of a hurricane passing farther out to sea. The cedar trees creaked and swayed in the wind beyond the library windows. The students had staggered off to bed, after the visitor from Woods Hole had finished his lecture on the explorations of the Alvin in the Cayman Trough, and Frank and Gunnar and Carol had shrouded themselves in their rain gear and left as well, sheltering the visitor between them. Ruby sat at one end of the long table, preparing bottles of fixative for their expedition the following morning, and Jonathan lay on the sofa writing notes. The boat was leaving just after dawn and they knew they ought to go to bed.

The wind picked up outside, sweeping the branches against the walls. The windows rattled. Jonathan shivered and said, "Do you suppose we could get a fire going in that old fireplace?"

"I bet we could," said Ruby, which gave both of them the pretext they needed to crouch side by side on the cracked tiles, brushing elbows as they opened the flue and crumpled paper and laid kindling in the form of a grid. The logs Jonathan found near the lobster traps were dry and the fire caught quickly.

Who found the green candle in the drawer below the microscope? Who lit the candle and turned off the lights? And who found the remains of the jug of wine that Frank had brought in honor of the visitor? They sat there side by side, poking at the burning logs and pretending they weren't doing what they were doing. The wind pushed through the window they'd opened a crack, and the tan window shade lifted and then fell back against the frame. The noise was soothing at first; later it seemed irritating.

Jonathan, whose fingernails were bitten to the quick, admired the long nail on Ruby's right little finger and then said, half-seriously, how much he'd love to bite a nail like that. When Ruby held her hand to his mouth he took the nail between his teeth and nibbled through the white tip, which days in the water had softened. Ruby slipped her other hand inside his shirt and ran it up his back. Jonathan ran his mouth up her arm and down her neck.

They started in front of the fire and worked their way across the floor, breaking a glass, knocking the table askew. Ruby rubbed her back raw against the rug and Jonathan scraped his knees, and twice they paused and laughed at their wild excesses. They moved across the floor from east to west and later from west to east, and between those two journeys, during the time when they heaped their clothes and the sofa cushions into a nest in front of the fire, they talked.

This was not the kind of conversation they'd had during walks and meals since that first time on the rocks: who they were, where they'd come from, how they'd made it here. This was the talk where they instinctively edited out the daily pleasures of their lives on the mainland and spliced together the hard times, the dark times, until they'd constructed versions of themselves that could make sense of what they'd just done.

For months after this, as they lay in stolen, secret rooms between houses and divorces and jobs and lives, Jonathan would tell Ruby that he swallowed her nail. The nail dissolved in his stomach, he'd say. It passed into his villi and out to his blood and then flowed to bone and muscle and nerve, where the molecules that had once been part of her became part of him. Ruby, who always seemed to know more acutely than Jonathan that they'd have to leave whatever room this was in an hour or a day, would argue with him.

"Nails are keratin," she'd tell him. "Like hooves and hair. Like wool. We can't digest wool."

"Moths can," Jonathan would tell her. "Moths eat sweaters."

"Moths have a special enzyme in their saliva," Ruby would say. This was true; she knew it for a fact. She'd been so taken by Jonathan's tale that she'd gone to the library to check out the details and discovered he was wrong.

But Jonathan didn't care what the biochemists said. He held her against his chest and said, "I have an enzyme for you."

That night, after the fire burned out, they slept for a couple of hours. Ruby woke first and watched Jonathan sleep for a while. He slept like a child, with his knees bent toward his chest and his hands clasped between his thighs. Ruby picked up the tipped-over chair and swept the fragments of broken glass onto a sheet of paper. Then she woke Jonathan and they tiptoed back to the rooms where they were supposed to be.

## Ⅲ Questions for Further Thinking

1. What factors might have caused Jonathan and Ruby to be together after they worked on the island for three weeks?

2. Do you think Jonathan and Ruby truly love each other when they are on the island?

3. What are the strategies that Jonathan and Ruby takes to handle their disappointment of each other after fifteen years of remarried life?

4. What is the attitude of the author? Do you think she is suggesting a moral criticism towards Jonathan and Ruby's choice?

5. What is the implied meaning of the title, "The Littoral Zone"?

## Ⅳ Appreciation

"The Littoral Zone" is another story focused on love in and is stemmed out of marriage. The two characters, Jonathan and Ruby, are professors who accept teaching jobs for three weeks at a research station on an island. Jonathan teaches botany, while Ruby teaches zoology. Not knowing each other before they arrive, they develop an unexpected extramarital affair during the last week on the island.

It might be reasonable to say that the tough living environment on the island, exhaustion from overwork, and loneliness combined help to link Jonathan and Ruby together. Starting from the conversation for relief, they first develop a feeling that is "more than friendship, but not yet love." It cannot be denied that they find comfort and pleasure in the conversations as colleagues. Nobody expects that their professional relationship might evolve into a sexual one, but when they stay on an isolated island, where their spouse, children, as well as social morality temporarily recede, the passion of love naturally sparkles into a flame.

Who is to blame? The author does not provide an easy answer to the question. However, the repeated usage of the subject "they," as well as the combined names of "Jonathan and Ruby" seems to suggest that the two characters are taking an equivocal stance when they have to face the sense of guilt brought about by their infidelity. One strategy they adopt to escape from children's curious questioning is to stress that "both of them admit ... " or "both of them agree ... " And the method they adopt to endure the disappointment of the remarried life is to remind each other by saying "do you remember ... " to ensure that they both feel the same way as they feel on the island. The passionate love is like the rise of the tide. There would be a moment when the tide recedes and the passion fades into the ordinary tediousness of commonalities.

One week on the island and fifteen years of disappointed remarried life seems to suggest the author's stance that passionate love is not as welcoming and sweet as people imagine. As the title suggests, with the natural recession of passion, the intensity of love will, in the end, fades into the ordinariness of marriage life.

## Ⅴ Writing Topic

在英文中,"passion"(激情)、"love"(爱情)和 "affection"(亲情)有不同的含义。很多基于激情的关系往往被当作真爱,从而诱使人们放弃原有的情感。试以该作品为例,讨论基于激情的爱得以产生的原因和可能引发的结果。

# Part Five

## *Utopian, Dystopian and Reality*

# Unit 13 "If I Were a Man" by Charlotte Perkins Gilman

## Ⅰ Introduction to the Author and the Work

Charlotte Perkins Gilman (1860 – 1935), is a prominent American writer of short stories, poetry, non-fiction, and a lecturer for social reform. Her best remembered work is her semi-autobiographical short story, "The Yellow Wallpaper", which she wrote after a severe bout of post-partum depression. She served as a role model for future generations of feminists because of her unconventional concepts.

While she is best known for her fiction, Gilman was also a successful lecturer and intellectual. One of her greatest works of non-fiction, *Women and Economics*, was published in 1898. As a feminist, she called for women to gain economic independence, and the work helped cement her standing as a social theorist. It was even used as a textbook at one time. Other important non-fiction works followed, such as *The Home: Its Work and Influence* (1903) and *Does a Man Support His Wife?* (1915). Along with writing books, Gilman established *The Forerunner*, a magazine that allowed her to express her ideas on women's issues and on social reform.

"If I Were a Man" is a short story which reflects the voice of the second wave of western feminist movement, which calls for equality and gender understand. The story is based on a young woman's subconscious thinking of becoming a man. Due to her wishes to be a man, Mollie Mathewson ends up becoming her husband, Gerald. With an androgynous image, Mollie Mathewson makes her bold defense for women.

## Ⅱ If I Were a Man[①]

"If I were a man ..." that was what pretty little Mollie Mathewson always said when Gerald would not do what she wanted him to—which was seldom.

That was what she said this bright morning, with a stamp of her little high-heeled slipper, just because he had made a fuss about that bill, the long one with the "account rendered," which she had forgotten to give him the first time and been afraid to the second—and now he had taken it from the postman himself.

Mollie was "true to type." She was a beautiful instance of what is reverentially called "a true woman." Little, of course—no true woman may be big. Pretty, of course—no true woman could possibly be plain. Whimsical, capricious, charming, changeable, devoted to pretty clothes and always "wearing them well," as the esoteric phrase has it. (This does not refer to the clothes—they do not wear well in the least—but to some special grace of putting them on and carrying them about, granted to but few, it appears)

She was also a loving wife and a devoted mother possessed of "the social gift" and the love of "society" that goes with it, and, with all these was fond and proud of her home and managed it as capably as-well, as most women do.

If ever there was a true woman it was Mollie Mathewson, yet she was wishing heart and soul she was a man.

And all of a sudden she was!

She was Gerald, walking down the path so erect and square-shouldered, in a hurry for his morning train, as usual, and it must be confessed, in something of a temper.

Her own words were ringing in her ears—not only the "last word," but several that had gone before, and she was holding her lips tight shut, not to say something she would be sorry for. But instead of acquiescence in the position taken by that angry little figure on the veranda, what she felt was a sort of

① https://www.libraryofshortstories.com/onlinereader/if-i-were-a-man.

superior pride, a sympathy as with weakness, a feeling that "I must be gentle with her," in spite of the temper.

A man! Really a man—with only enough subconscious memory of herself remaining to make her recognize the differences.

At first there was a funny sense of size and weight and extra thickness; the feet and hands seemed strangely large, and her long, straight, free legs swung forward at a gait that made her feel as if on stilts.

This presently passed, and in its place, growing all day; wherever she went, came a new and delightful feeling of being the right size.

Everything fitted now. Her back snugly against the seat-back, her feet comfortably on the floor. Her feet? ... His feet! She studied them carefully. Never before, since her early school days, had she felt such freedom and comfort as to feet—they were firm and solid on the ground when she walked; quick, springy, safe—as when, moved by an unrecognizable impulse, she had run after, caught and swung aboard the car.

Another impulse fished in a convenient pocket for change—instantly, automatically, bringing forth a nickel for the conductor and a penny for the newsboy.

These pockets came as a revelation. Of course she had known they were there, had counted them, made fun of them, mended them, even envied them; but she never dreamed of how it felt to have pockets.

Behind her newspaper she let her consciousness, that odd mingled consciousness, rove from pocket to pocket, realizing the armored assurance of having all those things at hand, instantly get-at-able, ready to meet emergencies. The cigar case gave her a warm feeling of comfort—it was full; the firmly held fountain pen, safe unless she stood on her head; the keys, pencils, letters, documents, notebook, checkbook, bill folder—all at once, with a deep rushing sense of power and pride, she felt what she had never felt before in all her life—the possession of money, of her own earned money—hers to give or to withhold, not to beg for, tease for, wheedle for—hers.

That bill—why, if it had come to her—to him, that is—he would have paid it as a matter of course, and never mentioned it—to her.

Then, being he, sitting there so easily and firmly with his money in his pockets, she wakened to his life-long consciousness about money. Boyhood—its desires and dreams, ambitions. Young manhood—working tremendously for the wherewithal to make a home—for her. The present years with all their net of cares and hopes and dangers; the present moment, when he needed every cent for special plans of great importance, and this bill, long overdue and demanding payment, meant an amount of inconvenience wholly unnecessary if it had been given him when it first came; also, the man's keen dislike of that "account rendered."

"Women have no business sense!" she found herself saying. "And all that money Just for hats—idiotic, useless, ugly things!"

With that she began to see the hats of the women in the car as she had never seen hats before. The men's seemed normal, dignified, becoming, with enough variety for personal taste, and with distinction in style and in age, such as she had never noticed before. But the women's—

With the eyes of a man and the brain of a man; with the memory of a whole lifetime of free action wherein the hat, close-fitting on cropped hair, had been no handicap; she now perceived the hats of women.

The massed fluffed hair was at once attractive and foolish, and on that hair, at every angle, in all colors, tipped, twisted, tortured into every crooked shape, made of any substance chance might offer, perched these formless objects. Then, on their formlessness the trimmings—these squirts of stiff feathers, these violent outstanding bows of glistening ribbon, these swaying, projecting masses of plumage which tormented the faces of bystanders.

Never in all her life had she imagined that this idolized millinery could look, to those who paid for it, like the decorations of an insane monkey.

And yet, when there came into the car a little woman, as foolish as any, but pretty and sweet-looking, up rose Gerald Mathewson and gave her his seat. And, later, when there came in a handsome red-cheeked girl, whose hat was wilder, more violent in color and eccentric in shape than any other—when she stood nearby and her soft curling plumes swept his cheek once and again—he felt a sense of sudden pleasure at the intimate tickling touch—and she, deep down with in, felt such a wave of shame as might well drown a thousand hats forever.

When he took his train, his seat in the smoking car, she had a new surprise. All about him were the other men, commuters too, and many of them friends of his.

To her, they would have been distinguished as "Mary Wade's husband," "the man Belle Grant is engaged to," "that rich Mr. Shopworth," or "that pleasant Mr. Beale." And they would all have lifted their hats to her, bowed, made polite conversation if near enough—especially Mr. Beale.

Now came the feeling of open-eyed acquaintance, of knowing men—as they were. The mere amount of this knowledge was a surprise to her—the whole background of talk from boyhood up, the gossip of barber—shop and club, the conversation of morning and evening hours on trains, the knowledge of political affiliation, of business standing and prospects, of character—in a light she had never known before.

They came and talked to Gerald, one and another. He seemed quite popular. And as they talked, with this new memory and new understanding, an understanding which seemed to include all these men's minds, there poured in on the submerged consciousness beneath a new, a startling knowledge—what men really think of women.

Good, average, American men were there; married men for the most part, and happy—as happiness goes in general. In the minds of each and all there seemed to be a two-story department, quite apart from the rest of their ideas, a separate place where they kept their thoughts and feelings about women.

In the upper half were the tenderest emotions, the most exquisite ideals, the sweetest memories, all lovely sentiments as to "home" and "mother," all delicate admiring adjectives, a sort of sanctuary, where a veiled statue, blindly adored, shared place with beloved yet commonplace experiences.

In the lower half—here that buried consciousness woke to keen distress—they kept quite another assortment of ideas. Here, even in this clean-minded husband of hers, was the memory of stories told at men's dinners, of worse ones overheard in street or car, of base traditions, coarse epithets, gross experiences—known, though not shared.

And all these in the department "woman," while in the rest of the mind—

here was new knowledge indeed.

The world opened before her. Not the world she had been reared in—where Home had covered all the map. almost, and the rest had been "foreign," or "unexplored country," but the world as it was—man's world, as made, lived in, and seen, by men.

It was dizzying. To see the houses that fled so fast across the car window, in terms of builders' bills, or of some technical insight into materials and methods; to see a passing village with lamentable knowledge of who "owned it" and of how its Boss was rapidly aspiring in state power, or of how that kind of paving was a failure; to see shops, not as mere exhibitions of desirable objects, but as business ventures, many mere sinking ships, some promising a profitable voyage—this new world bewildered her.

She—as Gerald—had already forgotten about that bill over which she—as Mollie—was still crying at home. Gerald was "talking business" with this man, "talking politics" with that, and now sympathizing with the carefully withheld troubles of a neighbor.

Mollie had always sympathized with the neighbor's wife before.

She began to struggle violently with this large dominant masculine consciousness. She remembered with sudden clearness things she had read, lectures she had heard, and resented with increasing intensity this serene masculine preoccupation with the male point of view.

Mr. Miles, the little fussy man who lived on the other side of the street, was talking now. He had a large complacent wife: Mollie had never liked her much, but had always thought him rather nice—he was so punctilious in small courtesies.

And here he was talking to Gerald—such talk!

"Had to come in here," he said. "Gave my seat to a dame who was bound to have it. There's nothing they won't get when they make up their minds to it—eh?"

"No fear!" said the big man in the next seat. "They haven't much mind to make up, you know—and if they do. They'll change it."

"The real danger," began the Rev. Alfred Smythe, the new Episcopal clergyman, a thin, nervous, tall man with a face several centuries behind the times, "is that they will overstep the limits of their God-appointed sphere."

"Their natural limits ought to hold'em, I think," said cheerful Dr. Jones. "You can't get around physiology, I tell you."

"I've never seen any limits, myself, not to what they want, anyhow," said Mr. Miles. "Merely a rich husband and a fine house and no end of bonnets and dresses, and the latest thing in motors, and a few diamonds—and so on. Keeps us pretty busy."

There was a tired gray man across the aisle. He had a very nice wife, always beautifully dressed, and three unmarried daughters, also beautifully dressed—Mollie knew them. She knew he worked hard, too; and she looked at him now a little anxiously.

But he smiled cheerfully.

"Do you good, Miles," he said. "What else would a man work for? A good woman is about the best thing on earth."

"And a bad one's the worst, that's sure." responded Miles.

"She's a pretty weak sister, viewed professionally," Dr. Jones averred with solemnity, and Rev. Alfred Smythe added, "She brought evil into the world."

Gerald Mathewson sat up straight. Something was stirring in him which he did not recognize—yet could not resist.

"Seems to me we all talk like Noah," he suggested drily. "Or the ancient Hindu scriptures. Women have their limitations, but so do we, God knows. Haven't we known girls in school and college just as smart as we were?"

"They cannot play our games," coldly replied the clergyman.

Gerald measured his meager proportions with a practiced eye.

"I never was particularly good at football myself," he modestly admitted, "but I've known women who could outlast a man in all-round endurance. Besides—life isn't spent in athletics!"

This was sadly true. They all looked down the aisle where a heavy ill-dressed man with a bad complexion sat alone. He had held the top of the columns once, with headlines and photographs. Now he earned less than any of them.

"It's time we woke up," pursued Gerald, still inwardly urged to unfamiliar speech. "Women are pretty much people, seems to me. I know they dress like fools—but who's to blame for that? We invent all those idiotic hats of theirs, and design their crazy fashions, and, what's more, if a woman is courageous enough to wear commonsense, clothes—and shoes—which of us wants to dance with her?

"Yes, we blame them for grafting on us, but are we willing to let our wives work? We are not. It hurts our pride, that' s all. We are always criticizing them for making mercenary marriages, but what do we call a girl who marries a chump with no money? Just a poor fool, that's all. And they know it.

"As for Mother Eve—I wasn't there and can't deny the story, but I will say this. If she brought evil into the world, we men have had the lion's share of keeping it going ever since—how about that?"

They drew into the city, and all day long in his business, Gerald was vaguely conscious of new views, strange feelings, and the submerged Mollie learned and learned.

## Ⅲ Questions for Further Thinking

1. In the story "If I Were a Man", Mollie Mathewson is described as a "true woman." What is the relationship between being a "true woman" and the stereotypes about women?

2. Why does the author have Mollie transformed into a man with an androgynous mind?

3. In describing the moment when Mollie is on the train chatting with other men, the subject is transformed from "Mollie" to "Gerald." How can we understand this shift?

4. What is your understanding of Gerald's defense for women? What would be different if it is Mollie who argued against those men's accusations?

5. When Mollie possesses both a man and a woman's consciousness, what is the literary meaning of being androgynous?

## Ⅳ Appreciation

As a story talking about gender stereotypes, *If I Were a Man* is suitable to be the initial story for this book to discuss the growth of women's self-consciousness in the early twentieth century. One of the reasons is that after more than a hundred years of feminist movements, gender stereotype is still quite prevalent even today. Thus, it is necessary to learn how to identify these stereotypes. In this story, Mollie is the stereotyped true woman. She is "little, pretty, whimsical, capricious, charming, changeable, devoted to pretty clothes and knows how to wear them well." As expected, she is also "a loving wife and a devoted mother." Correspondingly, Mollie's husband Gerald is the stereotypical man. He is big in size, strong in body, and brilliant in mind. This true woman image and true man image are the basic gender constructions of our society.

As suggested in the story, because of the fact that each is strictly confined only to his/her gender roles, both men and women turn out to be extremely ignorant of the other gender. When Mollie magically resides in Gerald's body, she is curious about Gerald's size, weight, and thickness of the body, which brings her a feeling of freedom and comfort. She is also amazed at the number of pockets a man's pant can have, which by allowing the small items of keys, pencils, documents, bill folders inside, carries a deep sense of power and pride. In addition, she is struck by the business, political, and professional knowledge that man enjoys in the society, which grants a sense of confidence and solemnity. Dazzled by the men's world, Mollie feels the competition between her feminine consciousness and the masculine consciousness.

From a man's perspective, Mollie perceives that men's knowledge of women is limited to their narrow observation of women's silly hats, endless dresses, diamonds, delicate sentiments, and the desire for mercenary marriages. The contempt for women's shallowness and delicacies are so widely popular among men.

The androgynous identity of Mollie allows her to detect the prejudices towards women. Because if each gender are confined to separate life spheres, it is impossible for men and women to reach a mutual understanding of each other's lives. After all, it is only made possible for Mollie, after possessing both feminine consciousness and masculine knowledge, to speak on women's behalf. Although the strong proclamation that "women are pretty much people" is more of an assertion than an act, it can be viewed as the start for them to make a difference from the domestic "home bird(s)" to fully developed human beings.

## Ⅴ Writing Topic

你是否设想过另外一种性别的生活？无论是更换身体，还是更换大脑，都在强调性别差异。那么，认可性别差异是不是解决性别对立问题的一种途径？

# Unit 14 "She Unnames Them" by Ursula K. Le Guin

## Ⅰ Introduction to the Author and the Work

Ursula K. Le Guin (1929 –2018) grew up in Berkeley, California. Her parents were anthropologist Alfred Kroeber and writer Theodora Kroeber, author of *Ishi*. She attended the Radcliffe College (becoming part of the Harvard University in 1999) and did graduate work at the Columbia University. Few American writers have done work of such high quality in so many forms. Her oeuvre comprises 21 novels, 11 volumes of short stories and novellas, 6 volumes of poetry, 12 children's books, 4 collections of essays, and 4 volumes of translation. Le Guin's major titles have been translated into 42 languages and have remained in print, often for over half a century. Her fantasy novel *A Wizard of Earthsea*, has sold millions of copies worldwide.

Le Guin's first major work of science fiction, *The Left Hand of Darkness*, was considered groundbreaking for its radical investigation of gender roles and its moral and literary complexity. Her novels *The Dispossesed* and *Always Coming Home* redefined the scope and style of utopian fiction. Le Guin's poetry drew increasing critical and reader interest. Her final collection of poems, *So Far So Good*, was published shortly after her death.

"She Unnames Them" is a short story in which a woman has gone about unnaming all the animals, and many of them are perfectly fine with that. Some of the more human-friendly pets, such as dogs and birds, were resistant to giving up their names. Yet others are happy to return their names. Her implied name is Eve (or Lilith), but it is never said, for she too, gives back her name to Adam, thanking him but acknowledging she doesn't need it. Adam accepts her decision with little second thought until it's time for dinner. She explains that she is going with "them," and it's here that she realizes it might be a bit complicated to actually communicate without words and to fully express herself—she is in new terrain and must tread carefully.

## Ⅱ She Unnames Them

Most of them accepted namelessness with the perfect indifference with which they had so long accepted and ignored their names. Whales and dolphins, seals and sea otters consented with particular alacrity, sliding into anonymity as into their element. A faction of yaks, however, protested. They said that "yak" sounded right, and that almost everyone who knew they existed called them that. Unlike the ubiquitous creatures such as rats and fleas, who had been called by hundreds or thousands of different names since Babel, the yaks could truly say, they said, that they had a name. They discussed the matter all summer. The councils of elderly females finally agreed that though the name might be useful to others it was so redundant from the yak point of view that they never spoke it themselves and hence might as well dispense with it. After they presented the argument in this light to their bulls, a full consensus was delayed only by the onset of severe early blizzards. Soon after the beginning of the thaw, their agreement was reached and the designation "yak" was returned to the donor.

Among the domestic animals, few horses had cared what anybody called them since the failure of Dean Swift's attempt to name them from their own vocabulary. Cattle, sheep, swine, asses, mules, and goats, along with chickens, geese, and turkeys, all agreed enthusiastically to give their names back to the people to whom—as they put it—they belonged.

A couple of problems did come up with pets. The cats, of course, steadfastly denied ever having had any name other than those self-given, unspoken, ineffably personal names which, as the poet named Eliot said, they spend long hours daily contemplating though none of the contemplators has ever admitted that what they contemplate is their names and some onlookers have wondered if the object of that meditative gaze might not in fact be the Perfect, or Platonic,

Mouse. In any case, it is a moot point now. It was with the dogs, and with some parrots, lovebirds, ravens, and mynahs, that the trouble arose. These verbally talented individuals insisted that their names were important to them, and flatly refused to part with them. But as soon as they understood that the issue was precisely one of individual choice, and that anybody who wanted to be called Rover, or Froufrou, or Polly, or even Birdie in the personal sense, was perfectly free to do so, not one of them had the least objection to parting with the lowercase (or, as regards German creatures, uppercase) generic appellations "poodle," "parrot," "dog," or "bird," and all the Linnaean qualifiers that had trailed along behind them for two hundred years like tin cans tied to a tail.

The insects parted with their names in vast clouds and swarms of ephemeral syllables buzzing and stinging and humming and flitting and crawling and tunneling away.

As for the fish of the sea, their names dispersed from them in silence throughout the oceans like faint, dark blurs of cuttlefish ink, and drifted off on the currents without a trace.

None were left now to unname, and yet how close I felt to them when I saw one of them swim or fly or trot or crawl across my way or over my skin, or stalk me in the night, or go along beside me for a while in the day. They seemed far closer than when their names had stood between myself and them like a clear barrier: so close that my fear of them and their fear of me became one same fear. And the attraction that many of us felt, the desire to feel or rub or caress one another's scales or skin or feathers or fur, taste one another's blood or flesh, keep one another warm, that attraction was now all one with the fear, and the hunter could not be told from the hunted, nor the eater from the food.

This was more or less the effect I had been after. It was somewhat more powerful than I had anticipated, but I could not now, in all conscience, make an exception for myself. I resolutely put anxiety away, went to Adam, and said, "You and your father lent me this—gave it to me, actually. It's been really useful, but it doesn't exactly seem to fit very well lately. But thanks very much! It's really been very useful."

It is hard to give back a gift without sounding peevish or ungrateful, and I did not want to leave him with that impression of me. He was not paying much attention, as it happened, and said only, "Put it down over there, OK?" and went on with what he was doing.

One of my reasons for doing what I did was that talk was getting us nowhere, but all the same I felt a little let down. I had been prepared to defend my decision. And I thought that perhaps when he did notice he might be upset and want to talk. I put some things away and fiddled around a little, but he continued to do what he was doing and to take no notice of anything else. At last I said, "Well, goodbye, dear. I hope the garden key turns up."

He was fitting parts together, and said, without looking around, "OK, fine, dear. When's dinner?"

"I'm not sure," I said. "I'm going now. With the—" I hesitated, and finally said, "With them, you know." And I went on out. In fact, I had only just then realized how hard it would have been to explain myself. I could not chatter away as I used to do, taking it all for granted. My words must be as slow, as new, as single, as tentative as the steps I took going down the path away from the house, between the dark-branched, tall dancers motionless against the winter shining.

## Ⅲ Questions for Further Thinking

1. What is the connection of this story to "Genesis"? Find the evidence to prove this connection.

2. Why does Eve unname the animals? What are the reactions of the animals?

3. What is the significance of having a name in this world?

4. When Eve tells Adam about her act of unnaming, what is Adam's reaction?

5. When Eve tells Adam "I'm going now. With the—", what was the meaning of having a pause?

## Ⅳ Appreciation

"She Unnames Them" is a feminist story that alludes to "Genesis." In "Genesis," God creates the world and living beings, including Adam and Eve. God takes one of Adam's ribs and creates Eve; thus, Eve is called a "woman," meaning she is taken out of man. It is Adam, the man of all men, who names the livestock, the birds in the air, and all the beasts on the land. Naming, then, is the first power exercise to shape the world. In "She Unanmes Them," Eve, the woman of Adam, is about to overthrow the old and make a new start by naming the world.

As the title suggests, Eve starts her work by unnaming all the living creatures she encounters. However, few animals care how they were called. They are accustomed to the fact that names are more useful to those other than themselves. They abandon their names in an equally careless way as they are named because naming is just a narrative game played by Adam, who stands at the top of the hierarchy.

When Eve unnames all the animals and herself, she expects that Adam, who named all the animals, would be outraged because of her revolutionary challenge. To her disappointment, Adam does not seem to care about what had happened. His casual inquiry of "When's dinner" seems to render the intent of her rebellion meaningless.

In the gender confrontation, if a man simply ignores the woman's challenge as if it were a children's game, was Eve's effort to subvert the world still a meaningful one? Eve seems to be not sure about that. By saying "I'm going now. With the—", she realizes demolition without providing a new naming system would mean to make the world anew almost from every corner of life. It would mean to grope ahead in the darkness. But still, she leaves without regret, with the achievement of the narrative of "I," which brings initiatives to her for the first time in life.

## Ⅴ Writing Topic

近年来，女性通过不断的努力和尝试，试图构建新的社会设定。但是，人们对夏娃能否从原有的语言体系中脱钩也存在疑问。这些努力和尝试也激发了性别对立。试讨论，女性是否有必要创建新的话语体系。

# Unit 15 "We Are the Crazy Lady" by Cynthia Ozick

## Ⅰ Introduction to the Author and the Work

Cynthia Ozick (1928– ) was born in New York City in a Russian Jewish immigrant family. She received a BA from the New York University in 1949 and an MA from the Ohio State University in 1950. Beginning with a novel *Trust*(1966), she has embarked on a journey in publishing essays, plays, stories, and novels, including *The Pagan Rabbi and Other Stories* (1971), *The Cannibal Galaxy*(1983), *The Messiah of Stockholm* (1987), *The Shawl* (1989), *The Puttermesser Papers* (1997), *Heir to the Glimmering World*(2004), *Dictation: A Quartet*(2008), *Foreign Bodies*(2010).

In 1972, Ozick published "We Are the Crazy Lady and Other Feisty Feminist Fables" ("We Are the Crazy Lady" for short) in *Ms. Magazine*. These witty autobiographical parables about intellectual women, very much in the tradition of Edith Wharton's *The Valley of Childish Things*, are as relevant today as they were then. But Ozick has scrupulously corrected a phrase in "Section Ⅵ: Ambition," that is, "Polemics are nearly always a bit skewed away from truth-telling, and here I have had a serious life lesson ... I'm afraid I inserted a bit of imaginary history—that—never was, in order to heighten an argument. No relative, or anyone else, ever changed me with being a childless housewife, a failed woman. Alas, I invented these nasty phrases ... I have vowed, though perhaps too late, to confine make-believe to stories and novels."

# Ⅱ We Are the Crazy Lady and Other Feisty Feminist Fables[①]

## ⅰ: The Crazy Lady Double

A long, long time ago, in another century—1951, in fact—when you, dear younger readers, were most likely still in your nuclear-family playpen (where, if female, you cuddled a rag baby to your potential titties, or, if male, let down virile drool over your plastic bulldozer), Lionel Trilling told me never, never to use a parenthesis in the very first sentence. This was in a graduate English seminar at the Columbia University. To get into this seminar, you had to submit to a grilling wherein you renounced all former allegiance to the then-current literary religion, New Criticism, which considered that only the text existed, not the world. I passed the interview by lying, cunningly, and against any real convictions. I said that probably the world did exist—and walked triumphantly into the seminar room.

There were four big tables arranged in a square, with everyone's feet sticking out into the open middle of the square. You could tell who was nervous, and how much, by watching the pairs of feet twist around each other. Professor Trilling presided awesomely from the high bar of the square. His head was a majestic granite-gray, like a centurion in command; he looked famous. His clean shoes twitched only slightly, and only when he was angry.

It turned out he was angry at me a lot of the time. He was angry because he thought me a disrupter, a rioter, a provocateur, and a fool; also crazy. And this was twenty years ago, before these things were de rigueur in the universities. Everything was very quiet in those days. There were only the Cold War and Korea and Joe McCarthy and the Old Old Nixon, and the only revolutionaries around were in Henry James's *The Princess Casamassima*.

Habit governed the seminar. Where you sat the first day was where you

① https://link.springer.com/chapter/10.1057/9780230604841_9.

settled forever. So, to avoid the stigmatization of the ghetto, I was careful not to sit next to the other woman in the class: the Crazy Lady.

At first the Crazy Lady appeared to be remarkably intelligent. She was older than the rest of us, somewhere in her thirties (which was why we thought of her as a Lady), with wild tan hair, a noticeably breathing bosom, eccentric gold-rimmed old-pensioner glasses, and a tooth crowded wild mouth that seemed to get wilder the more she talked. She talked like a motorcycle, fast and urgent. Everything she said was almost brilliant, only not actually on point, and frenetic with hostility. She was tough and negative. She volunteered a lot and she stood up and wobbled with rage, pulling at her hair and mouth. She fought Trilling point for point, piecemeal and wholesale, mixing up queerly angled literary insights with all sorts of private and public fury. After the first meetings, he was fed up with her. The rest of us accepted that she probably wasn't all there, but in a room where everyone was on the make for recognition—you talked to save your life, and the only way to save your life was to be the smartest one that day—she was a nuisance, a distraction, a pain in the ass. The class became a bunch of Good Germans, determinedly indifferent onlookers to a vindictive match between Trilling and the Crazy Lady, until finally he subdued her by shutting his eyes, and, when that didn't always work, by cutting her dead and lecturing right across the sound of her strong, strange voice.

All this was before R. D. Laing had invented the superiority of madness, of course, and, cowards all, no one liked the thought of being tarred with the Crazy Lady's brush. Ignored by the boss, in the middle of everything she would suddenly begin to mutter to herself. She mentioned certain institutions she'd been in, and said we all belonged there. The people who sat on either side of her shifted chairs. If the Great Man ostracized the Crazy Lady, we had to do it too. But one day the Crazy Lady came in late and sat down in the seat next to mine, and stayed there the rest of the semester.

Then an odd thing happened. There, right next to me, was the noisy Crazy Lady, tall, with that sticking-out sighing chest of hers, orangey curls dripping over her nose, snuffling furiously for attention. And there was I, a brownish runt, a dozen years younger and flatter and shyer than the Crazy Lady, in no way her twin, physically or psychologically. In those days I was bone-skinny, small, sallow and myopic, and so scared I could trigger diarrhea at one glance from the Great Man. All this stress on looks is important. The Crazy Lady and I had our separate bodies, our separate brains. We handed in our separate papers.

But the Great Man never turned toward me, never at all, and if ambition broke feverishly through shyness so that I dared to push an idea audibly out of me, he shut his eyes when I put up my hand. This went on for a long time. I never got to speak, and I began to have the depressing feeling that Lionel Trilling hated me. It was no small thing to be hated by the man who had written "Wordsworth and the Rabbis" and Matthew Arnold, after all. What in hell was going on? I was in trouble, because, like everyone else in that demented contest, I wanted to excel. Then, one slow afternoon, wearily, the Great Man let his eyes fall on me. He called me by name, but it was not my name—it was the Crazy Lady's. The next week the papers came back—and there, right at the top of mine, in the Great Man's own handwriting, was a rebuke to the Crazy Lady for starting an essay with a parenthesis in the first sentence, a habit he took to be a continuing sign of that unruly and unfocused mentality so often exhibited in class. And then a Singular Revelation crept coldly through me. Because the Crazy Lady and I sat side by side, because we were a connected blur of Woman, Lionel Trilling, master of ultimate distinctions, couldn't tell us apart. The Crazy Lady and I! He couldn't tell us apart! It didn't matter that the Crazy Lady was crazy! He couldn't tell us apart!

Moral 1: All cats are gray at night, all darkies look alike.

Moral 2: Even among intellectual humanists, every woman has a Doppelgänger—every other woman.

### ii: The Lecture, 1

I was invited by a women's group to be guest speaker at a Book-Author Luncheon. The women themselves had not really chosen me: the speaker had been selected by a male leader and imposed on them. The plan was that I would autograph copies of my book, eat a good meal and then lecture. The woman in charge of the programming phoned to ask me what my topic would be. This was a matter of some concern, since they had never had a woman author before, and no one knew how the idea would be received. I offered as my subject "The Contemporary Poem."

When the day came, everything went as scheduled—the autographing, the food, the welcoming addresses. Then it was time to go to the lectern. I aimed at the microphone and began to speak of poetry. A peculiar rustling sound flew up from the audience. All the women were lifting their programs to the light, like hundreds of wings. Confused murmurs ran along the walls. I began to feel very uncomfortable. Then I too took up the program. It read, "Topic: The Contemporary Home."

Moral: Even our ears practice the caste system.

### iii: The Lecture, 2

I was in another country, the only woman at a philosophical seminar lasting three days. On the third day, I was to read a paper. I had accepted the invitation with a certain foreknowledge. I knew, for instance, that I could not dare to be the equal of any other speaker. To be an equal would be to be less. I understood that mine had to be the most original and powerful paper of all. I had no choice; I had to toil beyond my most extreme possibilities. This was not ambition, but only fear of disgrace.

For the first two days, I was invisible. When I spoke, people tapped impatiently, waiting for the interruption to be over with. No one took either my presence or my words seriously. At meals, I sat with my colleagues' wives.

The third day arrived, and I read my paper. It was successful beyond my remotest imaginings. I was interviewed, and my remarks appeared in newspapers in a language I could not understand. The Foreign Minister invited me to his home. I hobnobbed with famous poets.

Now my colleagues noticed me. But they did not notice me as a colleague. They teased and kissed me. I had become their mascot.

Moral: There is no route out of caste which does not instantly lead back into it.

## ⅳ：Propaganda

For many years, I had noticed that no book of poetry by a woman was ever reviewed without reference to the poet's sex. The curious thing was that, in the two decades of my scrutiny, there were no exceptions whatever. It did not matter whether the reviewer was a man or woman: in every case the question of the "feminine sensibility" of the poet was at the center of the reviewer's response. The maleness of male poets, on the other hand, hardly ever seemed to matter.

Determined to ridicule this convention, I wrote a tract, a piece of purely tendentious mockery, in the form of a short story. I called it "Virility."

The plot was, briefly, as follows: A very bad poet, lustful for fame, is despised for his pitiful lucubrations and remains unpublished. But luckily, he comes into possession of a cache of letters written by his elderly spinster aunt, who lives an obscure and secluded working-class life in a remote corner of England. The letters contain a large number of remarkable poems; the aunt, it turns out, is a genius. The bad poet publishes his find under his own name, and instantly attains worldwide adulation. Under the title "Virility," the poems become immediate classics. They are translated into dozens of languages and are praised and revered for their unmistakably masculine qualities: their strength, passion, wisdom, energy, boldness, brutality, worldliness, robustness, authenticity, sensuality, compassion. A big, handsome, sweating man, the poet swaggers from country to country, courted everywhere, pursued by admirers, yet respected by the most demanding critics.

Meanwhile, the old aunt dies. The supply of genius runs out. Bravely and contritely the poor poet confesses his ruse, and, in a burst of honesty, publishes the last batch under the real poet's name. The book is entitled *Flowers from Liverpool*. But the poems are at once found negligible and dismissed: "Thin feminine art," say the reviews, "a lovely girlish voice." Also: "Choked with female inwardness," and "The fine womanly intuition of a competent poetess." The poems are utterly forgotten.

I included this fable in a collection of short stories. In every review, the salvo went unnoticed. Not one reviewer recognized that the story was a sly tract. Not one reviewer saw the smirk or the point. There was one delicious comment, though. "I have some reservations," a man in Washington, D.C., wrote, "about the credibility of some of her male characters when they are chosen as narrators."

Moral: In saying what is obvious, never choose cunning. Yelling works better.

### V: Hormones

During a certain period of my life, I was reading all the time, and fairly obsessively. Sometimes, though, sunk in a book of criticism or philosophy, I would be brought up short. Consider: Here is a paragraph that excites the intellect. Inwardly, one assents passionately to its premises; the writer's idea is an exact diagram of one's own deepest psychology or conviction; one feels oneself seized as for a portrait. Then the disclaimer: "It is, however, otherwise with the female sex ..." A rebuke from *The World of Thinking*, "I didn't mean you, lady." In the instant one is in possession of one's humanity most intensely, it is ripped away.

These moments I discounted. What is wrong—intrinsically, psychologically, culturally, morally—can be dismissed.

But to dismiss in this manner is to falsify one's most genuine actuality. A Jew reading of the aesthetic glories of European civilization without taking notice of his victimization during, say, the era of the building of the great cathedrals, is self-forgetful in the most dangerous way. So would be a black who read of King Cotton with an economist's objectivity.

I am not offering any strict analogy between the situation of women and the history of Jews or colonialized blacks, as many politically radical women do (though the analogy with blacks is much the more frequent one). It seems to me to be abusive of language in the extreme when some women speak, in the generation after Auschwitz, in the very hour of the Bengali horror, of the "oppression" of women. Language makes culture, and we make a rotten culture when we abuse words. We raise up rotten heroines. I use "rotten" with particular attention to its precise meanings: foul, putrid, tainted, stinking. I am thinking now especially of a radical women's publication, *Off Our Backs*, which not long ago presented Leila Khaled, terrorist and foiled murderer, as a model for the political conduct of women.

But if I would not support the extreme analogy (and am never surprised when black women, who have a more historical comprehension of actual, not figurative, oppression, refuse to support the analogy), it is anyhow curious to see what happens to the general culture when any enforced class in any historical or social condition is compelled to doubt its own self-understanding, when identity is extremely defined, when individual humanity is called into question as being different from "standard" humanity. What happens is that the general culture, along with the object of its debasement, is also debased. If you laugh at women, you play Beethoven in vain. If you laugh at women, your laboratory will lie.

We can read in Charlotte Perkins Gilman's 1912 essay, "Are Women Human Beings?", an account of an opinion current sixty years ago. Women, said one scientist, are not only "not the human race—they are not even half the human race, but a sub-species set apart for purposes of reproduction merely."

Though we are accustomed to the idea of "progress" in science, if not in civilization generally, the fact is that more information has led to something very like regression.

I talked with an intelligent physician, the Commissioner of Health of a middle-sized city in Connecticut, a man who sees medicine not discretely but as part of the social complex. He treated me to a long list of all the objective differences between men and women, including particularly an account of current endocrinal studies relating to female hormones. "Aren't all of these facts?" he asked, "how can you distrust facts?" "Very good," I said, "I'm willing to take your medically educated word for it. I'm not afraid of facts, and I welcome facts—but a congeries of facts is not equivalent to an idea." This is the essential fallacy of the so-called "scientific" mind. People who mistake facts for ideas are incomplete thinkers; they are gossips.

"You tell me," I said, "that my sense of my own humanity as being 'standard' humanity—which is, after all, a subjective idea—is refuted by hormonal research.

My psychology, you tell me, which in your view is the source of my ideas, is the result of my physiology. It is not I who express myself, it is my hormones which express me. A part is equal to the whole, you say. Worse yet, the whole is simply the issue of the part: my 'I' is a flash of chemicals. You are willing to define all my humanity by hormonal investigation under a microscope. This you call 'objective irrefutable fact,' as if tissue-culture were equivalent to culture. But each scientist can assemble his own (subjective) constellation of 'objective irrefutable fact,' just as each social thinker can assemble his own (subjective) selection of traits that define 'humanity.' Who can prove what is 'standard' humanity, and which sex, class, or race is to be exempted from whole participation in it? On what basis do you regard female hormones as causing a modification from normative humanity? And what better right do you have to define normative humanity by what males have traditionally apperceived than by what females have traditionally apperceived—assuming (as I, lacking presumptuousness, do not) that their apperceptions have not been the same? Only Tiresias—that mythological character who was both man and woman consecutively—is in a position to make the comparison and present the proof. And then not even Tiresias, because to be a hermaphrodite is to be a monster, and not human."

"Why are you so emotional about all this?" said the Commissioner of Health. "You see how it is? Those are your female hormones working on you right now."

Moral: Defamation is only applied research.

### Ⅵ: Ambition

After thirteen years, I at last finished a novel. The first seven years were spent in a kind of apprenticeship—the book that came out of that time was abandoned without much regret. A second one was finished in six weeks and buried. It took six years to write the third novel, and this one was finally published.

How I lived through those years is impossible to recount in a short space. I was a recluse, a priest of Art. I read seas of books. I believed in the idea of masterpieces. I was scornful of the world of journalism, jobs, everydayness. I did not live like any woman I knew. I lived like some men I had read about—

Flaubert, or Proust, or James—the subjects of those literary biographies I endlessly drank in. I did not think of them as men, but as writers. I read the diaries of Virginia Woolf, and biographies of George Eliot, but I did not think of them as women. I thought of them as writers. I thought of myself as a writer.

It goes without saying that all this time my relatives regarded me as abnormal. I accepted this. It seemed to me, from what I had read, that most writers were abnormal. Yet on the surface, I could easily have passed for normal. The husband goes to work, the wife stays home—that is what is normal. Well, I was married. My husband went to his job every day. His job paid the rent and bought the groceries. I stayed home, reading and writing, and felt myself to be an economic parasite. To cover guilt, I joked that I had been given a grant from a very private, very poor, foundation—my husband.

But my relatives never thought of me as a parasite. The very thing I was doubtful about—my economic dependence—they considered my due as a woman. They saw me not as a failed writer without an income, but as a childless housewife, a failed woman. They did not think me abnormal because I was a writer, but because I was not properly living my life as a woman. In one respect we were in agreement utterly—my life was failing terribly, terribly. For me it was because, already deep into my thirties, I had not yet published a book. For them, it was because I had not yet borne a child.

I was a pariah, not only because I was a deviant, but because I was not recognized as the kind of deviant I meant to be. A failed woman is not the same as a failed writer. Even as a pariah I was the wrong kind of pariah.

Still, relations are only relations. What I aspired to, what I was in thrall to, was Art, was Literature, not familial contentment. I knew how to distinguish the trivial from the sublime. In Literature and in Art, I saw, my notions were not pariah notions. There, I inhabited the mainstream. So I went on reading and writing. I went on believing in Art, and my intention was to write a masterpiece. Not a saucer of well-polished craft (the sort of thing "women writers" are always accused of being accomplished at), but something huge, contemplative, Tolstoyan. My ambition was a craw.

I called the book *Trust*. I began it in the summer of 1957 and finished it in

November of 1963, on the day President John Kennedy was assassinated. In manuscript, it was 801 pages divided into four parts: "America," "Europe," "Birth," and "Death." The title was meant to be ironic. In reality, it was about distrust. It seemed to me I had touched on distrust in every order or form of civilization. It seemed to me I had left nothing out. It was (though I did not know this then) a very hating book. What it hated above all was the whole—the whole—of Western Civilization. It told how America had withered into another Europe. It dreamed dark and murderous pagan dreams, and hated what it dreamed.

In style, the book was what has come to be called "mandarin": a difficult, aristocratic, unrelenting virtuoso prose. It was, in short, unreadable. I thought I knew this. I was sardonic enough to say, echoing Joyce about *Finnegan's Wake*, "I expect you to spend your life at this." In any case, I had spent a decade and a half of my own life at it. Though I did not imagine the world would fall asunder at its appearance, I thought—at the very least—the ambition, the all-swallowingness, the wild insatiability of the writer would be plain to everyone who read it. I had, after all, taken History for my subject: not merely History as an aggregate of events, but History as a judgment on events. No one could say my theme was flighty. Of all the novelists I read (and in those days I read them all, broiling in the envy of the unpublished, which is like no envy on earth), who else had dared so vastly?

During that period, Françoise Sagan's first novel was published. I held the thin little thing and laughed. Women's pulp!

My own novel, I believed, contained everything—the whole world.

But there was one element I had consciously left out. Though on principle I did not like to characterize it or think about it much, the truth is I was thinking about it all the time. It was only a fiction-technicality, but I was considerably afraid of it. It was the question of the narrator's "sensibility." The narrator, as it happened, was a young woman; I had chosen her to be the eye—and the "I"—of the novel because all the other characters in some way focused on her. She was the one most useful to my scheme. Nevertheless, I wanted her not to live. Everything I was reading in reviews of other people's books made me fearful: I would have to be very cautious; I would have to drain my narrator of emotive value of any kind, because I was afraid to be pegged as having written a "woman's" novel. Nothing was more certain to lead to that than a point-of-view seemingly lodged in a woman, and no one takes a woman's novel seriously. I was in terror, above all, of sentiment and feelings, those telltale taints. I kept the fury and the passion for other, safer, characters.

So what I left out of my narrator entirely, sweepingly, with exquisite consciousness of what exactly I was leaving out, was any shred of "sensibility." I stripped her of everything, even a name. I crafted and carpentered her. She was for me a bloodless device, fulcrum or pivot, a recording voice, a language-machine. She confronted moment or event, took it in, gave it out. And what to me was all the more wonderful about this nameless fiction-machine I had invented was that the machine itself, though never alive, was a character in the story, without ever influencing the story. My machine-narrator was there for efficiency only, for flexibility, for craftiness, for subtlety, but never, never, as a "woman." I wiped the "woman" out of her. And I did it out of fear, out of vicarious vindictive critical imagination, out of the terror of my ambition, out of, maybe, paranoia. I meant my novel to be taken for what it really was. I meant to make it impossible for it to be mistaken for something else.

Publication: Review in *The New York Times Sunday Book Review*.

"The review is accompanied by a picture of a naked woman seen from the back. Her bottom is covered by some sort of drapery.

Title of the review: "Daughter's Reprieve."

Excerpts from the review: "These events, interesting in themselves, exist to reveal the sensibility of the narrator." "She longs to play some easy feminine role." "She has been unable to define herself as a woman." "The main body of the novel, then, is a revelation of the narrator's inner, turbulent, psychic drama."

"O rabid, rotten Western Civilization, where are you? O judging History, O foul Trust and fouler Distrust, where?

"O Soap Opera, where did you come from?

(Meanwhile the review in *Time* was calling me a "housewife.") Pause.

"All right, let us take up the rebuttals."

Q: Maybe you did write a soap opera without knowing it. Maybe you only thought you were writing about Western Civilization when you were really only rewriting *Stella Dallas*.

A: A writer may be unsure of everything—trust the tale not the teller is a good rule—but not of his obsessions; of these he is certain. If I were rewriting *Stella Dallas*, I would turn her into the Second Crusade and demobilize her.

Q: Maybe you're like the blind Jew who wants to be a pilot, and when they won't give him the job he says they're anti-Semitic. Look, the book was lousy, you deserved a lousy review.

A: You mistake me, I never said it was a bad review. It was in fact an extremely favorable review, full of gratifying adjectives.

Q: Then what's eating you?

A: I don't know. Maybe the question of language. By language I mean literacy. See the next section, please.

Q: No Moral for this section?

A: Of course. If you look for it, there will always be a decent solution for female ambition. For instance, it is still not too late to enroll in a good secretarial school.

Q: Bitter, bitter! You mean your novel failed?

A: Perished, is dead and buried. I sometimes see it exhumed on the shelf in the public library. It's always there. No one ever borrows it.

Q: Dummy! You should've written a soap opera. Women are good at that.

A: Thank you. You almost remind me of a Second Moral: in conceptual life, junk prevails. Even if you do not produce junk, it will be taken for junk.

Q: What does that have to do with women?

A: The products of women are frequently taken for junk.

Q: And if a woman does produce junk ...?

A: Glory—they will treat her almost like a man who produces junk. They will say her name on television. Do please go on to the next section. Thank you.

### vii: Conclusion, and a Peek

Actually I had two more stories to tell you. One was about Mr. Machismo, a very angry, well groomed, clean man (what a pity he isn't a woman—ah, deprived of vaginal spray) who defines as irresponsible all those who do not obey him, especially his mother and sister. A highly morbid and titillating Gothic tale. The other story was about Mr. Littletable, the Petty Politician, at the Bankers' Feast—how he gathered up the wives in a pretty garland, threw them a topic to chatter over. A Bronx neighborhood where you can buy good lox, I think it was. Having set them all up so nicely, he went off to lick the nearest Vice-President of Morgan Guaranty.

But these are long stories, Ladies and Gentlemen. No room up there for another Woman's Novel.

## Ⅲ Questions for Further Thinking

1. Since Cynthia Ozick is a writer and intellectual, what makes it special when she illustrates the gender prejudices happening in academia?

2. If we read this essay carefully, we can find that "We Are the Crazy Lady" echoes with Virginia Woolf's *A Room of One's Own*. Find out the connection which suggests how obstinately the gender stereotypes exist.

3. Of those gender stereotypes discussed by Ozick, which of them is still prevalent today?

4. Do you have a criterion in judging a good novel? Do you think feminine qualities or masculine qualities spoil the greatness of a literary work?

5. Choose one of the five morals and elaborate on your understanding of it.

## Ⅳ Appreciation

In this essay, Cynthia Ozick picks up a few episodes to illustrate the stereotypes and prejudices she personally experienced as a woman and an intellectual in the years from the 1950s to the 1970s.

The first story is about how the distinguished professor, Lionel Trilling, the most famous figure in the New York Intellectuals, mistook her with another lady, who was labelled as "the crazy lady" because she dares to express her idiosyncratic ideas. Even though there are only a few women in the seminar, Lionel Trilling does not care to give a second look to distinguish Ozick from "the crazy lady." What disappoints her is the fact that gender discrimination is not only widely adopted by commoners but also top intellectuals like Lionel Trilling, a widely acclaimed humanist.

Two other examples of stereotypes concerning women's intellectual capacity were also commonly seen during the 1950s. One is that the host of a Book-Author Luncheon willingly changes Ozick's speech title "The Contemporary Poem" to "the Contemporary Home," because he does not trust that a woman was capable of discussing poems. Another one is that in an important seminar, she is arranged to sit with her colleagues' wives rather than with the other speakers. The two examples proves that nearly 50 years after Virginia Woolf accused the degradation of women's intellect, the stereotype that women are intellectually inferior to men is still popular in the public mindset.

The contempt towards women's intellect was almost omnipotent. Ozick continued to mock the reviewers who ignored the real qualities of the poem but made judgments simply on the assumed understanding of gender differences. To them, if the poem was written by a man, then it was of virile qualities; if it was done by a woman, surely, it would be full of feminine sensibility.

Because the society, in general, did not take women's writing seriously, Ozick, who hoped to follow Virginia Woolf and George Eliot to exhibit women's intellectual competency, determined to write a great novel as marvelous as that of Henry James. However, she seemed to fall into a pitfall that, if she expected to remove her feminine qualities, she was catering to men's standard of a great novel. When intellect is defined by males, the desire to be accepted and respected as great is to fit into men's standards. To be fairly judged as a writer rather than a woman writer, it requires a de-gendered criterion for literature writing.

"We Are the Crazy Lady" raises a question as to how women could act in response to the society that ignores their effort to become full humans. When time enters into the first half of the twenty-first century, we now have so many brilliant women writers and amazing writings. Looking back at the frustration and dismal experienced by Ozick, it can still remind us that every effort made by women of every generation deserves trying.

## Ⅴ Writing Topic

辛西娅·欧茨克(Cynthia Ozick)的这篇短文记录了她在二十世纪五六十年代美国文学界的一些亲身经历。其中,不乏学界和公众对女性学者的轻视。试比较欧茨克的经历与弗吉尼亚·伍尔夫在《一间自己的屋子》里对社会贬低女性智力活动的相关论述,以及爱丽丝·门罗在《办公室》中刻画的女性作家在租房写作时遭遇的偏见,并对女性在获取知识、进行智力活动方面可能遭遇的“社会结构性围困”进行讨论。

# References


BEARD M, 2017. Women & power: a manifesto[M]. New York: Liveright.

BRADLEY H, 2013. Gender[M]. Cambridge: Polity Press.

BUTLER J, 1989. Gender trouble: feminism and the subversion of identity[M]. London: Routledge.

BUTLER J, 2004. Undoing gender[M]. London: Routledge.

CAHILL S, 2002. Women and fiction: short stories by and about women[M]. New York: New American Library.

DE BEAUVOIR S, 1972. The second sex[M]. PARSHLEY H M, trans. New York: Penguin Books.

DE BEAUVOIRS, 1989. The second sex[M]. PARSHLEY H M, trans. London: Vintage.

FRIEDAN B, 1997. The feminine mystique[M]. New York: W.W. Norton & Company.

GILBERT S M, GUBAR S, 1984. The madwoman in the attic: the woman writer and the nineteenth-century literary imagination[M]. London: Yale University Press.

HALBERSTAM J J, 1998. Female masculinity[M]. Durham: Duke University Press Books.

HANSON S, GERALDINE P, 1995. Gender, work and space[M]. London: Taylor and Francis.

HOOKS B, 2000. Feminist theory: from margin to center[M]. London: Pluto Press.

IRIGARAY L, 1992. Je, tu, nous: toward a culture of difference[M]. London: Routledge.

LANSER S S, 1992. Fictions of authority: women writers and narrative voice [M]. Ithaca: Cornell University Press.

Martin W, 2004. More stories we tell: the best contemporary short stories by north American women[M]. New York: Pantheon Books.

MILL J S, 2007. On liberty and the subjection of women[M]. London: Penguin Classics.

MILLETT K, 1969. Sexual politics[M]. Urbana: University of Illinois Press.

OAKLEY A, 2019. The Sociology of housework[M]. Bristol: Policy Press, 2019.

ORGAD S, 2019. Heading home: motherhood, work, and the failed promise of equality[M]. New York: Columbia University Press.

RUSS J, 2005. How to suppress women's writing[M]. Austin: University of Texas Press.

SEDGWICK E K, 1985. Between men: English literature and male homosocial desire[M]. New York: Columbia University Press.

SHOWALTER E, 1977. A literature of their own: British women novelists from Brontë to Lessing[M]. Princeton: Princeton University Press.

SHOWALTER E, 2011. The vintage book of American women writers[M]. London: Vintage.

TONG R, 1998. Feminist thought: a more comprehensive introduction[M]. Boulder, Colo.: Westview.

WOLLSTONECRAFT M, 1987. A vindication of rights of women[M]. 2nd ed. New York: W.W. Norton & Company.

WOOLF V, 1963. Three guineas[M]. Pleasanton: Harvest Books.

YALOM M, BROWN T D, 2015. The social sex: a history of female friendship [M]. New York: Harper Perennial.

鲍晓兰，1995. 西方女性主义研究评介[M]. 北京：生活·读书·新知三联书店.

波伏娃，1998. 第二性[M]. 陶铁柱，译. 北京：中国书籍出版社.

伯克，2014. 性暴力史[M]. 马凡，等译. 南京：江苏人民出版社.

陈丽，2020. 空间[M]. 北京：外语教学与研究出版社.

邓利，2007. 新时期女性主义文学批评的发展轨迹[M]. 北京：中国社会科学出版社.

弗里德曼，2014. 图绘：女性主义与文化交往地理学[M]. 陈丽，译. 南京：译林出版社.

福柯，2016. 性经验史[M]. 佘碧平，译. 上海：上海人民出版社.

弗里丹，2005. 女性的奥秘[M]. 程锡麟，朱徽，王晓路，译. 广州：广东经济出版社.

戈德，墨菲，2013. 生态女性主义文学批评：理论，阐释和教学法[M]. 蒋林，译. 北京:中国社会科学出版社.

吉尔曼,2014. 她的国[M]. 朱巧蓓,王骁双,康宇扬,等译. 北京:北京时代华文书局.

金文野,2011. 中国现当代女性主义文学论纲[M]. 北京:中国社会科学出版社.

李小江,2016. 女性乌托邦:中国女性/性别研究二十讲[M]. 北京:社会科学文献出版社.

李银河,1997. 女性权力的崛起[M]. 北京:中国社会科学出版社.

李银河,2018. 女性主义[M]. 上海:上海文化出版社.

刘岩,等,2019. 性别[M]. 北京:外语教学与研究出版社.

孟悦,戴锦华,2018. 浮出历史地表:现代妇女文学研究[M]. 北京:北京大学出版社.

上野千鹤子,2015. 厌女:日本的女性嫌恶[M]. 王兰,译. 上海:上海三联书店.

隋红升,2020. 男性气质[M]. 北京:外语教学与研究出版社.

王金玲,2005. 女性社会学[M]. 北京:高等教育出版社.

伍尔夫,2009. 论小说与小说家[M]. 翟世镜,译. 上海:上海译文出版社.

张金凤,2019. 身体[M]. 北京:外语教学与研究出版社.


相关阅读书目请扫描二维码:

# 后 记

一直以来，英美文学方向的专业课都聚焦西方经典文学作品的选读。除阅读这些节选的经典作品之外，学生对其他作品的阅读非常有限。于是，2016 年暑假，基于多年对女性主义的研究和持续关注，我决定开设一门以阅读完整的短篇小说为主的英语文学赏析课程，将其作为文学选读课的补充。相比于节选的长篇作品，短篇小说更容易吸引学生，也能让学生更细致地把握小说的精巧构思和文字(考虑到原著的语言风格、时代特色以及作者的用词习惯，在编排中对相关内容予以保留)。在“短平快”的阅读时代，短篇小说更有利于达到教学效果。事实证明，这个选择是正确的。这门课不仅让学生们感受到了女性作家不同于男性作家的细腻文笔，还非常适合学生结合现实生活进行思考并展开讨论。开课以来，时常有学生跟我反馈这门课带来的思想转变和情感共鸣。每学期也会有非英语专业的学生选修和旁听，越来越多的学生从中受益。这既让我感动，也鼓励我把这门课上得更好。

随着这门课程的日益完善和课程资料的积累，教材编写顺理成章。在成书的过程中，我得到了浙江工商大学研究生院和外国语学院的大力支持与资助。在此，特别感谢李靖华老师、薛薇薇老师、陈帅老师给予的支持和建议。还要感谢我的学生，他们在这本教材的编写中承担了部分工作：姚一帆、温在满和陈易完成了相关作者的信息查询、文稿的电子化，以及文稿的核对；余知玖全程参与了教材的编撰，对英文赏析部分进行了非常细致的校对，并利用自己在国外学习的便利条件，极大地推进了部分文本的版权联系工作。感谢浙江工商大学出版社的编辑王英，没有她的坚持，本书难以顺利出版，在此谨致谢忱。

此外，也感谢选课的历届学生。他们对这门课沉浸式的讨论和积极反馈，让我有动力把这门课的讲义转化为教材，为学生提供一个既能满足其学习需求又能帮助其理解女性生活多样化的阅读文本。同时，学生的讨论与反馈，也让我紧跟时代，将传统教材数字化，为大家提供一种可以便捷地获取文本和相关文学材料的阅读方式。